ACCLAIM FOR

The Color of Hope

"In *The Color of Hope*, Kim Cash Tate weaves a powerful story that will shake you to the core. You will laugh, your heart will break, and, ultimately, you'll be uplifted by the many colors of hope."

—Stephanie Perry Moore, author and co-executive editor *of Sisters in Faith*

"Tackling difficult topics, the *Color of Hope* peels back the veneer of life in the South, turning over traditions and expectations between races, families, and churches. Tate's engaging storytelling and eloquent prose journeys us through the challenge of breaking through prejudice and hurt for the sake of love and faith. Tate is definitely a voice of influence in today's Christian fiction."

—Rachel Hauck, award-winning, best-selling author of *The Wedding Dress* and *Once Upon a Prince*

Hope Springs

"Tate expertly crafts an intriguing narrative that explores unrequited love, true faith, and the complicated politics of change in the Christian church."

—*Publishers Weekly*

"Kim Cash Tate draws us into a world where the dreams, desires, missteps, and matters of the heart we discover there mirror our own. She is a master at crafting characters who make you forget you're reading fiction. By the end of *Hope Springs*, you'll feel as if you're cheering on members of your extended family."

—Stacy Hawkins Adams, best-selling author of *Coming Home* and *The Someday List*

Cherished

"Tate's amazing ability to connect with the reader on both personal and spiritual levels elevates this novel far above the rest. Those looking for hope and encouragement will find it on the pages of this superb book."

—*Romantic Times* TOP PICK

"As I read Kim's book *Cherished*, the word that came back to me over and over again is grace. Kim has the gift of being able to tell a story so vividly that you forget that the characters she portrays are fictitious, and you experience deep empathy for them. You will find yourself in this story. More than that, you will discover for the first time or rediscover how deeply you are loved, valued, and cherished by God."

—Sheila Walsh, author of *Sweet Sanctuary*

Faithful

"The author skillfully ties the concept of sexual purity, whether married or single, to the idea of faithfulness on a spiritual level. . . . Readers will not be disappointed."

—Crosswalk.com review

"Kim Cash Tate's enjoyable novel is true to both the realities of life and the hope found through faith in Jesus. Romance meets real life with a godly heart. Hooray!"

—Stasi Eldredge, best-selling author of *Captivating*

The
Color of Hope

ALSO BY KIM CASH TATE

Hope Springs

Cherished

Faithful

The
Color of Hope

KIM CASH TATE

THOMAS NELSON
Since 1798

NASHVILLE DALLAS MEXICO CITY RIO DE JANEIRO

Published in Nashville, Tennessee, by Thomas Nelson. Thomas Nelson is a registered trademark of Thomas Nelson, Inc.

Thomas Nelson, Inc., books may be purchased in bulk for educational, business, fund-raising, or sales promotional use. For information, please e-mail SpecialMarkets@ThomasNelson.com.

Author is represented by the literary agency of The B&B Media Group, Inc., 109 S. Main, Corsicana, Texas, 75110. www.tbbmedia.com.

Publisher's Note: This novel is a work of fiction. Names, characters, places, and incidents are either products of the author's imagination or used fictitiously. All characters are fictional, and any similarity to people living or dead is purely coincidental.

Library of Congress Cataloging-in-Publication Data

Tate, Kimberly Cash.
  The color of hope / Kim Cash Tate.
    pages cm
  Summary: "Hope shines brightest when all seems lost"-- Provided by publisher.
  ISBN 978-1-59554-998-3 (pbk.)
  1. African American women--Fiction. 2. Teacher-student relationships--Fiction. I. Title.
  PS3620.A885C65 2013
  813'.6--dc23
                            2012047038

Printed in the United States of America

13 14 15 16 17 18 RRD 6 5 4 3 2 1

To Jesus, in whom lies all hope

Sanders Family Tree

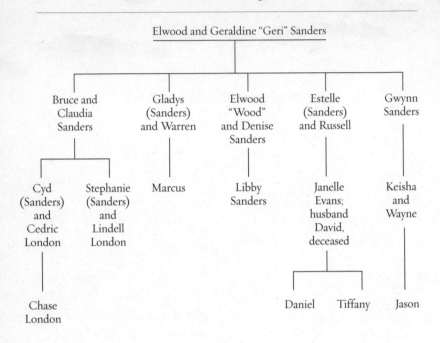

Elwood and Geraldine "Geri" Sanders

- Bruce and Claudia Sanders
  - Cyd (Sanders) and Cedric London
    - Chase London
  - Stephanie (Sanders) and Lindell London
- Gladys (Sanders) and Warren
  - Marcus
- Elwood "Wood" and Denise Sanders
  - Libby Sanders
- Estelle (Sanders) and Russell
  - Janelle Evans; husband David, deceased
    - Daniel
    - Tiffany
- Gwynn Sanders
  - Keisha and Wayne
    - Jason

Dillon Family Tree

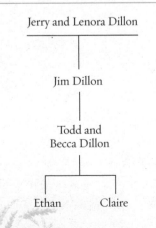

Jerry and Lenora Dillon

- Jim Dillon
  - Todd and Becca Dillon
    - Ethan
    - Claire

CHAPTER ONE
Tuesday, July 27

W e're making a huge mistake. I just know it.

Stephanie Sanders London stood with her husband, Lindell, in front of family and friends in the
activity center at Living Word Church, heart palpitating—or con-
stricting. Or whatever word fit the slow but sure panic that had
threatened all evening to overtake her and was about to make good
on the promise.

Lindell, on the other hand, had an odd glow.

"I'm still so overwhelmed by your support," he was saying. "I
never expected this." He paused, visibly moved.

Their pastor had asked them to say a few words to the crowd
who had come to say good-bye. Stephanie had spoken first, which
hastened the onset of whatever this was. She couldn't even remember what she'd said after acknowledging that they were leaving.

Lindell continued, "I became a doctor because I wanted to
help people. But candidly, I was also drawn to the lifestyle it would
afford. I never thought that one day the lifestyle wouldn't matter
and medicine would become ministry. But a one-month trip to

Haiti earlier this year changed my life. And now, because of you, I can alternate between practicing in the States and returning to Haiti on a regular basis. I can't thank you enough."

He turned to Stephanie to see if she had anything more to add. She looked out at her parents, Bruce and Claudia Sanders. Bruce had been surprised and moved that Stephanie had grown so close to his side of the family and would be planting herself in his Hope Springs roots. But he'd let her know how much he'd miss her. Looking at them now, it struck her that they might never live in the same city again. Her parents might never be a regular part of her life or her future children's lives. She shook her head at Lindell. If she opened her mouth now, the only thing she'd add would be a retraction of all their plans.

Lindell wrapped up. "This will always be home. You might not see us every week in the first service, fourth pew from the front, left side"—he chuckled with the rest—"but you'd better believe we'll be there in spirit. We love you, and we'll miss you."

Stephanie nodded her agreement as applause rang throughout the room. They walked down the steps of the riser, and Stephanie searched immediately for her older sister, Cyd.

"Stephanie! Lindell!"

They turned to see who was calling.

"You don't know me," a young woman said. "I'm new to Living Word, but when I saw the announcement Sunday at church, I wanted to come tonight. And I'm glad I did!" She regarded Lindell. "I'm in med school at Wash U and was so inspired by what you shared. It's radical, really, when you think about making a total life shift . . ."

Alarm bells went off in Stephanie's head. The only "radical" moves she'd ever made were things like wearing a dress with too much cleavage showing at her wedding rehearsal . . . which she only knew was radical by the feedback. Following-God radical was different. Harder. She needed baby steps. She needed her sister.

"Excuse me." Stephanie was glad Lindell had taken up the response. "I need to find someone, but it was nice to meet you."

She spotted Cyd a few feet over with her best friend, Dana. Stephanie tugged Cyd's arm. "Emergency. Now. For real."

Cyd was laughing, barely holding on to her rambunctious one-year-old, Chase. "I know! He's been in the dip, the punch, just got a fistful of cookies . . ." She rubbed noses with him as he giggled. "Why did I ever encourage you to walk?"

Dana pinched his cheek. "Auntie Dana understands, little man. You're just trying to have a good—"

"Uh, hello?" Stephanie waved her hands at them both. "Does *emergency* mean anything to you two?" She gaped at her sister. "As in, I desperately need to talk to you?"

Cyd gave her the momma look—which she'd always done, but now that she really *was* a momma, it had more umph. Thirteen years older, she'd actually always been like a second momma. "Steph, it's not an emergency."

"It *is* an emergency."

"I know what it's about."

Chase spied his dad across the room and lunged forward in Cyd's arms. "Da-da. Da-da."

Stephanie latched onto her nephew's hand. "You're just a little cutie, you know that? Auntie Stephy loves you." Chase was her soft spot, and she wouldn't be seeing *him* either, which brought her back to her angst. She looked at Cyd. "You do *not* know what it's about."

Dana laughed, wresting Chase from Cyd. "How about this? I'll take Chase to his da-da, and you go with Steph. In no time, you'll be wishing she was still here in St. Louis bombarding you with emergencies."

"I know, right?" Stephanie said.

Cyd gave them both a look.

The sisters walked out of the activity center. "Okay, what's the emergency?" Cyd said.

"I need to know if I'm crazy for going through with this move."

"I knew it." Cyd stopped in the hallway outside the center. "Yes. You are. Crazy for asking the same question week after week."

"No, it's *really* hitting me right now." Stephanie smiled at a couple just arriving. She lowered her voice. "I think we're making a mistake."

"Why?"

"*Because.*" Stephanie pulled her farther down the hall. "Lindell and I are leaving St. Louis where I've lived all my life—not to move to Chicago or DC or someplace else that makes sense, but to *Hope Springs*. I mean, when I say it I *sound* crazy. Why would I move to a little country town in North Carolina? Who *does* that?"

"You're doing it. Tomorrow."

"That's not funny."

"And Janelle did it last month when she moved *from* DC," Cyd said.

"Yeah, but she's got an excuse for her crazy. She's in love."

Stephanie and her cousin Janelle had cared for their ailing grandmother in Hope Springs earlier in the year while Lindell was in Haiti. Stephanie had been excited that God put it on both her and her cousin's hearts to relocate there. She'd also been excited that they'd be near another cousin, Libby, who lived in Raleigh. But now . . .

"Ever since Grandma Geri's funeral," Cyd said, "you and Lindell felt like God wanted you to do something different. You prayed and asked everybody and their momma to pray, even Pastor Lyles, which I've never seen you do." Cyd had moved from momma to exhortation mode. "And you both felt this was your answer. I understand the cold feet, but I just know God is leading you. Even if it feels crazy."

"It's more than cold feet. My heart is so out of rhythm, it might be a warning. What if we move to Hope Springs, and that's *not* what God was saying? That would be tragic."

Cyd almost laughed. "Oh, stop it. You had a great time down there."

"The *two months* I spent there were great, because I got to know Grandma, Janelle, Libby, and other family. *Living* there is another story. We've got more people in our church than they've got in the town." She started pacing. "I can't believe I told Lindell to do that fleece thing."

"I meant to ask where you got that idea," Cyd said.

Stephanie paused with pursed lips. "Where do you think I got it? Bible study."

"What Bible study?"

"My *personal* Bible study."

"Really?" Cyd smiled. She'd been encouraging Stephanie to study her Bible for years. "I didn't know you were doing that."

"Well, don't get happy. I didn't think the fleece thing would work."

"And not just 'work,'" Cyd said. "It was more than Lindell could've hoped."

Lindell had said chances were slim that he'd find something near Hope Springs since so many medical practices were downsizing or closing. But Stephanie suggested the "fleece" of contacting Dr. Richardson, a doctor in the little town who'd cared for many in her family. One call led to another, which ultimately led to an interview and an offer for Lindell to join a practice in nearby Rocky Mount. But they could only accommodate him part-time—which turned out to be perfect. Their church family at Living Word was making it possible for him to travel to Haiti one week per month as a medical missionary.

Stephanie sighed. "I just don't know why we took *that* as the sign we should go. Maybe it was meant to show us what's possible *here*.

Surely there's a practice in St. Louis that would allow him to work a part-time schedule and travel to Haiti." She threw up her hands. "But noooo, we ran with it before we had any idea what *I* would be doing in Hope Springs." She gave her sister a pointed look. "Why did you let me do that?"

"Why did *I* . . . ? You're the one who said it seemed clear."

"But you should've told me to wait until all the pieces were in place. I don't have a job yet, and we're moving tomorrow."

"Steph, you don't have a job *here*, you haven't in years." Cyd's eyes softened. "What's the real issue? The small town, lack of a job . . . or something else?"

Stephanie took a long breath and thought on it a moment. "This has been my safety net all my life . . . this church, my family, *you*. If I don't know the answer—which is most of the time—you're the first person I run to, no offense to Lindell." Tears slid down her face. "I don't want to live hundreds of miles from all of you. I *need* you."

Cyd took her into her arms. "I'm so proud of you."

"Why?" She sniffed on Cyd's shoulder. "For being a first-class coward?"

Cyd took a step back and looked her in the eye. "I've watched my little sister go from a self-centered, overconfident, impetuous brat—"

Stephanie rolled her teary eyes.

"—sorry, but you were—to a reflective, prayerful woman who wants to follow God, whatever it might mean. It seems crazy, you're scared, you have no idea what you'll be doing down there—but you and I both know you're still going."

Stephanie pouted. "Can't y'all just move there too? We can make room in Grandma Geri's house."

Cyd laughed softly. "It'll be hard enough trying to find room in Grandma's house for a few days this week." Her phone was ringing, and she pulled her purse off her shoulder and fished around to find it. "I'm so glad you scheduled the move the same week as the family reunion. We get to road-trip with you all, help you get settled, and hang out a few days with family. It'll be fun."

"Yeah . . . until I have to say another round of good-byes Monday morning." Stephanie gave a forlorn sigh.

"Oops." Cyd stared at her phone. "Missed call from Libby."

Stephanie's phone rang in her hand. "Now she's calling me. No need to wonder what it's about."

Cousin Libby, an event planner, had agreed to take over the planning of the Sanders family reunion, which for years had been handled by their parents' generation. The closer they got to the reunion, the more they'd heard from her. And it was always urgent.

Cyd nodded. "Libby might be the only one with more 'emergencies' than you right now."

Stephanie answered. "What's up, Lib?"

"Why is your team the only one who has yet to post pictures on the reunion site? I hope you know Team Bruce is in last place."

Stephanie gasped. "Last place? I'd better not tell Dad. He'll never live it down if he doesn't win—wait, what's this again? *Survivor* or *The Amazing Race*?"

"See, that's why I didn't want to do this. I knew people wouldn't take it seriously," Libby said. "I work hard to come up with fun new ideas to get people involved, and all I get is grief."

The Sanders family reunion was huge, with dozens of relatives beyond the offspring of Grandma Geri and Grandpa Elwood Sanders. But Libby had cooked up a team concept just for their branch of the tree to encourage participation. Stephanie's dad, Bruce, was the oldest of Grandma Geri's five offspring.

"Oh, ease up on the violins." Stephanie was smiling. "You know I'm one of the ones who talked you into doing this. Would've posted pictures, but mine are all packed up."

Cyd took the phone. "Mine are by the computer, ready to scan before we leave town tomorrow. Even got Dad to give me pics from when he was little. That's more points, right?"

"Team Bruce trying to come from the rear!" Libby exclaimed.

Stephanie was listening and grabbed the phone back. "Team Bruce not only coming from the rear but about to pass *your* team, especially when we get points for the basketball game. Both our husbands are playing." She cleared her throat. "No need to point out the obvious, but since you don't have a brother or a husband— and Uncle Wood's probably not playing—you'll get zero points for that one."

"*Wrong.*" Libby sang it. "Rules stipulate we can recruit team members for events, and Team Wood *will* have a b-ball player."

"Who?"

"Travis."

"Ooooh." Stephanie's eyebrows rose. "I won't even dispute this so-called rule you came up with. I just want to know what's up with Travis on Team Libby."

"He's on Team *Wood*, not Team Libby. And nothing's up with that. I asked him and he said yes."

"Mm-hm," Stephanie said. "I see I've got a lot to catch up on. The picture's looking a little different from when I was down there."

"Okay, well, gotta make some more calls."

"You can run but you can't hide."

Libby laughed. "When do y'all get here?"

"Loading up and hitting the road tomorrow. We'll stop some-where overnight. Probably get to Hope Springs late Thursday morning."

"The move-in crew will be assembled," Libby said. "Can't wait to see you!"

"You too, girl."

Stephanie hung up and glanced at Cyd, who appeared contem-plative.

"You mentioned Travis," Cyd said. "I was just thinking how challenging it must be to be a pastor in Hope Springs right now."

"Gee, thanks," Stephanie said. "Just when my mood lightens a little, you remind me of another downside to this move—the churches."

"I wouldn't call it a downside." Cyd was still pondering. "I actually think it's kind of exciting."

Stephanie frowned at her. "So . . . members of New Jerusalem and Calvary Church are complaining about a once-a-month joint service because they don't want to worship together." She gestured around them. "We happened to have grown up in this multiethnic church. Tell me what's exciting about stepping back into the sixties."

"But look what's happened there in just the last year. God switched up the leadership at both churches, bringing Todd and Travis back to pastor. Janelle just moved back and was instrumental in coming up with the joint service. And now you're moving down." Cyd nodded, clearly piecing it together in her mind. "There will always be people who resist change, but it's still exciting when God is at work. Who knows? Maybe this is why you're moving, to play a role in all of this."

"In the church thing?" Stephanie said. "I doubt it. I've never been active in anything churchwise."

"Doesn't mean you won't. You're more of a leader than you know."

Stephanie smirked at her sister. "I still think the whole move is crazy."

Cyd smiled. "Maybe crazy is just what Hope Springs needs."

CHAPTER TWO
Thursday, July 29

Libby took the Hope Springs exit early Thursday morning, her mind loaded with things to do, the first being, "Kick yourself for agreeing to oversee this reunion."

Her dad, Wood, and his twin sister, Estelle, had helmed it for decades. They'd begun planning this one as well, sending out notices to family members of the date and reserving a block of hotel rooms in Rocky Mount. But they lived out of state and had wanted for some time to pass the planning duties to the next generation. And when Libby pulled together a last-minute celebration of Grandma Geri's eighty-seventh birthday last spring, the prodding to take the reins of the annual reunion became unavoidable.

Her dad and Aunt Estelle had promised to stay in the mix, but once Libby got going, her ideas took on a life of their own. Planning was in her blood. And while she loved what those ideas had produced, the reunion as a whole had sucked too much time away from her real job—especially this week. She'd taken the entire week off, going back and forth between her apartment in Raleigh and Hope Springs.

She turned down Grandma Geri's street, catching herself for

still thinking of it that way. But how could she not? That's how she'd thought of it all her life. It would take a long time to get used to walking through the door of the family home and seeing Janelle and Stephanie living there instead of Grandma Geri.

Her foot tapped the brake a little as she approached Travis's place, and the butterflies swirled. They always swirled when she passed his house. She glanced over and saw the door ajar, with only the outer screen in place. Probably about to take his morning jog. Or maybe her cousin Marcus was up and about. To her surprise, the two of them had forged a tight bond after reconnecting at Grandma Geri's party. Marcus had asked Travis to mentor him spiritually, and Travis took it seriously. Next thing Libby knew, Marcus had been hired for a position at Hope Springs High and was staying with Travis until he got his own place.

Just as Libby realized her car had stalled, Travis opened the screen door and walked out, clad in Duke shorts and a T-shirt, arm muscles clearly defined. He looked even better than when they'd dated in college, though she wasn't sure what to think about that. Finding out he'd become a pastor had thrown off her equilibrium where he was concerned—and she hadn't quite gained it back.

"Good morning!" He was smiling. Always that smile. "You were stopping to say hello, right?"

He often chided her for driving past his house to get to her grandmother's and never stopping by. She smiled back "Yeah, that's it. I was stopping to say hello."

He laughed. "Now that you told that lie, you *have* to stop."

She pulled into the driveway behind his SUV and felt her heart hammering as she got out and walked toward him.

"You look nice," he said.

She glanced down at the shorts and shirt she'd thrown on. "I look bummy. This is reunion-prep-plus-help-Stephanie-move-in attire."

"You couldn't look bummy if you tried."

He gave her a hug, and quick as it was, it brought back memories. "You got a minute to come in?" he said.

"Sure." She smiled. "Janelle texted that she's making breakfast, but I'm sure she'll save me some."

"And you're smiling because you know I'm about to call Janelle and tell her to save *me* some. The most breakfast variety we've got here is Wheat Chex and Wheaties."

Libby followed him to the door. "I'm trying to remember the last time I was in your family's house. Had to be high school." Whenever she saw him, it was at Grandma Geri's.

"Those were the days," Travis said. "So many summer memories." He opened the door. "You and Janelle were a bad influence on Todd and me."

Libby needed only to give him a look. "Yeah, that's why Grandma Geri said you two were so bad she couldn't believe you both turned out to be pastors." She stopped short when she walked inside. "You have *got* to be kidding me." She looked at Travis. "You weren't too embarrassed to invite me in? Look at this place."

"What?"

Marcus emerged from the kitchen, a glass of orange juice in hand. "Hey, cuz." He surveyed the scene himself. "Yeah. What?"

She checked out the shirt on the arm of the sofa, the empty potato chip bag and glass on the floor, the carryout carton on the coffee table that had to have been from last night at least. "Y'all are slobs. I don't even want to see the kitchen. Definitely not using the bathroom."

"Aw, that's cold," Travis said. "I thought we were doing a good job keeping it straight."

Libby turned to Marcus. "I know Aunt Gladys taught you better than this. I've never seen a more spotless house than hers."

Marcus's face turned sheepish. "Actually I might've been spoiled, being the baby and the only boy. Between Mom and four older sisters, I escaped cleaning detail."

Libby shook her head, turning back to Travis. "And what's your excuse?"

He spread his hands. "I'm still trying to figure out what the problem is. It might not look exactly like it did when Mom was here, but it's not *that* bad." He donned a mischievous smile. "But your grandmother did say I needed a wife."

"When you find one," Marcus said, "ask her if she has a sister. I'm in my late twenties and wondering where all the good women are."

"Give me a break, little cousin," Libby said. "You've had girls after you from the time you were young, and Aunt Gladys had to tell them to quit calling her house late at night. You're just too picky."

"Oh really?" Marcus gave her a look. "Pot calling the kettle black?"

"I wouldn't say I'm *picky*." She thought a second. "Okay, maybe I am. But key difference—I'm not looking to get married."

"Does Omar know that?" Marcus added suddenly, "Where *is* Omar, anyway? You've been leaving him in Raleigh lately. Is he coming to the reunion?"

"Omar's not coming, no."

She'd brought Omar to a couple of family gatherings last spring, mostly to act as a buffer against her lingering feelings for Travis. But Omar started taking things too seriously. Plus—and she was only lately admitting this to herself—she no longer wanted that buffer.

Marcus swallowed the last of his juice and put the glass on the coffee table, then caught Libby's eye and took it to the kitchen. "Better get to work," he said. "Can't believe the kids'll be starting school in a week and a half."

"How does it feel, working at our parents' alma mater?" Libby called after him.

"In a word, weird." Marcus rejoined them, apparently pondering it. "If it weren't for this man right here, urging me to pray about applying—then urging me to take it—I would've stayed in Greensboro." He sighed. "Every school district has its politics, but small-town politics? *And* we're smack in the middle of this joint service thing?" He shook his head. "It's crazy."

"I know, man," Travis said. "I thought things would settle down over the summer, but it's only gotten worse."

Marcus opened the screen door. "I'll be back early afternoon to help Stephanie and Lindell move in."

"See you then," Libby said, heading to the door herself. She turned to Travis as Marcus left. "You coming too?"

"I'll be there. I can come earlier if you need me. Don't you need help setting things up outdoors?"

Travis had already been a big help in planning the reunion. He'd suggested the basketball game Saturday morning and another tourney on Sunday, and gave assistance whenever she came to town.

"That would be great." She looked at him. "Thank you for all your help with this."

"No need to thank me," he said. "Seems like I've been hanging out at Sanders family reunions all my life. I feel like I *am* a Sanders." He kept his gaze on her. "And if this is the only way I can get you to be nice to me again, I'll take it."

She swatted his arm. "You're saying I'm only being nice so I can get some tables set up?"

"And a basketball player."

She tried to swat him again, but he grabbed her hand and held it.

"It's nice," he said, "being friends again."

The touch of his hand stirred even more butterflies. "It is."

Neither broke the stare, and Libby could almost feel his arms pulling her close. And that kiss that used to drive her crazy. But he dropped her hand and stepped back, reminding her—that was the old Travis. She and "Pastor Travis" could be no more than friends.

He slipped on his shoes.

"Where are you going?" Libby asked.

"With you. Those Wheaties wore off an hour ago."

CHAPTER THREE

Charlotte Willoughby whisked her blond hair into a ponytail and slid her feet into her sneakers, making quick work of the laces . . . then rethought the ponytail, turning to the bedroom mirror. Sighing, she loosened her hair, grabbed a brush, tamed the wisps, and ponytailed it again. Then looked closer at her eyes.

Hmm . . . where was her makeup bag? She found it, laid out a few essentials, just for a light touch, then paused. Why was she doing this? Makeup, to coach a volleyball clinic at the high school? Except . . . she had a meeting before that, for which it wouldn't hurt to look decent. Not that she typically got dolled up for meetings either. But this one was a little . . . different.

She went to the laptop on her desk to reread the e-mail she'd just gotten.

Coach Willoughby,

Do you have a few minutes to meet this morning before your volleyball clinic? If not, no problem. We can schedule a time later today or tomorrow. Thanks.

She stared at his signature—*Marcus Maxwell, Assistant Principal, Hope Springs High School*—and her insides got a little jumpy. Again.

She should've said later today or tomorrow would be better. After all, it was last-minute, and she'd been in the middle of researching a job listing for a ministry in Charlotte when Marcus's e-mail diverted her.

She had an inkling what the meeting might be about; he'd already talked to her before about staying on as a P.E. teacher and assistant coach of girls volleyball. But any mystery surrounding the meeting wasn't the issue. Since he'd joined Hope Springs High at the beginning of June, just being around him made her jumpy.

She stared vaguely at her laptop screen. Was this a *crush?* Is this what it felt like? It'd been so long since she had one, if she ever had. Her only relationship had been with Jake, and they'd known each other practically from the womb—their families talked up a relationship between them as far back as she could remember. And over time it seemed a given that they would marry and live out their lives in Hope Springs, like their parents and their parents' parents. It was the easy thing to do, the expected thing. But when she learned this past spring that he'd cheated on her, ending it was surprisingly easy too. Almost a relief.

Now she was free to follow the stirring she'd been feeling to do life differently. College at UNC–Chapel Hill hadn't been that far away, but it felt like a different world. New church, new friends, new passions, like serving at a women's shelter and raising awareness for human trafficking. She'd been praying for a heart to embrace Hope Springs again, but with the breakup, she no longer had to. She resigned from her job at the high school, made plans to move in with college friends in Charlotte, and was praying God would show her what kind of out-of-the-box life she could lead.

But that was all before Marcus Maxwell came to town . . . Not that it mattered.

Charley logged off, shouldered her athletic bag, and descended the stairs. The front door opened as she hit the bottom step, and Grandpa Skip walked in.

"Mornin', Charley Warley." His gravelly voice made his silly nicknames sound sillier. "How's my best granddaughter?"

Charley smiled. "Best and only."

"Mere technicality." He closed the door. "Headed to the office, but had to stop by with some church news." He looked to his right. "Dottie in the kitchen?"

"I'm sure," Charley said. "When I came down for breakfast, she was baking up a storm for the nursing home."

Her grandfather led the way, pushing the swinging door that opened into the kitchen. Morning wouldn't be morning if he didn't cross the street from his house to theirs to talk news of the day and solve the world's problems, all in the space of a cup of coffee. He'd been a constant in Charley's and her brother's lives, even more so after their dad died six years ago.

Charley's mom removed a delicious-smelling tray from the oven and set it next to two others.

"Let me guess." Skip paused, inhaling. "Apple turnovers, dash of nutmeg, extra shot of cinnamon."

Dottie laughed. "You should know. This was one of Nancy's favorite recipes."

Charley grabbed a banana to go. "I'm headed to school, Mom," she said.

"Charley, wait a sec." Grandpa Skip poured a cup of coffee. "I want you to hear this too."

Charley turned, waiting.

"We had an elders' meeting last night," he said. "Decided to call a boycott of the joint service this Sunday."

"What?" Dottie pulled off her oven mitts. "You can't be serious."

"Dottie, you're not in favor of combining services any more than I am."

Charley leaned against the counter next to her mom. She'd been hearing rumblings about this all summer, mostly from her grandpa, but only with half an interest. She'd mentally checked out of Hope Springs weeks ago.

"I said I wasn't in favor of the *timing* of it," Dottie said. "Todd Dillon was only here a few months when he started this. We needed time to heal from his dad's sudden death, time to get to know Todd as our new pastor. But a boycott? I just don't see it."

"A boycott is how we end this thing." Skip took a seat at the table, blowing steam from his coffee. "The elders didn't attend last month, hoping we'd send a signal. But it got drowned out by all the people who showed up from outside of Hope Springs." He took a sip. "Now we're telling Calvary people outright, don't go."

"And what will Todd think?" Dottie said. "Won't this seem like a conspiracy behind his back?"

"How is it behind his back?" Skip said. "We told him up front we were opposed, and he went full-steam ahead. This Sunday will be the fourth one. It's got to stop."

Charley could feel her brows bunching into a frown. "But why? I don't think I've ever heard your problem with it."

"It's simple, Charley." Her grandfather sat back. "Calvary Church has existed for more than one hundred years as a bedrock of this town. Between your great-grandfather and me, there's been a Calvary elder in this family for more than half a century, and we've worked hard to maintain the church's integrity and position as a pillar in this community." He leaned forward, clearly agitated. "Todd's family has a long history with Calvary as well, and I can only presume he means well. But we didn't bring him on board as pastor to take us down this road—and we won't sit back and watch him do it."

"But . . . you say that like it's the wrong road." Charley rarely challenged her grandfather, but she had to say it. "The goal is to bring the two churches together, to foster unity, right? And it's only one Sunday a month. What could be wrong with that?"

"Charley, you're naïve," Skip said. "Pastor Todd and Pastor Travis grew up best friends in Hope Springs. They've been away for years, and now they're trying to import their big-city ideas into our town. It's clear to me the real goal is to somehow merge the two churches."

Charley almost asked what could be wrong with *that*, but she heard her brother calling from upstairs.

"Hey, Charley, don't leave without me!"

She looked at her mother. "Something wrong with Ben's car?"

"Probably on empty," Dottie said. "I told him I'm not giving him gas money. Still can't believe he got himself fired because he couldn't show up to work on time."

"So now it's my responsibility to shuttle him to football practice?"

Charley hadn't minded playing chauffeur when she started at the high school two years ago. She'd hoped the short drive would help them reconnect now that she was back from college. Instead, time spent in the car—and crossing paths at school—let her know that her once fun-loving kid brother had developed a funky attitude about almost everything. The loss of their father surely played a part and made her sympathize—when she wasn't about to throttle him. And he'd only gotten worse now that he'd turned eighteen, as if it gave him a license to do what he wanted.

"You only have to take me this morning." Ben's six-foot-three, two-hundred-plus pound frame entered the kitchen. "I'll have gas money after that."

Dottie looked at him. "From where?"

Ben got a glass of juice. "Don't worry about it, Mom. You wouldn't give it to me, so I asked someone else."

"Who? Kelsey?" Dottie asked.

He chugged the juice, grabbed a protein bar, and headed for the door, eyeing Charley. "Ready?"

Charley's gaze bounced from Ben to her mom, who was still awaiting an answer.

"Ben." Grandpa Skip stood. "I'm seeing a lot of disrespect from you lately."

Lately?

"Answer your mother's question," Grandpa Skip said.

Charley watched even more intently now. Her grandfather was tall and lean, his stature not very imposing. But he had a penetrating gaze that went well with the gravelly voice. The look alone was all the check she'd needed when she was young.

Ben sighed. "Yeah, it's Kelsey."

"You shouldn't be taking advantage of her like that," Dottie said. "She thinks you're committed to her, and what's going to happen if you break her heart? You know her mother and I are friends."

"Mom. Seriously. Can we not do this right now? I have to go."

Dottie sighed at him. "Fine. But we'll pick it back up later."

"The boycott as well," Grandpa Skip said. "I want my family on board. This is an important juncture in the life of our church."

"Oh, and, Charley, don't forget to call Connor about that date on Saturday."

"Connor Webber?" Grandpa Skip said. "Wonderful. That's a great family. Excellent addition to our town."

Charley sighed to herself. Were they really setting her up again, after Jake?

Ben looked puzzled as he and Charley left the house. "What boycott?"

Charley explained in the car.

Ben nodded easily. "Cool."

"You're just happy to get out of going to church."

"Exactly."

In five minutes they were at school, and Charley saw Kelsey waiting outside the building. Cute girl. Popular. One of their best volleyball players. She had everything going for her except, it seemed, common sense. She seemed to stay at Ben's beck and call.

She met them at the car. "Hey, Coach."

Charley got her athletic bag from the backseat. "Hey, Kels—Ben, really? Right out here in public?"

He had stepped out of the car, pulled Kelsey close, and kissed her.

Ben snickered. "What then? In private?" He tightened his arms around Kelsey. "Fine with me."

Charley cut her eyes at him, starting for the entrance, then glanced back. "Anyone else here, Kelsey?"

"Just Sam," she said. "Of course. Working on that serve."

"And you encouraged her." Charley paused. "Right?"

"Coach, seriously . . ." Kelsey gave her a look. "She can't play."

Charley knew that was the consensus among the girls in the clinic, especially those on the volleyball team. She had spied Sam's interest in volleyball during gym class last spring and encouraged her to take the clinic. But though Sam had worked hard to learn the fundamentals, she wasn't exactly a natural. Charley knew she couldn't micromanage the girls' interactions with one another, but something about Sam—her innocence, sweetness—made Charley want to rise up and defend her.

"I explained what this clinic was about from the beginning," Charley said. "Not just developing skills, but developing—"

"Confidence." Kelsey indulged her with a thin smile.

"The clinic ends tomorrow." Charley started toward the building. "I'm sure it would mean a lot to Sam if you told her how much her serve has improved."

Charley walked into the high school. In the echo of the empty halls, she could hear the faint sound of a ball being hit against the wall. But her thoughts shifted for the moment from volleyball to the administrative offices her feet were moving toward. She opened the outer door and, seeing no one, made her way past the administrative assistant's desk to the office of the assistant principal.

She peeked her head in and saw Marcus on the phone. He waved her in as he nodded at his caller. "Absolutely . . . No problem . . . That's fine . . . Okay, but I've really got to—"

He raised his hands apologetically, and Charley took a seat across from him, letting him know it was fine. Her eyes grazed piles of paper on his desk, looking for a spot to land—but kept flickering past him instead. What *was* it about him? The smile? Seemed his facial muscles naturally formed one, a nice one, as he talked. And the straight teeth definitely enhanced the smile. Was she weird for finding straight teeth attractive?

She checked herself, moving her eyes around the room. He hadn't put anything on the walls yet. No pictures on the desk. The view from his window was the parking lot. So . . . back to the piles of paper . . . *Maybe it's his eyes . . .*

"Really sorry about that." Marcus recradled the phone. "I know you don't have much time. But let me start this off properly." He stood, hand extended. "Good morning, Coach Willoughby."

She stood as well, noting the formality. It was part of the culture at the school to be sure. But having interacted with him at school for almost two months, she found herself wondering what his less formal side was like.

"Good morning, Mr. Maxwell. And no problem." She added as she sat, "But I can probably save some time if you're about to ask me to reconsider and keep my position here."

He had a curious look. "And if I am? What would you say?"

"I'd say, 'Sorry, I'm still leaving.'"

"Okay. Well, that's not my question . . . not exactly." He paused. "I want to know if you'll consider another position here."

Now Charley was curious. "What position?"

"Head volleyball coach."

"What?" She scooted forward. "Coach Nelson is leaving?"

"It happened quickly," Marcus said. "You know her husband's been out of work. He got a great offer from a Dallas company, and turns out Coach Nelson has friends who run a club volleyball team down there that makes it to nationals every year. She's excited to coach for them."

"And so . . . you're asking *me* to take over as head coach? I've only had two years' experience."

"But you played Division I volleyball, you know this program, and you're a natural instructor." Marcus clasped his hands. "You also have a love for the sport, which is huge."

How did he know all that about her?

He smiled. "And in case you're wondering, it's my job to know who's got talent in the building. I've not only heard great things about you, I've watched you work with those girls this summer. The fact that you still wanted to do the clinic after you resigned at the end of the school year tells me you have a love."

Charley sat back, letting out a sigh. "I can't believe this."

"Can't believe what?"

She looked up, realizing she'd said it out loud. "It's nothing. Just . . . hard sometimes, trying to figure out what God wants me to do." Her gaze moved to the pile of papers again as she took all of this in.

"I've had some experience with that myself recently," he said. "Can't say I figured it all out, but I landed here in Hope Springs, so I hope I got that part right." He shrugged a little. "What are you grappling with? That is, if you don't mind sharing."

"I don't mind," Charley said. "In a nutshell, I returned to Hope Springs after college only because of the guy I grew up dating. We got engaged, broke up this spring, and I figured now was my chance to spread my wings and do something different. Might sound weird, but I want to be part of something God is doing. So I decided to give up my teaching job and look for a ministry position, or maybe something missions oriented." She took a breath. "But I haven't found anything. And with this offer, I'm confused again."

Marcus nodded. "Mind if I ask a couple questions?"

"Shoot."

"And we can be real about God and faith and all that?"

Charley smiled. "So . . . you're a believer too?"

He opened a desk drawer and pulled out a thin, leatherbound Bible. "With all my heart."

Her own skipped a little. Maybe *that's* what it was about him. "Cool. And yes, we can be really real."

"Okay then," he said. "I'm assuming you were praying about what God wanted you to do?"

"Definitely."

"And you felt strongly that He wanted you to quit this job?"

Charley thought about that. "I felt strongly that I wanted my life to take a different direction, to be more mindful of my purpose. I want to make a difference, you know?"

"Absolutely," Marcus said. "That's awesome. But what I'm trying to understand is, did God lay the ministry thing on your heart, or did you 'figure'"—he smiled—"that was the best way to make a difference?"

The question struck her.

"And while you're thinking about that," he said, "could there have been a slight thought that it would be easier away from here, after the breakup?" He raised his hands partway, easy smile. "Just food for thought. You don't have to answer."

Charley gave a playful smirk. "Right. Just food for thought."

Marcus was right, of course, about the breakup. She'd spent all those weekends in Charlotte because she hadn't wanted to run into

Jake or his family. But the decision to move was something else. Or was it?

"Sounds like you're saying I should stay." Charley raised a wary brow. "But aren't you a little biased, since you need a coaching spot filled?"

"Nope." Marcus sat back. "Administrative hat is off. I'm talking to you solely as a brother in Christ. And I have no idea whether you should stay or go. I just don't want you to think you have to work for a nonprofit ministry to be part of what God is doing. God is at work everywhere." He gestured toward the door. "He's at work in what you do with those girls, because He's in *you*." The smile returned. "But if you're bent on getting out of Hope Springs, that's another matter."

Marcus's words rang in her ears as she entered the gym—and a volleyball sailed with force straight into the net.

"You've got the power down," Charley yelled. "Just gotta work on getting it over. You can do it."

Sam stood behind the baseline, head full of thick sandy-brown spirals bunched into a ponytail. Her hair, dominating her slight, five-foot-four frame, seemed to make the biggest statement. She nodded with a quick glance at Charley and focused on the ball in hand. Then she bounced it a couple of times, tossed it up a couple of times, and pounded it—into the net.

"That is so *dumb*."

Charley turned around. Three other girls had entered with Kelsey, talking among themselves.

"All that bouncing and tossing won't help you get it over the net," Tia said.

Sam lowered her head slightly. "I see other people doing that."

Tia looked at the others, mumbling, "Yeah, and those other people have skills."

Kelsey caught Charley looking at them and whispered to Tia. They moved on.

More girls arrived, and the chatter rose quickly as the girls talked end-of-summer pool parties and back-to-school shopping trips. Charley looked for Sam, wondering whether she'd found a pocket of conversation to at least listen to.

It took Charley a few seconds to spot her . . . practicing her hitting, alone. And for the first time this summer, she processed the scene differently, wondering if she was already where she belonged.

CHAPTER FOUR

W ho would've thought Ladies' Night Out would mean a Bible study?" Stephanie stepped out of the car in the parking lot of the Main Street Diner, noting the number of cars that had already arrived. "I remember hitting the clubs on Thursday nights."

"After all that driving and helping you move in, the only thing I was ready to hit was the bed," Cyd said. "But I've heard so much about Soul Sisters that I wanted to check it out while I'm here." She wagged her eyebrows at Stephanie. "Plus, I had to see where you used to work."

"Don't remind me." Stephanie walked toward the door. "Craziest couple of weeks of my life."

Janelle was at her side. "I wish Libby had come. Haven't been able to get her here yet."

Stephanie nodded. "Yeah, I tried to sell the whole Ladies' Night Out thing, but she wasn't buying."

Pastor Todd's wife, Becca, had ridden with them. The Dillon

and Sanders families had lived next door to each other for generations, and Todd and Becca had also moved "back" to Hope Springs
from St. Louis only the year before. "I'm trying to get Libby to come
to the joint service on Sunday," Becca said, "and not just because it's
being boycotted. I think she'd like—"

"Wait, what?" Stephanie's head whipped around. "Who's boycotting?"

"From what I understand, it's—"

"Hey, Stephanie's here! Welcome back, girl!"

They all turned to see Trina, Beverly, and Allison, all New
Jerusalem members who had been attending Soul Sisters since the
group's very first meeting.

Stephanie waved big, smiling. "Hey, good to see y'all!" She
hugged each of them. "This is my sister, Cyd."

"I remember," Trina said, hugging her. "We met briefly at your
grandmother's funeral."

"Sure did." Cyd hugged the others. "I remember your faces.
Good to see you again."

The group walked toward the entrance, chatting. The overhead
bell tinkled when Janelle pulled open the door. Stephanie walked in
and saw several new faces and many familiar ones.

"I've missed y'all!" she exclaimed, moving with wide-open arms
from person to person.

She traded a few words with each, then saw Sara Ann. One of
the few people born and raised in Hope Springs who'd never left, Sara
Ann had worked at the diner for many years. She'd been instrumental in getting Stephanie to fill in for those two weeks, and Stephanie
had come to admire her.

"Sara Ann!" Stephanie said. "How've you been?"

"Real good! So glad you're back." She was bubbly as always, ges-
turing around her. "So how do you like us on Thursday night?"

Stephanie took it in, nodding. "I like it a lot. We get the place all to ourselves."

"Yeah, we kinda outgrew Saturday mornings," Sara Ann said. "Since the diner closes at three, this solution was perfect. Lila is more than happy to let us use it."

"Except . . ." Janelle looked forlorn. "Coffee and water aren't the same as pancakes and sausage."

"True, true." Sara Ann smiled. "But my mouth is watering for fried fish tomorrow night. I'm excited about the reunion." She looked at Stephanie. "I always crash it."

"You've probably been to more Sanders family reunions than I have," Stephanie said. "It'll be my first one since high school."

"Wouldn't be the same without you, Sara Ann," Janelle said. She added quickly, "Matter of fact, I'm sure I can find some way for you to be on Team Estelle and boost our points."

"Really, Janelle?" Stephanie's hand flew to her hip. "I know your little team is on life support, but do you really want to go there with open recruiting? Because, as I recall, there's a talent show too." She looked to her left. "And Trina can sing."

Janelle narrowed her eyes at Stephanie.

Sara Ann had begun waving her hands. "Ladies, we can mingle some more at the end, but let's take our seats and get started."

Most of the women had already claimed their seats, purses holding their places. Stephanie, Janelle, Cyd, and Becca headed for an empty table for six just as the bell tinkled again, announcing another comer.

Janelle looked surprised, then popped over to hug the young blond woman and pull her toward their table, where Becca rose to greet her as well.

"Stephanie, Cyd," Janelle said. "This is Charley—"

"Oh my goodness, I *have* that." Stephanie pointed at Charley's red shirt with ALIEN in big letters on the front and I PETER 2:11

in smaller print beneath. "Except mine is black with white digital-looking letters."

"No way, that was the limited edition one," Charley said. "I tried to order it from the website, but it was sold out. You must've jumped on it early."

"Actually, I just . . . took one. Alien—Brian—is my brother-in-law."

"Shut. Up." Charley grabbed her forearm. "He's my absolute favorite Christian rapper. Saw him in Charlotte this May with his wife, heard their beautiful testimony." She paused. "You're serious, they're your fam—"

"Ladies . . ."

They glanced up and saw they were the only ones still standing.

"Uh, sorry, Sara Ann," Stephanie said, and she and Charley quickly sat down.

"You all know we're not big on formalities around here," Sara Ann continued, "but we *are* big on sisterhood"—she grinned—"so like it or not, we ask newcomers to introduce themselves." She turned to Stephanie's table. "And all our newcomers are at the same table, though you're not all new exactly. Tell us your name, where you're from, and how God led you to Soul Sisters. And, Stephanie, since you're already in a talkative mood, why don't you start?"

"Ha. Ha." Stephanie stood, smiling. "I'm Stephanie London, from St. Louis, moved to Hope Springs *today*—"

A round of cheers went up.

"—and I was at the very first Soul Sisters, as a server at the diner." She held up a hand. "Long story. Had to do with spiritual boot camp, God, and Sara Ann twisting my arm, but I survived. Barely." She grinned and sat down.

Cyd stood next. "I'm Stephanie's sister, Cyd, from St. Louis, in town for our family reunion. Steph and my cousin Janelle told me about Soul Sisters from the time it started, so I'm excited to finally come and meet everybody."

Charley stood. "Hey, I'm Charley Willoughby, born and raised in Hope Springs. I came to Soul Sisters back in March and the first part of April. But then . . . well, my fiancé and I broke up, and to be honest, I was kind of embarrassed and wanted to avoid all the questions."

"Girl, you don't need to be embarrassed around us," Beverly said. "I was wondering what happened to you. Even looked for you at the joint services. We've missed you."

Charley smiled. "I missed y'all too. I've been thinking through some things today, and Soul Sisters came to mind. That's what led me to come back."

"Well, I'm feeling good tonight," Sara Ann said. "Stephanie's a new resident of Hope Springs, Cyd's in town, and Charley's back." She scanned the group. "Any announcements or other housekeeping matters before we get started?"

Trina's hand went up. "Beverly mentioned the combined service. We've been praying for it from the beginning, and Pastor Travis and Pastor Todd even said Soul Sisters inspired it. But I'm afraid of what'll happen now that there's this boycott on Sunday."

"Who's boycotting?" another woman asked.

A few voices clamored at once.

Violet, a Calvary member in her seventies, stood, and the women quieted. "Skip Willoughby's the one who started it. Called me today and told me not to go. And I told him a thing or two in response." Ever full of spunk, she sat back down.

Willoughby? Stephanie couldn't help but glance at Charley. Had to be related to her somehow.

"Ladies, ladies!" Sara Ann tried to quell the noise, but so many pockets of conversation had erupted that her voice was barely audible. She walked closer to their table. "Becca? Could you say something? You probably know more than anybody here."

Becca hesitated. "That's why I *didn't* want to say anything, because I might be too close to the situation. But I'll try."

She got up and walked to the center of the tables, and the women grew quiet, probably thinking they were about to get some juicy tidbit.

"Sounds like a lot of you are upset about this." Becca had a calming way about her. "And understandably so. But we shouldn't be surprised. There was opposition from the beginning. The boycott is just the latest thing." She sighed. "Todd and Travis have suffered a lot of blowback from people in both churches. We know the real struggle is not flesh and blood, so let's keep praying. Todd is convinced that our prayers are the reason that more and more people are coming to the services from outside of Hope Springs. Boycott or no, let's pray for a packed house on Sunday."

"Amen!" rang out in the room as Becca took her seat.

"Thanks, Becca," Sara Ann said. "Sounds like we'll be doing a lot more praying than mingling at the end." Her eyes took a mischievous turn. "But right now, I'm wondering if everybody's ready to spend the next week focused on hospitality."

A couple of women groaned. "That's just not me," one said.

Sara Ann laughed. "Isn't that the whole point? To be like . . ." She cupped her ear.

"Him!" the women shouted.

Stephanie's brow creased. "What's that about?"

Janelle leaned over. "Our latest study—'Like Him.' Every week we focus on a different attribute of Jesus or a godly character trait."

"I'm just saying," the first woman insisted, "whenever I think about having people over, I get hung up on the food. I'm not good at cooking for people. By the time I go round and round with it, I just say forget it."

"Well, Soul Sisters to the rescue!" Sara Ann said. "Seriously, I need a lot of work in this area myself, but that's why we're doing this. Let's see what the Bible says about hospitality and look at some examples from Sarah to Martha." She turned to the table beside Stephanie's. "Then we've got a special treat. Trina's gonna come up and give us some tips." She smiled. "And if she did like I told her, she brought some recipes to share with us too."

Trina smiled, nodding. "Yes, ma'am, I did."

"The one for the lemon bars you made that time too?"

"You know it."

"Awesome!" Sara Ann pumped her fist, then picked up her Bible from the table. "Okay, y'all, turn to Romans 12 . . ."

⌒◦⌒

Stephanie had thought about it all during the time of closing prayer. When it ended, she turned to Charley. "We've given you another reason to stay away from Soul Sisters, haven't we?"

Charley looked surprised. "Because of talk about the joint service?"

"And your grandfather," Janelle said. "When somebody prayed for God to touch his heart, I thought, *I wouldn't blame Charley for taking this personally. She might never come back.*"

Charley shook her head. "I don't agree with what my grandpa's doing either, although I think that *he* thinks he's looking out for the best interests of Calvary." She looked around. "I'm glad I'm here. I didn't realize the service had been getting resistance on all sides, or all the praying you guys have been doing. I feel like I've been in a fog."

"You were, in a way," Janelle said. "You were engaged and thought you had a vision for your life. It takes awhile to see your way clearly to what's next after a sudden change."

"And you would know," Charley said. "You dealt with a lot worse, with your husband dying."

"Well . . . let's just say I understand," Janelle said. "How are you doing now, with the breakup and all?"

"Fine as far as the breakup," Charley said. "But still figuring out the 'what's next.' I've been planning a move to Charlotte."

"Sounded like I heard a *but* in there," Stephanie said.

Charley sighed. "You did. I'm a P.E. teacher and left my job at the high school this spring. But just this morning Mr. Maxwell, my assistant principal, offered me the head volleyball coach position, which is what I wanted. At least it was before I decided to leave."

"Mr. Maxwell . . . Marcus?" Stephanie asked. "He's our cousin."

Charley looked incredulous. "Okay, who *aren't* you related to?"

"Why did you leave your job?" Janelle asked.

"After the breakup, I wanted to do something different. Something God-sized. Leaving town seemed like the logical first step."

"That's funny," Stephanie said, "since I was feeling the same thing this spring and felt God leading me *here* to do something God-sized."

Charley seemed to take that in. "That's weird. Mr. Maxwell—Marcus"—she smiled—"basically said the same thing. Who would've thought God could be doing something here in Hope Springs?"

Janelle smiled. "I've actually been thinking about that very thing for a while—what God might be doing here. Seemed to start when Todd and Travis moved back and took over at Calvary and New Jerusalem. Next thing you know, a combined service is up and running. Then I relocate here, then Marcus, now Stephanie." She paused, taking it in. "*Something* weird is going on."

"Hmph." Stephanie glanced around the room. "All I know is, I'm looking at all these women in their thirties—Janelle, Becca, Sara Ann, Trina." She turned back to Charley. "How is it fair for God to move you out of town? I need another twentysomething around here. Plus, we rock the same music and the same shirt? Nope, you can't go."

Charley laughed. "This is so crazy. I literally have no idea what God wants me to do."

"Yeah, well, join the club," Stephanie said. "I'm here, but I don't know what He wants me to do here. I guess that makes the two of us doubly Soul Sisters or something."

"Which is kind of cool," Charley said. "Being clueless together."

Stephanie laughed with her. "Well, before God whisks you away, we should hang out. Our family reunion starts tomorrow night with a fish fry. You should come over." She snapped her finger. "You'd be helping me fulfill the hospitality charge too."

"Great idea," Janelle said. She put an arm around Charley. "And here's the deal. I'm inviting you to be on my team, Team Estelle—"

"Oh no you don't." Stephanie moved Janelle out of the way. "You would actually be more suited to Team Bruce."

Charley smiled. "What's the team thing?"

"The teams are named after our parents," Janelle said, "but we're just having fun with you. Not about coming, though—we'd love to have you."

Charley didn't hesitate. "That's actually something I'm not clueless about. I'd love to hang out with you all."

CHAPTER FIVE
Friday, July 30

S amara Johnston let herself into the house at five thirty, wondering if her mom would be home anytime soon. She'd spent much of her day at the school gym, thankful for the extra instruction Coach Willoughby had given her, even after the volleyball clinic had officially ended. Sam would miss that part— the coach's care and attention—but she wouldn't miss the other girls making fun behind her back. It was easier to stay to herself than to hang on the periphery, seemingly invisible. Not that it was anything new. Her sophomore year would start in a little over a week. There'd be more of the same.

Felt good in a way just to admit it. No false hopes. No rosy imaginings. In years past she'd told herself she'd find a good friend. She'd even pushed herself to make a friend, to speak in the halls, sit with different girls at lunch. But somehow, surrounded by laughter and camaraderie, she only felt isolated and heartbroken.

She'd never fit in. Would never have the latest styles in anything. She wasn't into dating or pop music or social media. And it didn't help that she looked different—her slight frame made her look more like a middle schooler, and her features were a hodge-podge. She couldn't count the number of times she'd been asked, "Are you black or white?" Was there a right answer? Would they like her if she were one or the other?

"Both," she'd say, and whoever was asking usually shrugged and moved on.

There was no doubt this year would be like all the others. The question was how long she could take it.

She opened her backpack and dumped the books she'd gotten from the library onto the coffee table—and heard her stomach rumbling. She headed to the kitchen, first taking her cell phone from her bag. Should she call her mother? Her prepaid phone had precious few minutes, but she wondered if her mom was bringing carryout. Or maybe she'd gone grocery shopping this afternoon. Sam had asked her to buy some fruit and vegetables, and chicken and fish, like Coach Willoughby recommended.

Her steps quickened to the refrigerator, but she sighed when she opened it. Same limited options as this morning. She dialed her mom but got no answer. So she boiled two hot dogs, sandwiched them with white bread, and ate on the sofa, burying herself in one of her new library books—Jane Austen's *Emma*.

A car door slammed suddenly, startling Sam, and she realized she'd fallen asleep. She jumped up and looked out the front window, hoping, and her heart fell. Hank, her mother's boyfriend, was with her. Couldn't she and her mom have a weekend together alone? She grabbed her book and dashed into her room, shutting the door. Moments later the TV and radio were blaring. How could they possibly listen to both?

Her door flew open, and her mother stood in the doorway. Petite like Sam, Teri was only in her early thirties. But with her long, straight dirty-blond hair, tired eyes, and drawn cheeks, she looked years older. "Sam, did you eat all the hot dogs?"

Sam looked up from her bed, propped up on an elbow. "Yes, but there were only two left."

"I told Hank I'd get him one, and they're gone."

Her mom blew smoke from a cigarette, clearly agitated. She always smoked more when she was nervous, and she smoked a lot when Hank was around.

Sam stared. "I'm sorry, Mom. I didn't know what else to eat, and I was hungry after volleyball and—"

"Why didn't you eat the fish sticks? I bought *those* for you."

"Mom, I don't even like fish sticks. I really wanted fresh fish or chicken or—"

"Sam, life is not about getting what you want all the time."

"Teri!" Hank called from the living room. "Where's the hot dog? It doesn't take that long, does it? And don't forget the mustard and relish."

Her mom sighed. "Now I've got to run to the store."

Sam wanted to ask her to bring back apples or bananas, but she stayed silent as her mom pulled the door shut.

She opened her book and found her page, trying her best to block out the noise . . . and let a tear slide onto her pillow.

CHAPTER SIX

Checkered tablecloths and scented candles adorned the picnic tables where the earliest arrivals were already chatting. Music streamed through an iPod connected to speakers that carried sound throughout the backyard. The welcome station—a new feature—was outfitted with a banner across the front that read "Welcome to the Sanders Family Reunion!" And the fried fish was already sizzling in a huge outdoor fryer, the delicious aroma permeating the evening air. The family's annual gathering had begun—minus one.

It hit Libby as she took it all in on her Grandma Geri's back porch—for the first time, her grandmother wouldn't be here. And she'd always been more than *here*, she'd been central. She and Grandpa Elwood Sanders had started this reunion almost forty years ago. They'd told the story a million times, how it started one year as a tribute to Grandpa Elwood's parents. Grandpa Elwood and his siblings surprised them by showing up with all of their kids and grandkids. They lamented that they'd never done it before, and Grandpa Elwood decided they wouldn't let a year go by without getting together. He and Grandma Geri oversaw the planning until they grew older and passed it down. But Grandma Geri remained a central figure, the one who knew every family member who showed up, no matter how distant the relation or how infrequently they came. The void would be palpable.

The screen door opened behind her, and Stephanie poked her head out. "You're wanted in the lab."

"I was just on my way in there," Libby said.

Ever since their parents had arrived in town—Libby's, Stephanie and Cyd's, and Janelle's—the moms, along with Aunt Gladys, had taken over the kitchen, as usual. The girls had taken to calling it "the lab" because these women were serious when it came to cooking up some food.

Stephanie opened the door wider, and she and Libby headed through a living area and around the corner to the kitchen. The aroma indoors was as enticing as the one outside. The women had been baking cakes and cobblers, and had also made several side dishes—boiled potatoes, green beans, potato salad, coleslaw, and rolls. As much planning as Libby had done, she'd be nowhere if she couldn't count on the love of cooking in her parents' generation.

Libby's mom, Denise, saw her walk in. "Sweetheart, you need to get going with the hush puppies." She was stirring the coleslaw. "You sure you don't want me to do it? It'll only take a few minutes."

Libby folded her arms. "I'm noticing there's been more than one offer to take this to-do item off my hands. Y'all think they won't turn out right, don't you?"

"I'm a little nervous," her mom said unapologetically. "You rarely cook, and I don't think you've fried anything a day in your life. I don't know why you're attempting to tackle this for such a large crowd."

She *wouldn't* be tackling it if it weren't for Travis. He'd made an offhanded remark that they'd never had hush puppies at the Friday night fish fry, and Libby immediately knew they would be a hit. She'd planned to ask her parents who could do it, the women or perhaps the men, since they could fry them outside while they fried the fish. But Travis had a third option—the two of them. It would be easy enough, he said, though he'd never done it. And it would be fun. Reminded her of the time they tried to fix lasagna while dating and never got further than the noodles that burned. The laughter was almost worth the awful smell.

"It'll turn out great, you'll see," Libby said, half convincing herself.

"When do you plan to mix the ingredients?" Aunt Gladys said. "Everything else is about done."

"We already did it, in Travis's kitchen, since the lab was taken." She made a face. "Had to make Travis and Marcus clean it first, though. Aunt Gladys, have you seen that pigsty they're living in? I told Marcus I know you taught him better than that. And Travis ought to be ashamed of him— What?"

Aunt Gladys looked amused, her eyes darting beyond Libby.

She turned. Travis had eased into the kitchen with the pans of mix they'd made, already shaped into puppies.

"So you're doggin' me behind my back, huh?"

Libby laughed. "No, I'm not. I told you to your face that place was a mess."

"I'll come over and clean it top to bottom for you and Marcus," Aunt Gladys said.

"Aunt Gladys!" Libby's look chastised her aunt. "That's their problem, people bailing out the poor bachelors. They need to learn how to clean for themselves."

Travis nodded at the pans in his arms. "You want to keep lecturing or get these puppies going?"

Libby smiled. "Let's head out."

"Holler if you need us," her mom said.

"We'll be just fine," Libby called back.

They went to an area of the backyard in which her dad and Travis had set up a small outdoor fryer earlier, a few feet away from the humongous fryer being used for the fish.

"Hey, look," Libby said, "Dad's got us ready to roll. Oil's piping hot."

Travis set the pans on a card table and picked up a bag that was sitting on the grass.

"Where'd that come from?" Libby asked.

"I put it over here before I went in the house," he said.

Travis lifted something out of the bag. Libby wasn't sure what it was until he slipped one part over his head and proceeded to tie the back. Then her eyes widened.

"You bought a grilling apron?" Libby bit her lip. "You're serious, huh?"

"You think it's funny?"

She gave her head an emphatic shake. "Nope."

"Because if you start clowning me . . ."

"Never."

"Good. Because you've got one too." He took hers out of the bag. "Turn around." Travis placed it over her head and tied the back. "Now we're official."

Libby looked at him. "You didn't have to do this, you know. Not just the aprons. Everything."

"I said I would help you this weekend, and that's exactly what I intend to do. Anyway, it's partly selfish. My mouth is already watering for these hush puppies."

Janelle was walking by as he said it. "As long as you don't get near the fish, we're good."

Travis picked up the tongs and aimed them at her. "Don't start, Janelle. You should be encouraging my budding skills."

"Whether they're budding is yet to be seen." She came closer, surveying their operation. "And actually, I'm wondering who sanctioned this idea of you and Libby cooking anything in mass amounts for actual people. It's kind of scary."

"Everybody's a naysayer." Libby wagged her finger at her cousin. "You just wait. You'll be fighting for seconds."

"Mm-hm." Janelle gave them a pointed look. "I'll give you this. You look cute in the matching aprons."

"You know it. Team Wood!" Travis bellowed.

Libby's dad heard and looked over. "That's right!" He pumped a fist. "Team Wood!"

Travis flexed his arms like he was entering a boxing ring, tongs still in hand.

Libby laughed, taking in the moment. It was all in fun, but they hadn't had this much fun in more than a decade. Much as she tried not to, her mind drifted to thoughts of whether the two of them could ever one day really be a team . . .

"People are arriving in droves now," he said.

"Yeah, we'd better get moving. The good thing is it won't take long."

Travis took the aluminum foil off of the first pan. "I think we're good to go."

Libby was suddenly apprehensive. "Did you pray?"

"Pray?"

"Over the hush puppies, that they'd turn out delicious—and wouldn't give anyone food poisoning."

Travis chuckled. "All right. Team Wood'll huddle up." He put an arm around her, and they bowed their heads. "Lord, you know the two of us can't cook . . ."

Libby smiled at the way he talked to God.

". . . but this task seemed easy enough even for us. I pray it turns out well, doesn't make anybody sick . . . And thank You for the friendship Libby and I are building again after all these years. Amen."

Her stomach got butterflies. "Amen."

"Ready or not," Travis said, lifting the tongs again.

He placed several hush puppies into the stainless steel basket, then lowered it into the oil to the tune of loud sizzles and crackling.

They saw Todd approaching from his yard to theirs, which were one for purposes of reunion activities.

"Hey, Libby," he said, "just got off the phone with Keisha. She's definitely not coming."

Libby sighed. "I know. I talked to her too. Thought I could persuade her when she vacillated a little, maybe at least come for Sunday. But she decided it would be too much." She added, "Of course Aunt Gwynn was a no from the beginning."

Aunt Gwynn, the youngest of Grandma Geri's children, had only returned to Hope Springs once since leaving as a teen, pregnant with Keisha, three decades ago. The families had learned only this year that Keisha's father was Jim Dillon, Todd's dad. Because they were an interracial couple, their parents pressured them to break up. And Aunt Gwynn had never forgiven Grandma Geri.

Todd looked disappointed. "I didn't get to spend much time with Keisha or her husband and son at Grandma Geri's funeral. I was hoping for that this weekend."

"Libby Lou!"

Todd moved on as Libby turned to see who was calling her. "Hey, Aunt Louise, you just get in?"

"Got here this afternoon," her great-aunt said. "Took a nap at the hotel, now here I am."

Travis hugged her. "Aunt Louise, you're looking well." He bent a little, looking at the boy beside her. "I know that's not Jamar. You've gotten so big. How you doing, young man?"

Jamar, who couldn't be more than four, scooted behind his grandmother.

Aunt Louise prodded him. "Boy, stop being so shy and speak up. These are your relatives."

Libby was sure Travis had been to so many reunions that some thought he was somehow related.

Aunt Louise eyed Travis. "I hear you're pastoring New Jerusalem now. You married yet?"

"No, ma'am."

"You know you need a first lady, don't you? Handsome man such as yourself . . . What's the problem?"

"Um . . . no problem. Just hasn't happened yet." He smiled. "I'm praying about it, though."

"Good, good!" She turned to Libby. "And what about you, Miss Libby Lou? You any closer to walking down the aisle?"

"I don't plan to get married," she said, her standard answer.

Aunt Louise waved her away. "Chile, you just wait. All it takes is one man to knock you off your feet."

Libby offered a thin smile and breathed a sigh of relief as other relatives came to greet Aunt Louise. Happily returning to the hush puppies, she lifted the basket from the oil.

"Travis, look. They look good, don't they? Deep golden brown." She scooped them with a slotted spoon into a pan lined with paper towels.

"I hope they taste as good as they look," he said.

Jamar was checking them out. "Can I try one?"

"Oh, so you *do* talk?" Libby smiled. "Tell you what. You give me a hug, and I'll give you one. You can be our first customer."

He wrapped his arms around her tight, and Libby laughed. She put three on a paper towel. "Let 'em cool off before you eat them, okay?"

"Okay. Thank you."

"You're welcome."

Libby put more into the basket, thinking about what Travis

had said. She glanced at him. "Are you really praying for a wife, Mr. I'm-Not-Ready-to-Commit?"

Travis looked at her. "Libby, that was a long time ago, in college."

"You didn't answer my question."

He shrugged lightly. "Sure. That's something I pray about." He paused. "Are you really planning *not* to get married?"

"Yep."

"You're just saying that."

"Oh, you can read my mind now?"

"Don't have to read your mind. I know you." He lowered the hush puppies into the oil. "Deep down, you have a very real desire for a committed relationship."

"That was a long time ago, in college."

Travis stared at her, and she knew they were both remembering that long-ago time.

"Libby . . . sometimes I wish we could—"

"These are good!" Jamar had returned, looking as if he wanted more.

"Can I get some?" his older brother said.

Aunt Louise was with them. "I tasted one of Jamar's," she said. "It was delicious. Are they ready to serve?"

"Really? You liked it?" Libby grinned. "Actually, we have to take them to the buffet table and everything will be served from there." She nodded toward the tented area.

"That's not gonna work."

Libby turned to see that Marcus had joined them—and was eating a hush puppy he'd apparently swiped.

"The line will be long," Marcus continued, "and when people find out how good these are, they'll go fast." He licked his fingers. "If you keep it over here, I can have as many as I want."

Travis laughed. "Spoken like a true hungry bachelor."

Marcus reached for another one, and Libby swatted his hand.

"I have to remain firm." Libby spoke as if it were a somber occasion. "As much as I love you all, I must guard the interests of the family as a whole. I'm sorry, but you'll have to fend for yourself at the buffet table. I wish you the best."

Marcus nodded slowly in defeat and stepped away, then darted back and stole another one.

"Boy!" Libby tried to swat him again, but he ran, hush puppy in hand.

She turned to Travis. "Can you believe it? We actually cooked something edible—and good!"

"Didn't I tell you? We're the team to beat!"

He high-fived her. And Libby's heart skipped when their hands clasped and came down together.

CHAPTER SEVEN

Charley guided her car into a makeshift parking lot on the gravel outside the Sanders' family home and let the motor run. She'd gone back and forth about whether to come. Seemed a fun idea when Stephanie and Janelle asked. She didn't know them well, but they were easy to like. Easy to connect with. Sort of like their cousin. And that's what was giving her pause.

She'd finally admitted it to herself—she had a crush on Marcus Maxwell. She couldn't stop thinking about their meeting yesterday, how their conversation flowed naturally to God and faith. She'd never had that with Jake. He'd been faithful about church on Sunday, but in the day-to-day, spiritual depth was lacking . . . which was fine until her walk with God deepened in college. From there the spiritual chasm between them increased, even as they planned their wedding—all the way to the breakup.

She'd vowed afterward to make faith "the main thing" when it came to guys. And Marcus had looks, personality, *and* that main thing. But so what? That's what she kept saying to herself. What difference did it make? It wasn't like he'd ever know she liked him. She wasn't the type to show it. And he seemed content to keep a professional wall between them. When they passed in the halls this morning, he was cordial as ever, but she was still Coach Willoughby. And his only other comment—while looking back, walking—referenced an administrative matter.

Another car pulled up beside her, and a family got out. Charley looked toward the house. The thought of seeing Marcus—especially a more personal side of him—was intriguing. But why encourage a silly infatuation? Either she'd be leaving town, so it wouldn't matter, or she'd be staying and it wouldn't matter, given the professional boundaries between them.

Or she wasn't his type, so none of it mattered.

Ugh. Charley, really? She shook her head, clearing her thoughts. She was being silly, all right, letting her mind dwell on this. She finally cut the engine and hopped out. Enjoy her time with Stephanie and Janelle—that's what she would do. And as she followed the sounds of music, laughter, and kids, she got excited about just that.

She entered the backyard, one that stretched a long ways left to right, and saw a lively atmosphere and people everywhere—at picnic tables, mingling, some dancing.

"Charley! Hey!" Janelle was waving from a welcome table.

Charley waved back as she walked over. "This is amazing." She hugged her. "I've never been to a family gathering like this."

Janelle smiled. "I'm told it's unique, but it's all I've known my entire life." She turned to the guy beside her. "Kory, this is Charley, one of my Soul Sisters. Charley, this is Kory . . ." She searched for words, then turned her puzzled look up at him. "How do I describe you? 'Boyfriend' sounds funny to me, at our age."

Kory chuckled. "First, nice to meet you, Charley." He shook her hand. "The problem is Janelle can't bring herself to say I'm the guy who met her at one of these reunions at eighteen, fell in love with her, and then was ignored and forgotten when we went off to college. But a decade and a half later, here we are. She finally agreed to date me."

"Are you serious?" Charley said. "That's how you met?"

"And that's about the only part of his story that's accurate," Janelle said.

Kory draped an arm around her. "So we're *not* dating?"

"Okay, I guess that part is true too."

"You *guess* it's true?"

Charley folded her arms, smiling at them. "You two are too cute."

Janelle put her arm around his waist, eyeing Charley. "I'll fill you in on the real details of how Kory ignored *me* after I went off to —"

"Coach Willoughby?"

Charley turned, her stomach doing a little flip. Marcus looked handsome even in casual shorts and an athletic tee.

"Hey, didn't know you'd be here," he said.

Handshake. Ever the professional.

"Hey, Mr. Maxwell." Charley tucked her hair behind an ear. "I didn't either, till last night. Janelle and Stephanie invited me."

Janelle folded her arms. "I get 'Coach' and 'Mr.' in the school building," she said. "But really? Y'all can't be Marcus and Charley on a Friday night?"

Marcus gave his cousin a sheepish smile. "A little formal?"

"You think?"

Another family walked into the backyard and headed for the welcome table.

"Marcus," Janelle said, "could you show Charley to the food and drinks and all that good stuff? Not sure where Steph is. I should only be a minute, until somebody takes our place."

Charley did a quick glance at the nearby crowd to see if she could spot Stephanie herself. Time with Marcus was exactly what she didn't need.

"Sure," he was saying, already leading the way. "So . . . *Charley* . . . it'll take a minute to get used to that." He smiled. "Didn't recognize you at first with the whole no-ponytail-or-sneakers look."

She glanced down at her skirt and sandals. "Well, I do clean up once in a while."

"Ha. Guess in my case, I went backward." He glanced at her. "How long have you known my cousins?"

"Not long. Met Janelle in the spring at Soul Sisters; just met Stephanie yesterday." She added, "But I'm looking forward to getting to know them better."

He nodded. "Which means you'd have to be near them, here in Hope Springs, which, in order for that to work, means you'd have to take the head coach position."

"Hmm . . . that wasn't Mr. Maxwell right there, was it? On a Friday night?"

"Uh, no. Not at all." He cleared his throat. "Just . . . okay, yeah, that was Mr. Maxwell." He laughed. "Promise. Marcus only, rest of the night." He paused. "But wait, I'm your brother in Christ too, right? I thought we had a vibe going yesterday, trying to figure out what God was doing in your life."

"Good save," she said. "We'll file that comment under brotherly advice."

They wove through pockets of conversation, Marcus patting people on the back or giving a nod, and stopped inside a tent area with long buffet tables filled with food. He passed her a sturdy plastic plate.

Charley held up a hand, smiling apologetically. "I should've told Janelle I'm not that hungry. I had dinner at home earlier."

"Oh. Janelle didn't warn you? You *have* to eat when you attend a Sanders reunion. It's, like, a law. Those who don't mysteriously disappear, never to be seen again."

Someone walked a pan of fresh fried fish by them. Charley followed it with her eyes to the buffet table.

"That smells really good," she said.

"I'm sayin'." He extended his hands like it was a no-brainer. "You can enjoy good food *and* keep your life. Win-win."

"All right, I'm sold," she said. "But I think I'll wait for Janelle or Stephanie."

Marcus took a glance around. "I don't know where Janelle went, and I still don't see Steph." He shrugged. "I'm a lame substitute, but I can join you."

"Did you eat already?" she said.

"I did, but I'm willing to get seconds just to be gracious."

She took the plate from him. "I've got to at least try that fish."

Marcus nodded. "That's the Sanders spirit." He got a plate himself and proceeded to pile it on.

"Wow. I thought you were just being gracious."

"Oh, I don't play." He scooped some butter beans and plopped them next to the potatoes and two pieces of fish. "I'll pack on a couple of pounds for the sake of being gracious."

She shook her head at him, following him to the second buffet as he added dessert. They stopped at the beverage station and got bottled water, then walked toward a picnic table that had space. Marcus introduced her to the others at the table—great-aunts and uncles—and they settled on the end.

Charley pinched off a piece of fish and tasted it. "Mmm, I love whiting. This is really good."

"I'm impressed," Marcus said. "I couldn't have told you what it was." He lifted a forkful himself. "So I know Coach Willoughby's résumé. But tell me about Charley. You grow up playing volleyball?"

She wiped her mouth with a napkin. "Started in middle school, played club through high school, then went on to college." She took a sip of water. "What about you? Did you play a sport?"

"Basketball. Point guard."

"In college?"

He nodded. "UNC-Greensboro." Smiling a little, he added,

"We've got a game tomorrow morning at the high school. Looking forward to hurtin' the older dudes in the family, but hoping the younger ones don't hurt me."

Charley laughed. "Sounds like fun. So you grew up in Greensboro?"

"Raleigh. But I was in Hope Springs a lot, right here at my grandmother's house. My mother grew up in this house."

"Janelle said she and Stephanie are the third generation to live here. That's pretty cool."

"Charley!" Stephanie walked up and took a spot next to her on the bench. "Sorry. Janelle came to get me, and I was in the middle of cheer practice."

"Cheer practice?" Charley asked.

Marcus gave Stephanie a look, then turned to Charley. "She's a traitor, cheering for the Over 30 team tomorrow morning."

"Excuse me," Stephanie said. "I might be in my twenties, but my husband is on that team, so that's where my loyalty lies." She hit Charley's arm. "Hey, you should join us. It's a ragtag group of cheerleaders, so it promises to be a riot."

"Hold it," Marcus said. "I know you're not talking about Charley cheering for the Over 30s. We need some Under 30 cheer support." He looked at Charley. "You got our backs, right?"

"I'd definitely have to go with my Under 30 peeps." She laughed. "But I've never cheered a day in my life . . . so enthusiastic hand claps will have to do. Actually, I was planning to go to the school tomorrow anyway, to start moving my things out of the gym office."

Marcus eyed her. "But you haven't made a final decision yet . . . have you?"

"It was final all summer," Charley said, "until you threw in that monkey wrench yesterday."

"He's throwing monkey wrenches into everybody's life," Stephanie said. "Approached me earlier today about subbing."

Charley's eyes got big. "Wow, really? I did hear there was a shortage of teachers."

"That's what Marcus said." Stephanie folded her arms. "And I said no. I don't do little kids if I can help it. Definitely don't do smart-alecky teens."

"You told me you would pray about it," Marcus said.

"Mm-hm. And no is still real strong in my spirit."

Charley laughed, almost spitting out the water she'd just swigged. "That's the answer I should've given him." She fist-bumped Stephanie.

"Oh, y'all are ganging up on me?" Marcus said. "I'm not worried because I know how to pray too—and I'm praying for both of you." He nodded like he had some inside track. "Don't be surprised when I'm fist-bumping y'all in the hallway on the first day of school."

"Don't be praying for me," Stephanie said. "Totally out of bounds and uncalled for. I don't need you trying to shake my inner resolve."

Marcus laughed and countered with a quick reply, but Charley barely heard—because she'd heard something else. That he was a praying man. And the thought that he might've prayed for *her* . . .

The plan wasn't working. Everything about this night was fueling her crush on him.

CHAPTER EIGHT
Saturday, July 31

Stephanie stood on the sidelines during a timeout, rallying cheers for the Over 30 team. "Forty-two seconds to go, and we're four points down. We've gotta pump up our guys! Let's do the last cheer I taught you."

Cyd gave her the same look she'd been giving the whole game. "I'm not doing another cheer. It's silly. Can't we just clap and shout 'Woo'?"

Stephanie eyed her sister. "You are so pitiful. Cedric's working himself to the bone, oldest one out there, and all you can give him is a sad ol' 'Woo.'" She shook a pompom at her. "Put some oomph into it, girl! Cheer on your man!" She shook her poms outward. "Go, Lindell! I see you, babe! You can do it!"

"Where'd you get those pompoms, anyway?" Cyd said. "I'm gonna burn those things."

Janelle laughed, shaking hers. "They're fun! We found them at the party store yesterday." She looked down at the three five-year-olds beside her—her daughter, Tiffany; Kory's daughter, Dee; and Todd and Becca's daughter, Claire. "Shake 'em, girls!"

The three shook their pompoms and shouted, always eager for fun.

"See," Stephanie said, "Some people don't have to be told twice."

"How about Libby?" Janelle said. "I see her poms going extra hard when Travis has the ball."

"So I saw," Stephanie said. "Heard her cheering extra loud for him too."

"Y'all are funny," Libby said. "It's not about Travis. It's about the Over 30s and Team Wood. And since we're counting points scored, I'm noting that Travis has the most points on the Over 30 team."

"True. But don't get excited." Stephanie glanced over to where the "older" guys were huddled up. "We've got Cedric *and* Lindell on our team, and their combined points give Team Bruce the win this morning."

"Uh, not exactly." Charley stood alongside them, pointing to the Under 30 team. "Marcus scored more than their combined points. Team Gladys won this round."

Stephanie gave her a look. "Yeah, with you cheering like a mad woman the whole time. I'm about to take back those pompoms I gave you. Sure didn't take you long to get into it."

"I know, it's fun! I was dead tired when I got here, but the game woke me up."

"Girl, you and me both. We were up another couple hours after you left at two!"

A whistle blew, the guys broke from their huddle, and Stephanie snapped back to cheer mode.

"Come on, y'all! Let's cheer our guys to victory!" She threw down her poms and started clapping, chanting, "Swish it, sink it, send it on in! Over 30s are here and ready to win!"

Family members stood in the bleachers, stomping as Stephanie repeated it two more times. About twenty to thirty of them had shown up; the Over 30s had the numbers advantage since the younger crowd liked to sleep in.

They all watched intently as Cedric inbounded the ball and passed it to Travis. Travis dribbled downcourt and passed to Kory. Kory took a shot, and it skidded around the rim and bounced back out.

"Awww!" sounded from Stephanie's cheer team, then, "Yesss!" when Kory rebounded.

"Dribble it!" Stephanie called to the cheerleaders. "Dribble it, pass it, we want a basket! Dribble, dribble, pass, pass, shoot, and score!" they yelled.

"D-E-F-E-N-S-E!" Charley yelled. "De-fense! De-fense!"

Marcus wouldn't let Kory get another shot, so he passed the ball out to Cedric, who took a chance on a three-point shot—and made it.

"Woooooo!" Cyd was jumping up and down. "Go, Ced, go! Go, Ced, go!"

"Oh, *now* you got some oomph in that 'Woo.'" Stephanie high-fived her sister. "Can't blame you. That was awesome! Team Bruce! Over 30s!"

One point down and twenty-seven seconds left, the Under 30s got ready to inbound the ball—then Marcus suddenly called a time-out.

"Why'd he do that?" Stephanie asked.

"He must've seen some defensive move he wanted to counter," Charley said.

Stephanie noticed more and more people, non–family members, coming into the gym and standing off to the side. She turned to Janelle. "Is something happening after this?"

Janelle looked toward the gym entrance. "Volunteers from New Jerusalem and Calvary come at ten to set up for the service tomorrow."

Marcus jogged over when the Under 30s huddle broke. Charley

handed him a hand towel and a water bottle. He wiped his face, took a swig, and exchanged a few words. Stephanie watched him jog back.

She looked at Charley. "This little refreshment stand you've got going . . . I'm noticing the only member of your team who's benefiting is Marcus."

"Well." Charley blushed. "Remember he asked if I would have his back? As I was leaving the house this morning, it hit me that I could offer more than cheer support. It was nothing to grab a towel and a couple bottles of water."

"Uh-huh." Stephanie eyed her. "I'm sure it was nothing."

Janelle was waving across the gym. "There's Trina. She must be on the setup committee."

Trina spotted the arm-waving and headed over. "Hey, y'all!" She doled out hugs. "How's reunion weekend? Are y'all having a blast?" She got to Charley. "Hey, you hanging out with the Sanders family?"

Janelle answered for her. "We had a great time last night," she said, "and tonight is our family dinner and talent show at a hotel in Rocky Mount, and there's a party afterward. I know it's last-minute, but you're welcome to come to the party if you can."

Trina smiled big. "Sounds fun. I'd love to." She looked out on the court. "Is the game over? I wanted to get here earlier, but I got caught up running errands."

"Only a few seconds left," Stephanie said. "It's been exciting." She paused. "You knew about the family basketball game?"

"Travis told me," Trina said.

Stephanie stole a glance with Janelle. Since when did Trina talk to Travis? Maybe he'd mentioned it in passing at church.

The whistle blew and the Under 30s got ready to inbound the ball again.

Libby had gone up into the stands for a moment, but at the

sound of the whistle, she hurried back. "Where's our cheer, Steph? Let's pump it up!"

Stephanie shook the questions from her head and shouted, "Aggressive!" Everyone knew what she meant and began chanting, "Be aggressive, B-e aggressive, B-e a-g-g-r-e-s-s-i-v-e, aggressive, B-e aggressive!"

The Under 30 team inbounded the ball, and Marcus got it right away. He made a fast break for the basket, but Travis stole the ball from him.

Libby pumped her fist, jumping up and down. "Go, Trav, go! Team Wood! Over 30s!"

Travis tried to pass to Kory, but Kory was being blocked, so Travis took it to the net and dunked it, beating the buzzer.

A thunder of cheers rose from the sidelines and bleachers. The cheerleaders ran out onto the court. Stephanie found Lindell and bear-hugged him. "Babe, y'all did it! Y'all did it!" He was covered in sweat, but she was too excited to care.

Cyd hugged Cedric. Janelle and the little girls tackled Kory. And Stephanie looked around for Travis. Libby was high-fiving him, and they shared an excited hug. Stephanie's gaze then moved to Trina, who was watching from the sidelines.

Travis held up his hands to get people's attention. "I hate to break up the celebration—believe me, it *will* continue throughout the day—but we need to set up chairs and equipment for service tomorrow. We older guys want to thank you for cheering us to victory." He wiped sweat from his brow. "If you have any Advil, we'd appreciate the donation."

Stephanie made her way to Libby. "Hey, Lib, why don't we all stay and help set up?"

"Steph, you know I'm not into the joint service thing. Plus, I've got a lot to do to get ready for tonight, which includes a quick nap." Libby already had her purse on her shoulder, car keys in hand. "I'll meet y'all back at the house." She stopped to say something to Travis and was gone.

Stephanie couldn't help it. Her eyes followed Trina as she approached Travis. They didn't hug, but the way she smiled at him, the proximity between them, the flow of conversation . . . there was a familiarity there.

Janelle joined Stephanie. "Are you seeing what I'm seeing?"

"Yep." Stephanie sighed. "You've been down here this summer. Had you noticed anything between them?"

"Not really." Janelle had her eyes on them. "I've seen them talking at church, but Travis is friendly with everybody, so I didn't think twice about it. But now . . ."

Stephanie sighed again. "You know Libby's falling for him again, much as she refuses to admit it."

"I know." Janelle turned to Stephanie. "But remember that talk we had with Libby in the spring? She knows she and Travis can never be together while she's running from God. He's a *pastor*. And he wants to be married. His wife will be someone who loves the Lord. Libby knows that."

"In her head," Stephanie said. "Doesn't stop her heart. She and Travis were right there with the rest of us, up half the night."

"This thing with Trina is probably nothing," Janelle said. "They're just friends."

Stephanie glanced at them again, now helping with setup. "You just had to invite her to come tonight, didn't you?"

"I felt bad," Janelle said. "I knew we couldn't invite all of the Soul Sisters, but once she saw that Charley had come, my mouth just started moving." She added, "But that was before we knew about her and Travis . . . or . . . whatever we want to call it." She sighed. "If Trina comes, this could be a mess."

"I don't think it's an *if*." Stephanie glimpsed them laughing. "She's coming."

CHAPTER NINE

In the ballroom of the Rocky Mount Hilton Saturday night, Libby waited anxiously. She'd surprised the family by showing a video produced for the occasion, compiled of reunion photos and footage taken over decades of time. Priceless memories from the earliest years got them laughing and talking as hairstyles and clothing on the screen revealed changing times. Babies now grown and relatives now deceased drew comments of wonder and reflection. The latter were especially poignant, as the music changed and they remembered those who had passed, including Janelle's husband, David. There was a photo of him at a reunion only four years ago, smiling big as he held baby Tiffany in his arms, little Daniel at his feet.

But none of this would compare to what was coming. The video appeared to be ending now, the music fading, and then—

"How's everybody doing?"

Gasps sounded around the room and everyone leaned forward as Grandma Geri stared straight at them. She was sitting up in her bed, pillows propped behind, wearing the frailness of her last weeks.

"I bet y'all are in Rocky Mount, eating hotel chicken that don't taste near good as mine." A raspy laugh made Grandma Geri cough a little. "Y'all thought I wouldn't be there to complain about it this year, didn't you?"

Laughter broke out around the ballroom. Grandma Geri was known for saying what she felt, though her delivery was a little labored now.

"Well, I don't have long. And I know you know that 'cause I'm dead if you're watching. But I asked Libby to tape this message for me and not to tell anybody till she showed it." She leaned forward a little. "Wood, you spank her for me if she told."

Libby's dad looked at her from the other side of the table. He had tears in his eyes, as did Libby.

Grandma Geri continued, "In this family, we've had good times and sad times. We've done right, and we've done wrong. Amen?"

Heads nodded. "Amens" sounded.

"But one thing we always done—hold to His unchanging hand. It ain't just a song. It's what we do. I don't want none of y'all to forget that. We ain't nothing without the good Lord."

She paused, and more "Amens" filled the space.

"I got to go. I'm tired." Grandma Geri coughed. "I love you. But I'd be lying if I said I miss you. I told y'all I wanted to be with my Jesus and my Elwood, and that's just where I am." She held up her hand in a wave. "I'll see you when you get here. All right, Libby, turn that thing off."

The screen went black, and no one moved. Libby wouldn't have known if they did anyway, because her head was lowered, tears streaming down her face. She'd seen the video a handful of times, but it had never hit her like this.

Travis leaned over and put an arm around her. "I miss her too."

Libby missed her, and that was surely part of it, but there was more . . . even if she couldn't put her finger on it.

At the table next to them, a voice started, "Hold to His hand, God's unchanging hand . . ."

Travis immediately stood, adding his voice. "Hold to His hand, God's unchanging hand . . ."

Seconds later the whole room was on its feet, which was quite a sight with a sea of olive-colored reunion shirts.

Travis led them into the first verse. "Time is filled with swift transition, Naught of earth unmoved can stand . . ." Everyone knew the next part: "Build your hope on things eternal, Hold to God's unchanging hand."

Hands clapping now, they launched into the chorus again, "Hold to His hand, God's unchanging hand; Hold to His hand, God's unchanging hand. Build your hope on things eternal; Hold to God's unchanging hand."

Libby hadn't sung that song in years, but the words were there. And she felt them. On her feet with the rest, she sang the chorus one last time. They ended with a hand clap of praise and took their seats.

Wood walked to the podium. His booming voice made him the natural emcee at these gatherings, and he'd played that role effortlessly tonight. Right now, though, he seemed at a loss for words.

"Wow," he said finally. "I wasn't expecting all this. But I should've known Mama would have the last word, even moving us to praise." He paused as people chimed in their agreement. "We all know how much her presence is missed here this year. We've talked about it throughout the weekend. Hearing her voice one last time . . . that was . . . really special."

Libby looked on, filled with emotion.

Wood looked over at his daughter. "I want to thank you, Libby, for producing such a splendid video. It'll be a family treasure always. And I have to add that this entire evening has been incredible. I know you worked hard pulling together all that talent for the talent show, even coaxing family members who *never* get up here to unveil their hidden talents." He paused. "I'm proud of you, sweetheart. You went above and beyond this evening."

Family members rose around the ballroom, giving her thunderous applause. Embarrassed, Libby waved it away, which made them clap all the more.

When they settled down, Wood continued, "The good news is the night isn't over. The DJ is set up and ready to go, so let's get the party started. But don't party too much." He looked out over the crowd. "Where are my pastors?"

Travis and Todd waved their hands.

Wood grinned. "They're expecting to see every last one of y'all at the combined Calvary– New Jerusalem service tomorrow."

The music kicked in and tables emptied as people got up to mingle or dance. Libby remained seated, turning over her father's comment. She'd said she wouldn't attend the service. But many in the family would. Couldn't she treat it as a reunion event and just go? Suddenly she kind of wanted to. Travis was preaching tomorrow, and he'd been asking her to go for months. She nodded to herself, letting it jell. This weekend really did seem like a turning point for the two of—

She felt a tug on her arm and looked left. It was Travis. "Remember this song? We've got to go out there for old times' sake."

Libby tuned in now. She loved that song, a midtempo from the late nineties. But she wouldn't budge. "Travis, I'm tired. I didn't get a nap today."

"Come on, we have to. This was our song."

The butterflies stirred, along with a cavalcade of memories. She let him pull her to her feet and walk her by hand to the dance floor. The weariness melted as they transported themselves back in time, doing the same dances they'd done in college. It got silly when

Janelle and Kory moved beside them and the couples went *way* back, doing some version of the waltz that probably wasn't the waltz at all.

Libby and Travis glided across the floor, hands clasped outward, his other on her waist. As the song ended, Travis and Kory dipped the women far back, to cheers and applause. They laughed as they left the floor, and Libby wondered how many in his congregation knew this side of him, the silly Travis. But then, they knew a side she didn't . . . which reminded her . . .

She looked into his eyes. "I'm thinking about coming to the service tomorrow morning."

He stared at her, his eyes soft. "I would love that. What made you change your mind?"

Libby shrugged lightly. "I think this weekend has changed me a little."

"How so?"

She hesitated, not fully sure of the answer herself. "I don't know. I just feel like I'm finally beginning to—"

"Hey, Libby, can you come here a minute?" her dad called from a few feet away. "People are asking how they can get a copy of that video."

"Okay, Dad." She looked at Travis. "Be right back."

Libby walked to the table where her father and a few others were gathered.

Aunt Gladys spoke up. "We can't stop talking about that video, Libby," she said. "We're wondering if we can get copies and how much it would cost. I think most of us want one."

"Sure," Libby said. "I should've made that announcement. If I know how many to order—"

Out of the corner of her eye, Libby noticed a woman arrive, the same one who had come to the gym that morning. She appeared to be a friend of Janelle and Stephanie—and Travis. He saw her first and went to greet her.

"Um," Libby continued. "Yeah, if you give me an idea of how many you need, I'll let you know the price."

"Wonderful," Gladys said. "That's a keepsake for sure."

Libby glanced at Travis and the woman as she joined Janelle and Stephanie. She didn't know why, but she felt a little jumpy inside.

"Who's that?" Libby asked.

Janelle and Stephanie turned. "Oh, Trina's here," Janelle said.

Libby was curious still. The woman was pretty and lively—and touchy-feely. "Who's Trina?"

"She attends New Jerusalem," Janelle said, "and Soul Sisters. Steph and I invited her."

Libby's insides settled somewhat. A member of his congregation. Of course they'd be friendly.

They walked over to her.

"Welcome to the Sanders family reunion, Trina," Janelle said. She hugged her, then Stephanie did the same.

"Yeah," Travis said, "their welcome is worth more than mine, since they're actual family."

"You've been to more reunions than I have," Stephanie said. "You might be adopted, but you're as much family as any of us."

Trina smiled. "Travis was telling me he's been coming since he was a young boy."

Libby extended her hand. "I don't think we've met. I'm Libby Sanders."

Trina shook it. "Nice to meet you, Libby. Trina Wheeler."

"You live in Hope Springs?" Libby asked.

"Wilson," Trina said. "I heard about Pastor Travis and New Jerusalem last fall and started coming." She smiled at him. "He's made a huge difference in my life."

There was an awkward silence until Janelle jumped in. "It's great that you could come hang with us tonight."

"I actually won't be able to stay." Trina looked at her watch.

"When you invited me earlier, I completely forgot my brother asked me to come to this jazz club where he's playing tonight—oh, and he invited you again too," she said, touching Travis's arm, "but I told him you'd be at the reunion this weekend." Hardly catching a breath, she turned back to the rest. "Anyway, it's not far from here, so I decided to stop by real quick and say hello." Pouting, she added, "But I need to run already."

Libby heard words of parting and something about seeing Trina tomorrow—and she may have said good-bye herself—but it was all a fog. She left the ballroom right after Trina, heading a different direction. To where, she didn't know. She simply walked the hall until she saw a little enclave to the left with a grouping of empty armchairs. Taking one facing the wall, she sat and lowered her head.

How could she have been so stupid? Did she really think there was a chance for her and Travis? She hadn't actually *thought* it, but it was there, lurking. Libby felt the sting of tears in her eyes. She knew Travis couldn't be with her. He was a pastor. He loved God, lived for God. Libby hadn't lived for God in years, if ever. But tonight she'd felt herself turning . . .

So naïve. Just because she and Travis spent time together, she thought it meant something? That her life was changing?

"Libby, can I talk to you?" Travis took the armchair next to hers.

She crossed her legs away from him.

"Libby." He leaned on his thighs. "We need to talk."

Libby wiped her eyes and sat up, looking away from him. "You could've told me, Travis."

"Told you what?"

"That you were seeing someone."

"I'm not seeing Trina."

Libby looked at him. "It's obvious the two of you spend time together."

"Because we went to a concert?"

She glanced away.

"Can we back up?" Travis said. "Why do you care? Aren't you seeing Omar?"

"What does *that* matter? It's not serious. He's not even with me this weekend."

"Which brings me to my other point. You say you don't want a committed relationship. So I repeat—why do you care if I'm seeing Trina? Why are you upset?"

She fought to contain another surge of emotion. "Because I thought we were rebuilding a friendship between us."

"Libby, we are. And I can't tell you how much it means to me."

She stared at her hands, tears sliding down her face.

"Tell me, Libby. What's on your mind?"

Libby swiped the tears and looked hard at him. "You know what's on my mind? Déjà vu. Fifteen years ago I was sitting in my dorm room telling myself what a fool I was to have feelings for you. And guess what? It was after finding out you were seeing someone else."

"So you're upset because you have feelings for me, right now?"

She looked away. "I'm not answering that."

"I will." Travis tugged her hand so she'd look at him. "I admit I have feelings for you."

Libby couldn't respond. She simply stared at him.

"This isn't déjà vu, Libby. In college I didn't commit to you because I was foolish. But now . . . it's a different reality."

"Because you're a pastor."

He shifted, looking more intently at her. "It's not just that," he said. "I'm committed to Jesus. I want to obey His Word, and that means the woman with whom I pursue a relationship must also be committed to Jesus." He sighed, glancing down a moment. "But reconnecting with you these past few months awakened old feelings—maybe even new ones." He paused again. "I thought we could be friends, but the last thing I want to do is hurt you again."

Why can't I stop these stupid tears?

She stared into her lap. "So . . . are you at least thinking about pursuing a relationship with Trina?"

"It's a possibility," he said, and the frankness of it hurt. He quickly added, "But this isn't about Trina, and it really isn't about me. It's about you, Libby. Your soul. Your eternity." He paused. "I told you at the fish fry that deep down I think you do want a committed relationship. And the only relationship that'll satisfy that desire is Jesus."

"Yeah. Thanks, Pastor. Nice way to write me off."

"Don't do that, Libby. You know this is from the heart."

She did know it. She just didn't know what to do with it.

She stood and turned to go.

"Just like that?" he said. "That's how we're leaving this?"

Libby looked at him. "I don't have anything else to say."

"Are you . . . still coming to the service tomorrow?"

Right. So I can watch you and Trina? "I'll pass."

His eyes fell. "What about the reunion? Should I stay away the rest of the weekend?"

"I wouldn't tell you that."

He looked at her. "But you'd prefer it."

She stared into his brown eyes. Didn't he know what she would truly prefer? Tears threatening once more, she walked away.

CHAPTER TEN

Charley had her hand on the door handle before the car came to a complete stop. "Thanks for dinner, Connor," she said. "I had a nice time."

Connor shifted his BMW to park, idling by the front curb of Charley's home. "So did I," he said. "But it's not even late. You sure you don't want to catch a movie or something?"

Charley nodded. "I'm sure. Appreciate the offer, though."

He leaned on the console. "Did I do something wrong?"

"What do you mean?"

"I hope you don't take this the wrong way," he said, "but I'm used to women showing a little more interest. If anything, I'm the one trying to cut the evening short. But I like you, a lot."

He eased closer, touched her hair. Charley flinched.

"See." Connor pulled back. "I feel like I keep doing the wrong thing with you."

Connor was cute and obviously used to getting his way.

"It's not you; it's me," Charley said. "Busy weekend, got a lot on my mind." She smiled, popped open the door. "Thanks again. Really. I enjoyed it."

"Next weekend?"

"Actually, I'll probably be out of town."

She stepped out, closed the door, and heard his engine roar off as she opened her front door. Heading upstairs, she glanced at her watch. Already late—later than she wanted to be, anyway. She slipped out of her skirt and top and into the olive green reunion shirt and khaki capris waiting on her bed.

Stephanie had gotten her the shirt and insisted she wear it—after insisting she come. Friday night and Saturday morning with the Sanders family had seemed enough to wear out her welcome, so Charley had tried to beg off. But it was hard to resist the tag team persuasion of both Stephanie and Marcus. The three of them seemed to click, especially after hanging out until two in the morning. Still, she read nothing into Marcus's end of the invitation. He was inviting her to hang with all of them, not just him. Though in her brief moments with just him, they'd seemed to have their own bit of chemistry . . . or was she imagining it?

She dashed into the hall bathroom to freshen her face and heard her mother's bedroom door open.

Dottie stopped in the bathroom doorway. "I didn't know you were back, honey. How did it go?"

"Fine." Charley pressed powder on her forehead and nose.

"You liked him?"

She shrugged. "He's okay."

"Just okay?" Dottie's disappointment showed. "He seems like a great guy, certainly on his way careerwise. And our families get along well, which is a plus . . ."

"I'm sure it's all true, Mom." Charley assessed her eye shadow. "He's just not my type."

"How can you tell after one date? Shouldn't you— Wait, are you heading back out?"

"Rocky Mount Hilton," she said. "The Sanders family is gathering there tonight."

"Sounds like you're having a great time at this family reunion," she said. "It's been a long time since I've seen Gladys and Estelle. Tell them I said hello."

"Actually, you could tell them yourself. I hear a lot of the family's going to the joint service tomorrow. It'll be a good time for you all to catch up."

"Oh, I haven't had a chance to tell you. I decided not to go tomorrow."

Charley turned. "What? You're boycotting?"

"I'm not *boycotting*. I don't like that term. But I've been talking to a few other Calvary friends. The consensus is that our church is in a transition phase, and the best thing right now is to focus inward and make sure our own house is in order, so to speak." She hesitated slightly. "Grandpa Skip wants me to make sure you're on board too."

"I'm sorry to disagree, Mom, but I really want the joint service to succeed," Charley said. "And being around Pastor Travis last night made me want to hear more from him. I'm looking forward to hearing him preach tomorrow."

Dottie was quiet a moment. "I don't think there's a right or wrong in this. We just have differing opinions about the best course."

"Maybe," Charley said. "I haven't really been paying attention or praying about it until now. I don't know if there's a right or wrong, but I'm really wondering what God's heart is in all of this."

❧

It was close to ten when Charley entered the hotel ballroom, lights dim, music playing. She took a deep breath as she glanced around, feeling the flutters. *You're not looking for Marcus; you're looking for Stephanie or Janelle.*

A cheer went up, and Charley walked toward the mass of olive green shirts on the dance floor. Rows of people were doing a line dance—and having a ball. Cyd and Cedric were especially into it, causing another cheer to go up as they turned toward one another, did a fancy dance move, then rejoined the line. Charley spotted Janelle and Kory, Stephanie and her husband, and Marcus—just as he spotted her.

Marcus smiled as he stepped sideways with the crowd, motioning for her to join them.

Charley's eyes widened, her head answering a vigorous no.

He two-hand urged her.

She two-handed no.

He said something to Stephanie, and they broke ranks and came for her.

Charley backed up, laughing. "Nope, nope, nope. I'm not making a fool of myself. I don't know that dance."

"It's the Cha-Cha Slide," Stephanie said, grabbing an arm. "Girl, they got me out there, and I never get it right. You'll look good next to me."

Marcus had her other arm. "I forgot to mention . . . there's the rule about eating, and there's one about doing the cha-cha . . . All guests have to try it."

She didn't know if it was the infectious beat or his infectious smile that did it.

"I'll try it," she said. "But if you laugh . . ."

"Me?" He pulled her by the hand. "Never."

The three of them took a spot near the edge of the floor, Charley in between. Marcus jumped right back in, moving backward. Stephanie joined in, but by the time Charley caught on and took a step back, they were doing a hop and stomping a foot. Next thing she knew, the line had made a quarter turn.

Charley turned as they were moving left. "Marcus, I can't get this. It's going too fast."

"Just follow what the guy's saying on the song," he said.

Charley nodded. Instead of focusing on the line dancers, she focused on the words. When the guy said, "To the left," she went left. When he said, "Take it back," she went back. Then she hopped forward with the line but started laughing at Stephanie—who was sliding left instead of right—and missed the cha-cha part.

They quarter-turned again, and Charley felt herself getting the hang of it. Her moves more fluid, she put some flavor in the hops and stomps—and got to try the cha-cha.

"I see you!" Stephanie called over. "Shake what your mama gave you, girl!"

Charley laughed again but kept moving so she wouldn't fall out of rhythm. Two quarter turns later, they added new moves—a criss-cross, a "Charlie Brown" thing, which she skipped, and a hand clap. Then she heard the guy say, "How low can you go; can you go down low; all the way to the floor . . ."

She didn't know what got into her, but she had to try it. What she didn't know was that she'd be one of few who would. Most stopped midway and cheered as she made her way down "to the floor."

"Look at you," Marcus said. He did a double-time clap to the beat to urge her on.

"This is fun!" Charley said—then her knee locked as she tried to come back up.

She almost keeled over, but Marcus grabbed her hand and pulled her upward. She clung to his arm, off balance still, mostly because she couldn't stop laughing.

"I think I'm done," she said. "But I gave it a try!"

He walked her off the floor. "You more than gave it a try. You get mad props from me, Coach Willoughby." He smiled at her. "Thought you said you couldn't dance."

"I said I didn't know *that* dance."

They sat at the nearest table, which was empty at the moment, and continued to watch the dance floor.

Marcus looked at her. "Glad you came tonight. I was beginning to think you changed your mind."

Charley could feel her heart racing. "I didn't think I'd be this late, but . . . I kind of had a date tonight."

Marcus's brows knit. "How do you *kind of* have a date?"

"When you go as a favor to your family and can't wait for it to be over."

"Ahh, okay." He sat back, crossed a leg onto his knee. "So, you haven't been seeing anyone seriously since your breakup?"

"No. What about you?"

"Nah." He glanced down, fingered a program on the table.

"Sounds like there's more to it."

"It's just . . . ironic." He shrugged. "I tended to date a couple women at a time—"

"Oh, only a couple?"

He glanced at her. "Not proud of it. Just being honest." He continued, "But now that I'm getting serious about my relationship with God and thinking differently about relationships with women, I find myself in Hope Springs . . . with no single women."

"No single women?" She hoped she didn't sound presumptuous. She quickly added, "Aren't there plenty at New Jerusalem?"

"Okay. *No* single women might've been a slight exaggeration." He smiled. "Maybe it's just part of the new thing happening with me right now—I'm not really looking. I'm enjoying this season of just . . . learning. The discipleship I'm getting from Travis is incredible."

Charley nodded. "I can imagine." She glanced around. "Where is Travis, anyway?"

"He was here earlier." He looked around too. "Guess he left. Probably getting ready for service tomorrow."

Another cheer went up when the music changed. The younger set was flocking to the floor, starting a different line dance.

"What's this one called?" Charley said.

"The Wobble." Marcus grinned at the sight, then cupped his hands around his mouth. "I see you, Cedric! You and Cyd show the young folk how it's done!"

Cedric waved at him, not missing a beat.

Stephanie came off the floor and collapsed in a seat next to Charley. "Don't encourage him, Marcus," she said. "Cedric doesn't seem to realize he's in his forties. Basketball this morning, dancing all night . . . he's gonna have a heart attack out there."

Charley smiled. "Stephanie, you seem really close with Cyd and Cedric."

Stephanie watched them on the floor. "Definitely. I hate they'll be leaving first thing Monday morning."

"Yep," Marcus said. "When the family reunion's over, everybody's gone, and you and Lindell are still here, that's when it'll hit you—you live here."

"Everybody won't be gone," Charley said. "She lives with Janelle and the kids, and you're right up the street."

Marcus nodded agreement. "True."

"Yeah, but it'll still hit me," Stephanie said, "and I'll be wondering what's next." She grew thoughtful. "I talked to Lindell about your proposition, Marcus. And I *am* praying. I know you need an answer soon."

"I'm praying too." Charley looked at Stephanie. "Have to admit it's crossed my mind how cool it would be to work in the same building. All the friends I grew up with are gone."

"Girl, I didn't even grow up with a lot of friends. I have this thing about getting too close to people." She paused. "But there's something about you." She nodded slightly. "You keep it real. I like you."

Marcus eyed the two of them. "Should I leave so you two can have your girl-bonding moment?"

"No," Stephanie said. "True girl bonding only happens late-night when Spanx come off—speaking for myself on that one—and hair is looking crazy." She turned to Charley. "Speaking of which, you should stay at the house tonight. Then you can ride with us to the service in the morning . . . if you're going."

"Definitely going," Charley said. "But don't you have a house full?"

"That's what makes it fun, long as you don't care about little things like getting a good night's rest."

"Sleep's overrated." Charley smiled. "I can run home after this and get my things."

"Awesome." Stephanie stood as the DJ switched to a slow song. "I see my hubby calling me to the dance floor." She waved back at him. "My feet are killing me in these wedge sandals, but that's our song."

Charley laughed as Stephanie wobbled her way over, then looked at Marcus.

"Don't feel that you have to keep me company," she said. "I'll be fine."

"I don't think I could move if I wanted to." Marcus stretched out his legs under the table. "Lack of sleep is catching up to me." He smiled. "It's a good tired, though. I don't know when I've laughed as hard as I laughed last night."

"Yeah, y'all get crazy after midnight."

"*Y'all?* Who started all the 'You might be from Hope Springs . . .' jokes?"

Charley laughed. "I thought up some more today too."

He stared at her a moment. "You're different from what I thought."

She gave him a look. "Not sure I want to know what that means."

"I mean, I knew you were a nice person, but whenever I'd see you, you were about business, heading to the gym, getting it done. I never would've pictured you cracking jokes or seeing 'how low can you go.'"

"All blame goes to you and Stephanie for bringing out that side of me."

"I'll take my share, then." He paused. "I like that side of you."

She let her gaze fall on the dance floor, telling herself to take caution, not to read anything into what Marcus said or did. He was a nice guy. This was casual conversation. It meant nothing.

She only needed to steady her beating heart long enough to listen.

CHAPTER ELEVEN

Sunday, August 1

E yes barely open, Stephanie entered the kitchen earlier than planned Sunday morning for the sole purpose of telling everyone to be quiet. She'd gone to bed at five, counting on at least four hours of sleep. But as much as she'd tried to bury her head under the pillow, she couldn't escape the rising voices in the kitchen—and it was only seven.

"Could y'all *please* keep it down in here?" Through half-shut lids, she could make out Cyd—with Chase on her lap—Becca, and Aunt Gladys at the kitchen table. "Are you aware there's such a thing as a *whisper*?" Stephanie said the last word in a hushed voice in case they needed a demonstration.

"I'm sorry, it's my fault." Becca had on her robe. "I knew somebody'd be up over here. I had to see what y'all thought about the morning paper."

Stephanie rubbed her eyes and came closer. "What's in it?"

Cyd turned it around so she could read it. It was *The Rocky Mount Sentinel*, and the headline below the fold on the front page read LOCAL QUEST FOR UNITY STIRS DIVISION, RACIAL TENSION.

Stephanie leaned over and skimmed the first few lines. "Oh my goodness, they're talking about Calvary and New Jerusalem?" She snatched up the paper.

"Yes, ma'am," Aunt Gladys said. "Keep reading."

Stephanie turned the page to see how long it was. "This is, like, a whole profile of Hope Springs and the churches."

"I learned a lot I didn't know," Becca said. "It's quite sobering."

Stephanie slid into a seat at the table, eyes back on the front page, and read aloud. ". . . 'known for its quaint, small-town feel . . . people still don't lock their doors at night . . . but there's a dark thread that runs through the history of the town.'" She looked up. "Dark thread?"

"Mm-hm," Aunt Gladys said. "Keep reading."

"Oh my goodness!" Stephanie looked at Cyd. "Did you read this?"

Cyd helped Chase spoon up some applesauce. "About the Hope Springs man who participated in the Greensboro sit-ins of 1960?"

"Yes!" Stephanie continued reading. "Says he was attending North Carolina A&T, heard about the sit-ins at Woolworth, and joined in with his classmates, and came home to Hope Springs that weekend. 'My family and I were awakened in the night when a brick came crashing through the living room window. All the men in sheets on horseback, yelling. I'd never been that scared in my life.'" Stephanie felt the hair rising on her arm. She looked up. "Can you all believe this?"

"You're not surprised, are you?" Cyd said. "That's what Jim Crow was about down here in the sixties, maintaining segregation at any cost."

"But this happened not far from right *here*." Stephanie pointed at the table. "This is so eerie."

"Can y'all lower your voices in here?" Libby stood in the kitchen doorway looking as half-present as Stephanie had a few minutes before. "I'm really trying to catch up on some z's."

Stephanie turned to her. "Libby, did you know there was a Klan raid near here in 1960?"

"You're surprised?"

Stephanie sat back and stared. "Okay, Cyd said that too. Why are y'all acting like this is nothing?"

"Steph, it's not that it's nothing," Aunt Gladys said. "It's just not surprising, especially for me. I lived Jim Crow. I remember when we couldn't eat at the Main Street Diner. And don't get me started on all the mess that went on when they started changing up the schools."

"Question." Libby lifted a finger, yawning. "Why are we having such an uplifting conversation early Sunday morning?"

Stephanie picked up the paper. "The joint worship service made the front page. They're talking about how these new young pastors at Calvary and New Jerusalem want to change the status quo but have run into opposition."

"Are you serious?" Libby came and looked over Stephanie's shoulder.

"They're saying the opposition is based on racial prejudice," Becca said, "and telling about a history of opposition here to bringing black and white people together."

"It's even more pointed than that," Cyd said. "The article touches on the tension that surrounded school integration and quotes an anonymous source who says Skip Willoughby was on record as being against it. Then they quote another anonymous source who says he was the one who called the boycott."

"Todd was bothered by the picture it painted of Skip," Becca said. "But at least the reporter went to Skip personally for a quote. His objections in the paper are the same ones he's given from the start. And they've never been based on race."

"Well, he'd never *say* it, not to Todd," Aunt Gladys said. "But hear me when I say that's his number one reason."

"Aunt Gladys, shh," Libby said. "Charley's sleeping in there. And anyway, you can't be slandering the man like that."

"Call it what you want," Aunt Gladys said. "I know way more history than they got in that article. But I'll say this . . ." She took a sip of coffee. "I'm all for the boycott."

"What?" Stephanie looked at her. "Why?"

"Becca, you know I love you and Todd, always loved his family— but we've got our own style, our own way of doing and being. Church is the one place we can have to ourselves to do and be."

Stephanie pointed at the paper. "They do make the point that both Calvary and New Jerusalem members are joining in the boy-cott. Here's a quote from a New Jerusalem member: 'I admire Pastor Travis for attempting it. But bottom line, if we have to change who we are and what we do to accommodate white people—which we do every other day of the week—no thank you.'"

Cyd sighed. "I wish people could see our church in St. Louis. Living Word has been multiethnic from the beginning, and that's what I love about it. The love, the unity, the bond in Christ . . . it's a beautiful picture of what heaven will be like one day."

Becca nodded. "That's the vision Todd and Travis have. They've been praying that members of both congregations would catch that vision. In fact, they're praying together right now at the house, after seeing this." She sighed again. "I wonder what effect this article will have on the service this morning."

Stephanie had been listening to the conversation and scanning the article simultaneously. "Listen to the end of the article," she said. "'Martin Luther King Jr. famously noted that eleven o'clock Sunday morning is the most segregated hour in America. Unlike schools or lunch counters, there's no court decree or law that can change that. If there is to be change in Hope Springs at eleven o'clock this morning—and every other Sunday morning—perhaps it will require a change of heart.'"

⁓✺⁓

Several carloads made the less-than-two-mile drive from the Sanders' household, pulling into the high school parking lot. Given the boycott, Stephanie wondered if they'd be among the only cars there. But with a full fifteen minutes to go before the start of service, the lot was teeming with vehicles.

"Wow." She gazed out of her backseat window.

Lindell was beside her. "Looks like turnout hasn't been affected."

"Yes, it has." Marcus was driving. "Never had to hunt down a parking spot like this. Somebody even took my reserved spot. This is way more people than usual."

Charley nodded from the passenger seat. "I bet that article drew a lot of people."

"Did you call home to see how your family was taking it?" Stephanie asked.

"Yeah, right before we left," Charley said. "Mom said Grandpa was livid about the way he was portrayed. Wonder what he'll say when he hears all these people showed up."

Marcus found a spot, and they all hopped out.

Lindell looked around. "What happened to the rest of our caravan?"

"They probably went to the other side of the lot," Stephanie said. "We'll catch them inside."

Stephanie walked inside with her mind on church, but as they passed the administrative office and classrooms, she began to take notice of the actual school. Soon these spaces would be filled with students. *Lord, do I have a place here? Would I even know how to connect with the kids?*

Two ushers stood outside the gym doors, handing out programs.

Stephanie whispered to Charley, "I'm assuming that guy's from Calvary? I'm a little surprised."

"I'm surprised to see him too," Charley whispered back. "He's a longtime member." She glanced around. "I see more Calvary members than I expected to, but a lot of the people you might think are from Calvary . . . I've never seen before."

Charley and the Calvary usher greeted one another. He looked as surprised to see her as she was to see him.

The four of them walked into the gym, where seats were filling rapidly. Stephanie looked for Cyd and Cedric, or Janelle and Kory, or even her other relatives who'd come, but couldn't spot them.

"I see some empty seats over there," Charley said.

They followed her to a row three-quarters of the way back. A teenage girl sat alone on the end, with a few seats between her and another couple in her row.

"Sam, hey, good morning!" Charley said. "Mind if we sit by you?"

"Good morning, Coach," she said, moving her legs aside for them to pass. "Morning, Mr. Maxwell."

"Good morning, Sam." Marcus smiled. "I think this is the first time I've seen you without a volleyball in your hands."

Sam smiled. "Yes, sir."

Charley introduced Stephanie and Lindell to Sam, then took the seat beside her, followed by the rest.

Stephanie glanced around and saw Todd and Travis mingling. When her little nephew Chase took off across the gym, she spotted Cyd, who carted him back to a seat across the aisle. Janelle, Kory, and the kids were with them.

"So you attend New Jerusalem?" Charley was asking.

"No, ma'am," Sam said.

"Oh, I'm sorry," Charley said. "Have you been attending Calvary, and I've somehow missed you?"

"No."

Stephanie didn't want to be rude, but she looked at the girl again. Sam was fair-skinned; if Stephanie had to guess, she'd say mixed.

Sam played with her purse strap. "We don't go to church. My mom says she doesn't feel welcome at either one." She glanced tentatively at Charley, then back to her purse. "I saw the article in the paper this morning, and since it was both churches together at school . . ." She shrugged. "I figured it'd be okay for me to come."

Stephanie's brows bunched. "Sam, I hope you don't mind my asking, but why wouldn't your mom feel welcome at either church?"

"I'm not really sure," she said. "She's never told me the whole story."

"I'm really sorry to hear that," Stephanie said. "I'm glad you came today."

"Thank you." Sam stood. "Excuse me. I want to go to the restroom before it starts."

Stephanie's eyes followed after her, noting her plain, worn jeans—genuinely worn, not designer-worn—and fitted shirt—but not designer-fitted. Sam tugged it down self-consciously. Everything about her seemed self-conscious.

"I don't know why," Stephanie said, "but my heart goes out to that girl."

"She's a great kid, going into tenth grade," Charley said. "Nice. Polite. Kind of stays to herself, though."

"Marcus mentioned volleyball. She's on the high school team?"

"No," Charley said. "She came to my summer clinic, and she's got a love for it, but I'm not sure if she's ready to try out."

Travis was walking by and stopped to shake hands.

"Are you as surprised as we were by the turnout?" Lindell asked.

Travis nodded. "Definitely. A lot of people read the morning paper and came from neighboring towns to support what we're doing. And I'm sure some are here out of curiosity. I believe God is at work even in that."

Todd came to the microphone up front. "Good morning," he said. "Could everyone take your seats, please? I want to say a few words before we get started."

Sam slipped back in and took her seat.

When the gym quieted, Todd said, "I think most of us are aware of the article in this morning's *Rocky Mount Sentinel*. Pastor Travis and I pondered whether to address it in the service. We decided to do so briefly." He paused, looking out at the crowd. "We've known from the beginning that there would be controversy surrounding the joint worship service. Ultimately, we moved forward because Pastor Travis and I felt a deep conviction that this was what God was calling us to do."

Something in Todd's delivery struck Stephanie, as if he were feeling the weight of it all—the article, the boycott, and who knows how many personal messages he was getting. He wasn't this sober when he gave the message at his own father's funeral right before Christmas.

Todd continued, "This is our fourth combined service, and I have to admit that I thought by now we'd be on the upswing. If I'd imagined the type of news article I'd want to see, it would be one in which our churches served as a model of what was possible everywhere. I'm a little disappointed that instead, our state of affairs was likened to 1960s Jim Crow. I'm disappointed that there are more people here from outside of Hope Springs than there are those who live here."

Lindell elbowed Stephanie. "Is it just me, or is this a different spin than Travis had?"

"But we're so thankful to those who have supported this vision from the beginning," Todd continued. "And we're thankful to those from neighboring towns who have come out to support us." The praise and worship team—a combined ensemble from both churches—had come up beside him. "We're about to begin our time of praise, and later in the service we'll have a special time of prayer, asking God to give us His vision going forward."

Stephanie elbowed Lindell back. "Is he saying the vision of unity and love might change? Seems like we just need to pray like that article suggested—that people have a heart to catch that vision."

She glanced the other direction at Sam. "This might be more important than we realize."

CHAPTER TWELVE

Libby was ready for the reunion to be over. She loved her family and was glad everything had turned out so well, but she was also glad there were only a few hours remaining. Only a few hours, and she'd be back in Raleigh, away from Travis.

She knew he'd be at Grandma Geri's house today. The Sanders family wouldn't let Travis stay away if he wanted to—and according to Marcus, he'd tried. He'd gone home after church and said he'd relax there the rest of the day. But Libby's dad, of all people, called him. She heard him herself.

"Didn't you say you were playing in the volleyball tournament for Team Wood? . . . Well, where you at, son? We need you!"

Travis was at the house and ready to play in the blink of an eye. *Team Wood. Whatever.*

A knock sounded on the bedroom door. Janelle poked her head in. "Can I come in?"

Libby propped herself up on an elbow. "It's your room."

Janelle closed the door and sat beside her on the bed. It was their familiar routine during family events, though it was weird that Grandma Geri's room was now Janelle's.

Janelle eyed her. "At first I was coming to drag you outside for the volleyball tournament—my team is out, by the way; you *know* Charley is killin' out there—but now I'm here for another reason. What in the world is Omar doing here?"

Libby sat up. "He's out there?"

As she said it, her phone dinged, and she grabbed it from the nightstand. A text from Omar: Just got here.

Libby got up to go meet him.

"Um, excuse me." Janelle looked at her from the bed. "You didn't answer my question. What's Omar doing here? You were adamant about not wanting him to come. 'He's getting too serious' and all that."

Libby shrugged. "I changed my mind."

"Don't try it, Lib. This is me. You know I already know. I just want to hear you say it."

"Say what?"

"You invited Omar to get your mind off of Travis." She continued before Libby could comment. "And it's not right. You shouldn't play with Omar's feelings like that."

Libby waved away her concern. "I'm not playing with anybody's feelings. Omar knows we're just friends." She paused. "But I have a question for you. Why didn't you tell me about Travis and Trina?"

Janelle frowned slightly. "There was nothing to tell. Still isn't, far as I can see."

"Come on, Janelle, you heard them last night. They've been out together. You go to church with them, and she's in your Soul Sisters group. You had no idea they were friends?"

"I knew they knew each other, of course," Janelle said. "But no, I had no idea they'd been out or anything like that." She eyed Libby. "And you care because . . . ?"

She rolled her eyes. "That's the same thing Travis asked me."

Janelle scooted to the edge of the bed. "We haven't had a moment alone to talk about that. What happened between the two of you?"

Libby sat back down with a sigh. "Nothing really. Just me making a fool of myself again, in tears, halfway admitting I have feelings for him as he let me know we could never be together."

Janelle looked stunned. "You were crying?"

"I just said that."

"You care about Travis more than I thought." She put a hand on Libby's shoulder. "Libby, I'm sorry. I wish we'd never invited Trina last night. It ruined the weekend for you."

"It was best," Libby said. "I'm glad I know. Wasn't like me anyway to start fantasizing about a relationship with him—as if it could ever go anywhere." She shook her head. "He and Trina can pursue their happily-ever-after."

Janelle looked at her.

"What?"

"You're the reason you and Travis aren't together."

"What's that supposed to mean?"

"Unless I'm totally clueless, Travis has feelings for you too. But you're the one who drifted from the Lord, stopped going to church, started living however you wanted to."

Libby stared at the floor.

"If you'd stop running from commitment—and I mean commitment to God—maybe you and Travis could begin to build something."

Libby's phone dinged again. She looked at it. Where are you?

"That's Omar," Libby said. "I have to go."

She headed for the door as another knock sounded, and then Stephanie poked her head in.

"Hey, they're calling for everyone to come out," Stephanie said. "Tournament's over, and they're awarding trophies."

"I thought you were handling that, Libby," Janelle said.

"I told my dad I wasn't up to it. He said he'd do it."

The three of them went out the back door, along with others who'd been inside escaping the heat. During the volleyball tournament, barbecue ribs and chicken were cooking on the grill. The inviting aroma hit them the moment they stepped outside. Once the winners were awarded their trophies, they'd all feast.

The backyard was crowded, as it had been Friday night. Libby snaked her way through, looking for Omar, and ran into Travis instead.

He touched her arm as she passed. "You weren't going to speak?"

She barely looked at him. "Didn't see the point."

"So all the progress we made becoming friends again, we'll just take twenty steps back?"

"However many steps it takes," Libby said.

"Oh, there you are."

Libby cringed inside when she heard Omar's voice. All these people, and she's caught between *these* two?

She turned and smiled. "Hey, glad you could make it."

Omar hugged her. "All I needed was an invitation." He spoke in her ear. "You know I wanted to be with you all weekend."

Libby took a step back. "You remember Travis, right?"

"Of course." Omar extended his hand. "Good to see you again, Pastor."

Travis shook it. "You as well."

"Okay, everybody, listen up." Wood waved his arms on the top step of the back porch so people could see him. "I don't have a microphone, so I need silence."

It took a good two minutes for the noise to quiet down, especially from the kids playing on the swing set.

"Libby came up with a great idea to start a volleyball tournament this year," Wood said. "And yes, I'm bragging on my baby girl again, because I could tell even from the barbecue pit that everybody had big fun!"

A round of cheers went up.

"Competition was stiff," Wood continued. "Seven teams signed up, and they came to *play*. But there can only be one victor—"

A group that included Marcus and Charley started cheering and pumping their fists.

Wood gave a hearty laugh. "They call themselves the Crush, and it's obvious why."

The Crush roared again.

"Winner of the first annual Sanders Family Reunion Volleyball Tournament is . . . the Crush! Come on up and get your trophies!"

Marcus, Charley, and five more players ran up, fists pumping, and collected the trophies Libby had bought from a supply store.

"Now, wait a minute," Wood said. "We're not done. I need Marcus and Charley to stay here. And I want my sister Gladys to come up."

People started buzzing, wondering what was up.

"A lot of you may not know," Wood said, "but we had our own little competition among Grandma Geri's kids. Each of us had a team, and we've been giving out points all weekend based on participation in events and so on. And frankly, you know me . . . I wanted to win."

Family members laughed and shouted back at him.

Wood continued, "For the record, I'm very proud of my team. Libby and Travis racked up most of our points this weekend." He scanned the crowd. "I don't know where they are, but a big shout-out to Team Wood!"

Travis and Libby waved at him. Neither shouted back. She could feel Omar staring at her.

"But I have to congratulate Team Gladys, because the basketball game yesterday and the volleyball tournament today put them at the top. Marcus and Charley, you are two serious athletes." He turned to the crowd. "Let's give a big round of applause to these athletic dynamos."

Marcus and Charley high-fived one another as applause went up. Gladys hugged them both.

Wood raised his hands to quiet everyone. "But wait . . . *wait* . . . there's one problem. Team Gladys has the most points *at the moment.* And even though there's nothing left to do but eat—no points for that—there *is* something that might knock them out of the number one spot. I think everyone will agree that we *have* to award big points for this." He paused for effect, grinning. "Kory, come on up!"

Libby snapped her head around, looking for Kory. *What in the world . . .*

Kory emerged from the crowd with a grin of his own, joining Wood on the top step.

When the chatter died down, Kory began. "I was eighteen years old when I came to my first Sanders family reunion. It was there that I met Janelle."

Everyone looked to see where Janelle stood in the crowd.

"I don't know how it was possible, but by the end of that weekend, after endless conversation and getting to know the spirit within, I had fallen in love with that girl."

Janelle was dabbing tears.

"We lost touch," Kory said, "and I thought Janelle would forever be a distant memory. But our paths have crossed again. And my love for her has only grown deeper and wider." He stopped to gather himself. "Estelle and Russell, can you come up here?" He smiled. "I've already had a long talk with them about this." He looked to the front row. "My daughter, Dee, and Janelle's son and daughter, Daniel and Tiffany, come on up—I talked to them too."

Laughter rose, but it was soft laughter.

When they had all gathered on the porch, Kory walked down the steps and into the crowd. He led Janelle by hand to the porch landing. Then he held out his hand, and Janelle's father passed him a small box. Kory went down on a knee.

Janelle was in tears, and Libby realized she was too. She couldn't hear the words clearly, but she had no doubt what Kory had said as Janelle blurted, "Yes," and he took her into his arms.

The family celebrated with applause, cheers, and tears. Slowly, the crowd broke, many making their way to congratulate Janelle and Kory.

"You okay?" Travis said.

Libby swiped the tears. "Fine."

Omar took her hand. "Walk with me a minute."

When they found space to themselves, Omar stopped and turned to her. "Looks like I've missed a lot this weekend."

Libby looked at him. "I don't know what you mean."

"I thought you didn't want me here because you'd be busy with reunion festivities." His eyes bore into hers. "But that wasn't it at all. You've been busy with Travis."

"Where'd you get that from?"

"Team Wood? You asked Travis to be on your team and not me? I thought I was the one you've been seeing."

"Okay, really, Omar? You're questioning me?" *Why does this happen every time?* "Travis has been coming to these reunions since he was a boy. My family knows and loves him. He helped with the planning, so I simply asked if he wanted to be on the team."

"Your *family* knows and loves him. That includes you, right?"

Libby sighed. "Omar, I'm not doing this. I'm not in the mood. I didn't invite you so you could grill me."

"Why *did* you invite me, Libby? Looked like there was some tension between you and Travis. Something happened, so you called your runner-up, Omar?"

"It wasn't like that."

"I think it was exactly like that." He looked at her, shaking his head. "You know what? You told me you didn't want a commitment, and I was fine with that. I didn't plan to get my feelings involved, but I did. I actually cut other women back to spend time with you. And to be honest, with all the time we spend together, I thought you'd come around. But I won't let you play me like this."

Emotion welled up again. Was he about to walk away? Libby could hear her Raleigh friends telling her she was crazy not to commit to Omar, that he was handsome, made good money, and treated her well . . . and if she didn't want him, she needed to get out of the way so somebody else could have him. But she didn't want to get out of the way. She liked having him in her life, even if only a part of it.

A light entered Omar's eyes. "I just realized what you said . . . that Travis has been coming here for years. You two have a history, don't you?"

"A long-time-ago history. We dated in college."

"Okay." Omar laughed a little, but there was no humor in it. "All this time I knew you weren't ready for 'commitment,' which I always took to mean you weren't ready for marriage. But I thought I was still special to you. I thought I was the main guy in your life. But that's Travis's spot."

"No, Omar, it's not Travis's spot." Exasperation filled her voice. "Can we just . . . move on and forget all this?"

He stared into her eyes. "No. We can't. I'm headed back to Raleigh."

Her heart sank. "Aren't you going to eat? We have ribs and chicken and—"

He held up his hand, taking a step back. "I'm good. Take care, Libby."

"I'll see you later this week?"

He shook his head, turned, and walked toward his car.

Libby couldn't breathe. Should she go after him? Reassure him? She sighed. Reassure him of what? Her noncommittal stance?

Suddenly, in the midst of a gathering of over a hundred people, she felt desperately alone.

CHAPTER THIRTEEN

C harley began making the rounds early evening, saying good-bye. Most of the Sanders family she still didn't know, but from hanging out at Grandma Geri's house, she'd gotten to know those family members in particular—and was proud of herself for learning the names of aunts, uncles, and innumerable cousins.

Charley hugged Janelle and Kory again. "I'm so happy for you two," she said. "So beautiful, the way you did it, Kory. I'm a sucker for love stories. And after all you've been through."

In one of the late-night conversations, Janelle and Kory had shared more of their story. Charley couldn't believe Kory's wife had left him for another man, then returned a year later—after he and Janelle had found one another again—when that other man left her. Janelle refused to stand in the way, insisting Kory try to reconcile. Though reluctant, he did try, only to watch his estranged wife leave again weeks later.

"I didn't think I could love again." Janelle clasped Kory's hand. "Words can't even describe."

Stephanie walked by, and Charley stopped her. "Hey, let me get my hug."

"Are you leaving?" Stephanie said. "I thought you wanted to tell me something."

"I did," Charley said, "but there hasn't been a good time. I'll call you." Then she waved the idea away as quickly as she'd said it. "Never mind, I can't wait." She grinned. "I told Marcus I'm taking the coaching position!"

Stephanie's eyes widened. "No way! You're staying? What made you decide?"

"It started with that newspaper article," Charley said. "I hate to say this, but I'd never heard much about what life was like in the sixties in Hope Springs. Gave me a real perspective for the way things are today, and why this joint service is so important. Then when Pastor Travis preached on God accomplishing His purpose through us . . . I felt this stirring, almost an urgency, that this is where I needed to be."

"Wow." Stephanie nodded. "I would say I'm surprised, but I know that feeling." She hugged her. "Now I can admit I pulled a Marcus—I was praying for you."

Charley gave her a skeptical look. "What did you pray?"

"That God would keep you here." She held up her hands in defense. "But I said only if it's His will."

"Uh-huh. Turnabout is fair play." She spotted Cyd in the distance. "Let me finish my good-byes to everybody who's leaving town." She smiled. "I can see you any ol' time."

Charley hugged Cyd, Cedric, and Chase, who were leaving early in the morning. Next she swung through the kitchen, saying good-bye to the aunts who'd cooked up a ton of good food, including breakfast that morning. Then, remembering her overnight bag in Stephanie and Lindell's room, she doubled back.

The bedroom door was slightly ajar, and Charley heard voices as she entered, though those speaking couldn't see her. When she realized the voices belonged to Stephanie and Marcus—with her name in the conversation—she couldn't help it. She paused where she stood.

"She just told me," Stephanie was saying. "I'm so pumped she's staying."

"Me too," Marcus said. "Definite plus for the volleyball program."

"And maybe a plus for someone else?"

Marcus hesitated. "What do you mean?"

"Oh, just thought maybe I detected a little teeny something between the two of you. You needn't confirm or deny, but if I'm right, I'm tickled pink."

Charley's jaw dropped. Stephanie detected something? On both their parts?

"A little teeny something?" There was a lightness in Marcus's voice. "I like Charley a lot," he said, "but not in the way you're thinking. More like a sister."

"Mm-hm. That's why you hung out over here till all hours of the night, two nights straight, talking to her. I may be many things, but I ain't crazy."

Marcus was quiet a moment. "You know . . . maybe I need to be honest with myself. From what I've seen so far, Charley has a lot of qualities I want in a woman. Maybe you did detect a little something. It's just . . ."

"What?"

Charley was sure she could hear her heart hammering.

"Whenever I see myself with someone, it's a black woman. That's what I happen to prefer. Is that wrong?"

"Marcus, I thought you were bringing me my purse!"

The sound of Aunt Gladys's voice startled Charley, causing her to step back—and into the door. She headed quickly into the living room, realizing she still needed her bag. Her feet kept moving anyway. She'd get it tomorrow. She just needed to get out of—

Someone grabbed her hand and turned her around, and she wished her heart hadn't fluttered. Marcus.

"Please tell me you didn't hear that," he said.

"I heard enough."

He sighed. "I didn't mean—"

"There's nothing to say, Marcus. Really. Everything's cool."

He looked at her. "But I can't leave it like this, Charley." He tried to make eye contact, to no avail. "Can we talk a few minutes? We could go for a walk."

Charley tried to stifle her emotions. He had no clue what she'd been feeling all weekend, so no clue how much it hurt. She needed to keep it that way.

She shrugged. "Sure, I've got a few minutes." She turned slightly toward the back door, and he opened it, holding it as she walked past.

They moved through pockets of people, out of the lighted back-yard, and up the street. They'd never had a moment alone like this, and Charley's senses were on hyper alert—aware of his slow gait, the fresh scent from his shower, the brush of his arm when he drifted too close. Why *now* was she feeling drawn to him more than ever? What a joke.

"This is so awkward," Marcus said. "I'm really sorry. I never would've said that if—"

Charley held up a hand. "Marcus, I know. And please, you don't have to apologize. I think we all have a certain image in our heads of our ideal mate."

He walked in silence a few feet. "But as soon as I said it, I was sort of convicted." He paused. "Just last night I was telling you God has me thinking differently about relationships. So it hit me, Am I thinking like God wants me to think, or like I was raised to think?

She glanced at him. "How were you raised to think?"

"You want me to be frank?"

Charley nodded.

"Mom always said, 'Don't bring home no white girl, especially not one with blond hair and blue eyes.'"

Charley felt a stab. "Aunt Gladys said that? But she's been so nice to me."

"It's not that she doesn't like white people. It's just, when it comes to marriage . . ." He turned toward her. "Your parents never said anything to you about interracial dating?"

"There was never a reason to," she said. "They promoted a relationship with Jake from the time I was young." She shrugged. "I honestly don't know what my mom would think."

He looked at her. "What about you?"

"It's not on the list of what's important to me. Maybe that's unrealistic, I don't know."

They rounded the bend and continued on for several yards, passing Travis's house.

"What *is* important to you?"

"That he have a heart for God. That's my main thing right now."

They walked in silence awhile.

Charley paused in the middle of the street. "I'd better start back. I have a lot to do in the morning, especially now that I've got a new position to think about."

"Which I'm still really excited about. But . . . I feel like the dynamic has changed between us."

"Not really." She started a slow trek back to the house. "Just maybe back to the way it was before Friday night."

"But why? I feel like we became friends this weekend. How did the conversation with Stephanie change things?"

Charley couldn't think of a quick answer, not one she wanted to reveal, anyway.

He stopped walking. "Charley, seriously, I'm trying to understand. We're not friends now? It's not like I said anything negative about you. I said I liked you."

She laughed a little, but it held no humor. "Yeah, like a sister. But if I were black . . ." She cringed the moment it came out of her mouth. "Forget I said that. I really don't want to talk about this anymore."

She walked a little faster than before, with Marcus keeping pace, silent. She almost wished he would defy her, keep talking. Part of her wanted to know more of what he was thinking, more about those words to Stephanie. *"Maybe you did detect a little something."*

But her saner self was raising the professional wall, hoping they never broached this subject again.

CHAPTER FOURTEEN
Thursday, August 5

I t might've taken a couple of days longer than expected, but by Thursday, after the dust from the reunion had cleared, everyone had gone, and she'd sufficiently caught up on sleep, it hit Stephanie—Hope Springs was home.

No carryout on Friday nights from her favorite local restaurants. No radio stations she had any interest in hearing. No department or boutique stores a mile away to drop in on when she was happy, sad, or mad—or Smoothie King or Ted Drewes frozen custard. And no impromptu visits with her parents or Cyd and Cedric. But she had a new normal she was enjoying—daytime kitchen table chats with Janelle and Becca.

Except "enjoy" might not be the best word for today. They were a little on edge, awaiting Todd's return from a meeting with his elder board.

"It's been two hours," Stephanie said. "How much could there have been to say?"

Becca sipped some sweet tea. "Maybe lots. Todd said he'd never heard Skip so angry. I've been really praying for God to take control of that meeting. Nothing good comes from anger."

Janelle looked over her shoulder from the sink. "I've been praying too. This is such a pivotal time." She sprayed one of the dishes from lunch and put it in the rack. "I can't get that newspaper article out of my mind. When you think about where this town has been and where we are today, there's been significant change . . . everywhere but the church. That's crazy."

"It's been weighing on Todd's mind too," Becca said. "Gave him a different perspective as to why it was so hard for his dad and your Aunt Gwynn to be together. Things were really ugly back then."

"And we're still experiencing the effects all these decades later," Stephanie said. "I knew nothing could get Aunt Gwynn to the reunion, but I thought for sure Keisha would come."

"Me too," Janelle said. "But at the same time, I can see why she didn't. She was overwhelmed at Grandma's funeral, inundated with questions about who she is and how she fits in the family." She rinsed a glass. "People meant well, but who wants to go through that? I hope she was serious about finding another time to come when she can just visit with us."

"Todd's hoping for that too," Becca said.

The screen on the side door slammed and lots of little feet came pattering inside. Claire, Tiffany, and Dee had been running around outside, but now they stood shoulder to shoulder before the grown-ups, grinning.

Janelle and Becca cast an amused glance at one another, waiting.

"Mom, we have a fabulous idea." Tiffany looked at the others, as if wondering how she should share this wonderful news. "You know how me and Claire are starting kindergarten at Hope Springs Elementary Monday?"

Janelle sat down at the table. "Yes, in fact, I do."

"Well . . ." Tiffany smiled at the others. "You say it, Dee."

Dee looked tentative. "We were wondering . . . since I'm

starting kindergarten too . . . if I could go to school with Tiffany and Claire."

"Oh, I love that you girls want to go to school together," Janelle said. "But, Dee, sweetie, you live in Rocky Mount, and you have to go to the school in your neighborhood."

Dee pouted. "But I don't want to go to that school. I want to be with my friends."

"I've got *another* idea, Miss Janelle!" Claire said. "You and Mr. Kory could get married, like, today. Then he and Dee could move in, they'd be living *here*, and she could go to school with us." She grinned at her solution.

Becca looked at her daughter. "Claire, you're—"

"Oh, could you?" Dee was all over it. "Can you ask Daddy?"

Janelle was smiling. "Dee, as soon as your daddy gets here after work, I promise I will ask him if we can get married today so you two can move in."

"Yayyy!" the girls said, running back out.

"Don't slam the screen door," Becca called. "Ethan is taking a—"

It shut with a loud clap.

"Just think," Janelle said, "this time next week our little girls will be in a classroom."

"It's really hard to believe," Becca said.

"So much will look different around here next week," Stephanie said. "The kids will be in school, Lindell will be in Haiti, Janelle starts her job"—she looked at her cousin—"which should be pretty cool."

"It's only part-time, but I'm kind of nervous," Janelle said. "It's been so long since I've been accountable to anyone on a job."

Stephanie tossed her a look. "Oh yeah, and you've got such a mean boss."

"That part *is* pretty cool," Janelle said. "I'm gonna love being Travis's assistant."

"*Executive* assistant," Becca added. "You two know each other so well. It'll be a great fit."

"Only problem is I don't know how long I can do it. Kory and I haven't set a date yet"—she smiled—"assuming it won't be today. And we haven't talked about whether we'll live in Rocky Mount, Hope Springs, or someplace else."

"What?" Stephanie looked at her like she was crazy. "Y'all *better* live in Hope Springs. Don't play with me."

Janelle laughed. "That'll be my vote. Anyway, I think I'm more excited about your job than mine, Steph."

"Girrrl, I think I lost my mind. Did I really tell Marcus I'd do it?" She aimed a finger at them both. "One of you drugged me."

"I think it will be perfect for you," Becca said. "I'm already praying."

"On that we agree," Stephanie said. "I'll need tons of prayer. Shoot, if I'm gonna substitute teach, I should've asked whether they needed anyone at the elementary school. That's more my speed." She thought about it. "Nah. They're both treacherous."

"Did Marcus say where you'd be assigned?" Janelle asked.

"Not yet. But I said don't give me math or science . . . or history . . . or English . . . or home ec . . ."

Janelle threw a napkin at her. "I will rejoice as God uses you in ways you haven't even imagined."

The screen door opened again, and heavier feet made their way into the kitchen. Stephanie expected to see Todd, but Travis walked in with him. None of the women said anything. They looked, and waited.

Todd and Travis pulled out chairs and sat, looking somber, unhurried. After a few seconds Todd sat back and cleared his throat.

"You may as well all hear this at once," Todd said. "There won't be any more joint services."

The women all spoke at once.

"What?"

"Why not?"

"Honey, what happened?"

"I won't get into everything that was said in the elder meeting," Todd said. "But the bottom line is that Calvary was being cast in a bad light. Although there were members of both churches who opposed the service—for various reasons—that newspaper clearly had an agenda to paint certain Calvary members as racially prejudiced. In particular, Skip Willoughby. I didn't like the tone when I read it, and Skip was understandably incensed."

Todd stared downward for a moment, then looked back at them. "He reminded me that I was hired to shepherd Calvary, and to carry on the tradition of my father and grandfather to uphold its standing in the community. I can't be a Lone Ranger, going against my elder board, men who are in place to help guide me and the church." He sighed. "I agreed it would be best to forgo any more joint services for now. My focus will be on Calvary alone."

Stephanie was sure Janelle and Becca were as stunned as she. No one jumped to speak. Which wasn't to say that Stephanie had no response. There was a lot she could say.

"Todd . . ." Becca paused, taking her time. "I honestly don't think you were being a Lone 'Ranger. There were a lot of people from Calvary at those first three services. I think they succumbed to the pressure of a small few who opposed it." She quickly added, "But even if you *were* being a Lone Ranger, you prayed long and hard about this. You felt convicted to make a change as you studied the Word. As a leader, sometimes you have to go it alone if it's God's will."

"Becca, you really can't," Todd said, "not when you've got a hierarchy to answer to, and this one's got a lot of history behind it. Skip's been on the elder board for decades. If I go it alone, they'll just fire me."

"Todd, I have a question," Janelle said. "I get that you were hired to shepherd Calvary—but the part about being hired to carry on tradition and uphold the church's standing in the community . . . where is that in the Bible?"

"Actually, Scripture says for the sake of tradition, people *neglect* the commandments of God." Travis was subdued. "But I said I'd keep quiet. Todd is already mad at me."

"I don't know why you keep saying that," Todd said. "We just agreed to disagree, that's all."

The women glanced between them, waiting.

"Go on and tell them," Todd said. "We're all family here."

Travis leaned forward. "I just asked Todd, what if Skip Willoughby's objections are in fact about racial prejudice? It's not much of a stretch, given his history. I just wanted to know how that would affect Todd's decision."

"And I said we can't hold people's pasts against them," Todd said. "There are many people who held to certain beliefs and attitudes in the sixties who've changed. That's what forgiveness in Christ is about." His eyes were weary.

"Okay," Travis said, "but you haven't answered my question."

Todd steepled his fingers and sighed. "I can't go there. I don't even want to assume one of my elders could think that way."

Silence descended on the room.

"We've got Soul Sisters tonight," Becca said. "They've been praying every week from the beginning about this. Can we update them?"

"Sure," Todd said. "It's no secret. The joint worship service on first Sundays is no more."

Travis was beginning to think he and Trina had lingered too long. It had seemed like an innocuous enough outing. He'd run into her at church as he was putting the final touches on his message for tomorrow. She'd come to make copies of a flyer for the choir picnic. A gourmet cook, she liked to tease him by asking his plans for dinner. As usual, he had none, and she admitted the same, so it seemed like no big deal when she said they should grab a bite.

But from there it snowballed. Instead of someplace local—his thought—they drove forty minutes to a new hot spot in Raleigh—Mama Jay's—new, at least, to the nation. Featured on a cable show as the place to go in the area for soul food, it was known for its long waits. Travis had never been, though he'd heard Libby rave about it, which was why he offered up other options when Trina suggested it. The last thing he wanted was to run into Libby while dining with Trina.

But Trina had never been either, and after a lot of back-and-forth, she kept coming back to Mama Jay's. He decided he was being paranoid. Libby was probably working an event tonight anyway. So they came—and loved it.

Travis balled his paper napkin and tossed it onto the wooden table beside his empty bowl of peach cobbler. "Now that I've eaten enough to waddle out of here, I guess we'd better head back."

"Don't say that." Trina finished her Diet Coke. "I had the nerve to get mac-and-cheese *and* candied yams, and I don't waddle well."

She smiled, and a single dimple showed. Travis had found himself noticing more of her features lately, and her style. At church she usually wore a casual skirt or slacks and a top. Today she wore blue jeans and a funky tie-dye shirt. She wasn't showy. Didn't overdo. He liked that.

She scooted back a tad in her chair, then paused. "I enjoyed this," she said. "I feel like I'm getting to know more of Travis the man instead of just Travis the pastor."

He smiled slightly. "I don't know if that's a good thing or a bad thing. Some people don't want to see their pastors as real people."

"I can imagine it would be hard to let down, so to speak."

"It is." Travis relaxed again. "I think I put up boundaries without realizing it. The only people I'm probably totally *me* with—live and unedited—are the friends I've known most of my life."

"Like Pastor Todd and Janelle?"

"Exactly." Libby entered his mind as well.

"So . . . just trying to see where I fit in your boundaries . . ." Trina smiled, her hair falling partially over her face. "How often do you go to dinner like this with members of New Jerusalem?"

"If you're talking females . . . never." He knew the statement needed follow-up. "I'll be straight with you. This is different for me, having a new female friend in this stage of life. I've never negotiated this terrain as a pastor. Actually," he added, "I made it a personal policy not to date anyone in my congregation"—he threw up his hands—"not that this is a date; I don't know how this happened. But seriously, I'm not sure how a new female friend in the congregation would work. Although I *am* sure it could get complicated."

"It's weird for me too, if that helps," Trina said. "I find myself watching what I say and how I say it because you're a pastor. Like, can I say *dang?*" She chuckled. "Oh, and I had to kick myself for Saturday night."

"Why?"

"I mentioned that my brother invited you to the jazz club," she said. "As soon as the words were out of my mouth, I thought, *Oh no, what if he didn't want people to know he went to a jazz club?* My only relief was that I said it was an invitation, and maybe they'd think you didn't go."

"You were safe with that crew," he said. "It wouldn't strike them as inappropriate that I went to a jazz club." *That was the least of it.*

"Oh, good."

"But to your other point," Travis said, "please don't feel you have to watch what you say or how you say it. I'd rather you be yourself." He gave a wry smile. "And I'll try to be myself."

Trina's eyes were warm. "I like that."

Travis let his gaze fall to the water glass. He took a final sip, then stood, shelling out a few dollars for a tip. "Ready? I think we pay up front."

The restaurant was crowded still. They moved past the tables to the front and saw a long line of people waiting to enter. There was a line to pay as well, so they got behind the last person.

"This is amazing," Trina said, looking around. "I wonder what it was like before they got national exposure."

"From what I heard, it's been a popular spot for a while. Probably not *this* popular, though."

As they moved up in line, Travis glanced around. Lots of different people, old and young. His eyes passed over the carryout line—and he turned swiftly back around, glad it was their turn. Travis paid—they'd debated that earlier—and made his way to the door. But the way to the door was past the carryout line.

It would be silly to pretend he didn't see her. As he came closer, he saw her eyes dead on him. But she didn't appear to be alone. A guy behind her was saying something to her, though they could've simply struck up friendly conversation. They were both nicely dressed.

Trina tapped him. "Isn't that Janelle's cousin? The one whose basketball team you were playing for?"

He nodded. "Yes, that's Libby."

Trina was closest as they approached. "Hey, Libby, good to see you again," she said.

"Good to see you too, Trina." Libby's eyes dusted him. "Travis." She gestured to the guy beside her. "This is Barry. Barry, Trina and Travis."

Barry gave enthusiastic handshakes. "Nice to meet you," he said.

"Likewise," Travis said.

He glanced at Libby. Didn't she and Omar just break up on Sunday? No one told him, but it had seemed obvious by how abruptly he left. Didn't take long for Libby to find a replacement. Or maybe she'd been seeing this Barry all along.

"You come here often?" Trina asked.

"I do," Libby said. "I don't live very far, and I love the food."

"It was our first time." Trina smiled at Travis. "And it was delicious. I wish I lived closer."

Libby replied with a thin smile. Moving up in line, she said, "Have a safe trip back."

"Thanks," Trina said.

Travis nodded good-bye to them both and walked silently to Trina's car. As Trina pulled out of the parking space, his phone buzzed with a text. He took it from his belt clip and looked at it.

Really, Travis? I know I told u I get carryout from Js most Sat nights. U had to come HERE w/ur girlfriend?

He sighed, his head knocking against the headrest.

Trina pulled onto the main road, glancing at him as he typed out a reply.

You nvr told me that. But I apologize. Didn't mean for that to happen.

He pointed a finger at Send but decided to add a footnote.

Was that your new boyfriend?

He sent it and immediately wished he could snatch it back. Didn't take long for Libby's reply to appear.

My COLLEAGUE & I worked a wedding 2day & his WIFE was waiting in the car. Njoy the rest of ur date.

Travis stared at the phone, then typed one more message.

I apologize again. Wasn't my place to ask.

He waited a moment to see if she would reply, but there was nothing.

Trina glanced at him. "Everything okay?"

Travis put the phone away. "Depends on which Travis you're asking . . . Travis the man or Travis the pastor."

❧

Libby entered her apartment and kicked the door closed behind her. She walked into the kitchen, dropped her purse and carry-out satchel on the counter, then walked back to her bedroom. Collapsing on her bed, she let out a tired sigh. Weddings were long days, and this one was especially long. A swanky affair two hours away at the waterfront in New Bern, there were ten attendants on each side, close to five hundred guests, and a popular local band. Thankfully, most everything came off without a hitch, but it was still long—and it didn't help that she'd spent much of the time battling thoughts of whether she ever wanted to be a bride herself.

She kicked off her heels and rubbed her feet, picturing the beautiful bride today. She was twenty-five, almost ten years younger than Libby, and deliriously happy. For now. Libby had seen too many fairy-tale weddings that ended in ugly separations. She knew too many people her age who were single because "the one" to whom they'd pledged undying love somehow became the wrong one. No doubt she'd become a cynic. Better to keep men at a safe distance, deal with them on her own terms . . . but her own terms weren't exactly yielding the best results.

This was the first weekend in a long time that she had no one to call and talk to. No one to catch a movie with. No one to enjoy Saturday night carryout with.

And she certainly wouldn't enjoy it right now. She hopped off the bed and began peeling off her pantsuit, irritated afresh. She still couldn't believe Travis came to *her* restaurant with someone else. She'd been talking up Mama Jay's to him for months, telling him he needed to check it out. For him to go without her—on a date, no less—felt like a kick in the gut.

And he had the nerve to ask if Barry was her boyfriend?

She threw on a pair of yoga pants and a T-shirt and headed back to the kitchen. *Why did he ask that?* She lifted her baked chicken from the bag, then the fried corn and black-eyed peas. *Was he just curious . . . or did he care?* She got a plate and spooned out a serving of each. They always gave her extra, and often it was even better the second day. She put it in the microwave to warm and leaned against the counter as she waited.

So what if he was curious, and so what if he cared? She had to get Travis out of her mind. That's why she didn't go to Hope Springs after the wedding, as Janelle and Stephanie had asked. She hadn't wanted to run into Travis. *Ha!* What a joke that she'd run into him in Raleigh.

The microwave stopped as her cell phone began ringing. She

thought of letting it go to voice mail. But what if Travis had just gotten home? What if he wanted to talk about what happened? Didn't mean she had to listen, but . . .

She found her phone in her purse and frowned at a number she didn't recognize. *If this is one of those telemarketers . . .*

"Hello?"

"Hello? Libby?"

"Yes, this is Libby. Who's this?"

"This is your aunt Gwynn."

It took a moment for Libby to grasp it. Her aunt rarely called her own siblings, let alone anyone else in the family. Libby couldn't recall ever speaking with her by phone.

"Aunt Gwynn? Hi. I'm . . . surprised to hear from you."

"I thought you might be." Her tone wasn't exactly casual, but friendly. "You included your number in that package you sent."

"Oh, right. So you got it?"

Libby had done a mass mailing of the DVD she'd had made for the reunion. She sent it to everyone who'd requested and paid for one. But as she packaged them up, Aunt Gwynn came to mind, and she mailed one to her in New Jersey.

"I received it, yes. And I don't know what made me watch, but I did." She paused. "I've never been to a Sanders reunion."

Her aunt's every word seemed weighty. Libby took a seat at her small kitchen table. "And I don't know what made me send it," she said. "I didn't know if you'd appreciate having a piece of family history . . . or not."

She braced herself for the latter. What if Aunt Gwynn was calling to let her know how much she *didn't* appreciate it? It was clear from Grandma Geri's eighty-seventh birthday party that her aunt had no problem letting her true feelings be known.

"It took me places I didn't expect to go," Aunt Gwynn said. "Seeing my brothers and sisters through the years, and their kids, and *their* kids, and all the great-aunts and uncles and *their* families . . . I've been on the outside of such a long-standing family tradition."

Libby waited. There seemed to be a lot on her aunt's heart, and she wanted to hear it all.

"I was able to go years and years without facing the past, even my own family," Aunt Gwynn continued. "And in a few short months, Jim died, then Momma, and now, it seems like the past keeps coming at me." She grew quiet for a moment. "I want to thank you for sending it. I was sad that I didn't know my nieces and nephews, including you. And when I read what you said in that note . . ."

"That I saw a lot of myself in you?"

"Yes. What did you mean by that?"

It was easy for Libby to write it when she was almost positive she wouldn't get a response. "I, um . . . I can be straight with you?"

"Anything else would be a waste of time."

Libby smiled a little. Forthrightness had to be a family trait. "Okay, here goes. I was surprised that after so much time had passed, your life was still very much affected by that one relationship, which of course produced Keisha. You never got married, and you said you've never loved anyone else. It seemed sad, if you want to know the truth, like you decided you weren't going to take the risk to really live again."

"Guess you couldn't be much straighter than that." Aunt Gwynn's tone was easy. "Now what part of all that reminds you of your own life?"

"Well. Mine doesn't involve an interracial romance. Or pregnancy. Or parents who said we couldn't be together." She paused, hearing herself. "Okay, now mine sounds trivial compared to yours."

"If it's on your heart like this, it's not trivial," Aunt Gwynn said. "I'm listening."

"It's just that . . . I dated this guy in college, and we both said we weren't looking for anything long-term and serious. But we were together all the time, got along well. He was a daily part of my life. And then . . ." Her breath caught. "Then I dropped by one day and a friend of mine opened the door, *his* door, like she belonged there. It knocked the wind out of me. After months and months together, he could so easily get with someone else? I wasn't special at all? And the worst part was that . . ."

A tear slid down her face. She'd never admitted this to anyone, not even Janelle. "I'd fallen in love with him." She flicked the tear away, wanting to move along. "Since then, I've been determined not to give my heart to anyone else. You could say I've committed myself to being uncommitted. So, kind of like you, that one relationship has affected everything else, because I don't want to risk getting hurt. And I'm wondering if I'll look up in twenty years and be where you are, bitter and alone."

"You think I'm bitter?"

"Sorry. It does seem that way."

"So the young man from college," Aunt Gwynn said. "You parted ways like Jim and I did, never to see each other again?"

"Not exactly," Libby said. "We went years without contact, then I saw him last December"—she paused, realizing the irony—"at Jim's funeral."

"At *Jim's* funeral?"

"Guess I left out part of it. The guy's name is Travis, and he grew up in Hope Springs. I've known him most of my life. He moved back to Hope Springs last fall to pastor New Jerusalem."

"Interesting," Aunt Gwynn said. "I understand Jim's son, Todd, is pastor at Calvary now. Sounds like a sea change happening in Hope Springs, with two young pastors. Okay, and what's the current story with you and Travis? Did you ignore one another? Patch things up?"

"It took awhile," Libby said, "but with Grandma Geri getting sick and passing away—she loved Travis, by the way—he and I became friends again and . . ." She sighed. "I won't bore you with all that."

"Or is it that it's too painful?"

Libby stared at the table. "You're right. See, you're getting to know your niece better." She smiled faintly. "At the reunion we broke off the friendship because once again I realized I had feelings for him, and he admitted the same for me. But it can't go anywhere because, like I said, he's a pastor now. And I'm not with the whole faith/God/church thing . . ."

"So we do have some things in common."

"That's where you are too?" Libby had thought they might be like-minded in this.

"I couldn't understand how my parents and Jim's parents—people of God, and a pastor in the case of Jim's dad—could be so dead set against us because of the color of our skin. I knew that wasn't in the Bible, and I said if this is what it looks like to be a person of faith, I want no part of it. And that's where I remained until . . . well, really until this summer."

Libby sat up. "What happened this summer?"

"Keisha's been praying for me a long time. She said I was bitter too. And she was upset about the things I said at Momma's birthday gathering. Talk about giving it straight . . ." She paused. "I wasn't ready to receive it at the time. Didn't go to my own momma's funeral, as you know—and Keisha told me what she thought about that too." She sighed. "Anyway, she got me to visit her church. I haven't been going regularly, but I have to admit it's making an impact."

Libby felt strangely let down. She wanted her aunt to understand where she stood with not going to church, and even affirm it.

"Libby?"

"Yes, I'm here."

"What would you think about taking a trip up here?"

CHAPTER SIXTEEN

Sunday, August 8

Charley hopped in the shower Sunday morning, resolved to stay home from church. News of the discontinuation of the joint services had hit her hard. She'd been praying for just the opposite, had even talked to her grandfather early in the week. He'd never attended one of them himself, so she told him how beautiful it was to see the unity and fellowship between the churches.

But his mind was fixed. And by the end of the week, he was practically giddy when he reported that the elders meeting with Pastor Todd had yielded the result he wanted. Calvary would no longer participate in a joint service with New Jerusalem. He'd even indicated that today's service would be a celebration of sorts, at least among those who'd been opposed to it.

Charley couldn't bear it. How could she look forward to worshiping with people who had boycotted an actual church service just last week? She'd decided to have her own personal boycott today and informed her mom last night.

But her thinking changed in the shower. As she prayed through her frustration, it occurred to her—Calvary wasn't the only church in town. It was almost silly that it hit her the way it did, as if she didn't know. But she'd never regarded New Jerusalem as an option until now. In all her thoughts that God was calling her to do something different, she was seeing more and more that the "different" was right before her, right in Hope Springs.

She stepped out of the shower, grabbing her towel, excited to call Stephanie and tell her. It didn't escape her that Marcus would be there too. But she'd seen him all week at school, as they prepared for the arrival of students tomorrow, and she'd kept their interactions brief and light. She'd do the same today.

She slipped on her robe and walked out of the bathroom—and stopped short. Her mother was standing outside her brother's bedroom, knocking.

"Ben, is Kelsey in there?" she said. "Unlock the door. *Now.*"

Charley's eyes widened. Did he sneak Kelsey into his room? The two had been downstairs watching a movie last night, and Kelsey had fallen asleep. Charley's mom called Kelsey's mom to say she could sleep over, on the sofa.

Ben opened the door and stepped out, looking disheveled in a shirt, shorts, and bedhead. He closed the door behind him.

Dottie looked at him, the look that said she was beside herself. "Exactly what is going on, Ben?"

Ben sighed. "Mom, calm down. Nothing's going on. Kelsey woke up in the night and couldn't get back to sleep. So we finished watching the movie, then fell asleep in here. That's it."

"And I'm supposed to believe that?"

"It's the *truth*, Mom." Ben ran his fingers through his hair. "I know how it looks, but can't you just trust me? You always assume the worst."

Charley eyed her brother. *With good reason.*

"I want to trust you, Ben," Dottie said. "After all you've been taught, I want to believe you wouldn't dare do something improper—right under my nose, no less."

"That's what I'm *saying*, Mom. I'm not that dumb. I'd be asking to get caught." He glanced back at the door. "I'll tell Kelsey she needs to get home . . . and we can all get ready for church."

"Oh. Right." Charley shook her head. "Now you want to go to church."

Ben cut his eyes over at her. "Butt out, Charley. This has nothing to do with—"

"Actually, it does, Ben." The words spilled out of her. "Kelsey is one of my players, and I care about the well-being of my girls. I care about you too. What you're doing is not—"

"We didn't *do* anything."

"Listen," Dottie said. Her gaze drifted beyond Ben to the door, then back at him. "Just . . . yes, tell Kelsey she needs to get home right now." She paused, then sighed. "I don't even know what to . . . We'll talk about this later, Ben."

Ben quickly disappeared into his room. Charley, shaking her head, moved toward hers.

"Charley, I'm hoping you changed your mind about going to church this morning," her mom said.

Charley turned. "Actually, I did. I'm going to New Jerusalem."

"What? But, Charley, that's not our church. Don't you think you might feel . . . out of place?"

Charley shrugged. "It'll be cool. I'll be with Stephanie and Janelle."

"You know your grandfather won't be pleased. He's looking forward to Calvary members coming together for worship this morning."

"Mom, I'm twenty-four. I can't worry about what Grandpa thinks. I feel like, more and more, I just want to know what God thinks."

Charley pulled away from the house at the same time as her mom and Ben, both cars headed for Maple Street. She'd gotten voice mail when she tried to call Stephanie and Janelle, which, she decided, was a good thing. They were sure to be surprised—since Charley was surprised herself by the idea. She'd much rather get their reaction in person than over the phone.

She needed to make only two turns between her house and Maple. Felt weird to pass the church she'd been attending her entire life, save for college. She saw familiar faces as people strolled down the sidewalk, heading inside. From her rearview mirror, she saw her mom slow behind her and parallel park.

With the churches only two blocks apart, Charley began to see a different wave of people strolling down the sidewalk, heading into New Jerusalem. She glanced down at what she was wearing. Though many at Calvary wore suits and dresses, she tended to dress down, a carryover from the church she attended near campus. Would her casual skirt and flat sandals fit the dressy garb she was seeing here?

She blew out a slow breath. *It's not about dress. It's not about anything but Jesus.* That's where she wanted her focus to be.

Charley had to turn up a side street to find a parking spot. She cruised two blocks and found one that her Corolla could maneuver into. She grabbed her Bible and got out.

"Parking must be real tight when Calvary folk have to come way down here."

Recognizing the voice immediately, she turned. Marcus had stopped in the middle of the road, his window rolled down.

"I'm worshiping at New Jerusalem today."

He paused, as if waiting for a punch line. "Seriously?"

"Seriously. Hey, are Stephanie and Janelle already here?"

"No. I was at the house before I headed here, and they were still getting ready."

Charley pointed. "You've got cars behind you."

"Let me park real quick," he said. "Be right back."

And what? I'm supposed to wait?

She'd noticed this from Marcus all week, signs of their newfound familiarity. Like texting an update on her request for new uniforms instead of sending an e-mail. Or snagging a carrot cake cupcake for her, made by the civics teacher and quickly raided by faculty, because she'd enjoyed carrot cake at the reunion. The cupcake was delicious, and she would've missed it otherwise, but still . . . She wished he'd pretend the weekend never happened.

Just as she wished she'd walked up the sidewalk and into the church building instead of waiting.

Marcus came toward her now, in beige slacks, a striped button-down shirt, and a tie, which she tried not to notice.

"So what brought this New Jerusalem thing on?" he asked as they walked.

She stared ahead. "Trying to live outside the box, I guess."

They walked in silence, then he glanced at her. "So . . . will you ever go back to being Charley?"

"I'm Charley right this moment."

"Not the easygoing, smiley, kinda crazy Charley."

"We all have different sides to our personalities." She focused on her sandals.

"Except I already know how easily I connect with your *other* side, so this remote one seems strange."

Their late-night conversations from last weekend, the laughter, the sharing—all of it came to mind as they rounded the bend and drew closer to the church. Charley knew her attitude must indeed seem strange. How was he supposed to know she'd been crushing on him? She turned to him finally, feeling a need to say *something*, but her eyes landed on a group of women in the distance who were staring at her. Her head fell a little, and she tucked her hair behind her ear.

The closer they got, the harder the women stared, until they were mere feet from one another.

"Really, Marcus?" one of them said.

Marcus looked at the speaker, obviously surprised, then turned to Charley. "Excuse me a second."

He went over to the women, who kept glancing over at her. Charley rummaged in her purse, for what she didn't know. She felt a mint near the bottom. That would do.

"What did they say?" she asked when he returned.

"Nothing. It's cool."

She looked at him. "Marcus, I want to know."

He hesitated, then, "She said she didn't know I was the type who paraded blond chicks on my arm."

Charley's eyes were wide as they approached the steps to the church. "I wasn't on your arm. We were, like, two feet apart, just walking." She looked at him. "What did you say?"

"I said, 'And I didn't know you were the type who paraded rudeness, so I guess we both learned something.'"

"You didn't.'"

"I did." Marcus was clearly bothered by it. "I can't believe she came at me like that."

Charley was about to comment, but just then she spied Stephanie and Lindell coming toward them.

"I thought I was seeing things," Stephanie said when she got closer. "Did you run down here to say hey and run back? Or are you here for real, for real?"

Charley smiled. "I'm here for real, for real."

"Cool!" Stephanie hugged her.

The same three women walked by, eyeing them.

Stephanie's hand went to her hip. "What was that about?"

"Cuz, you don't even want to know," Marcus said.

Lindell ushered her forward. "More like she doesn't *need* to know. My wife will go there."

"I'm trying to get better, though, babe," Stephanie said.

"I know, babe."

They entered the vestibule and waited for an usher to show them to their seats. Charley continued to receive stares, even if only brief, but she also got waves when women from Soul Sisters spotted her. She'd gone again last Thursday and enjoyed it even more.

The usher escorted them to the pew, and as they filed in, Charley had Marcus on one side, Stephanie on the other. Travis was standing at the end of a pew talking to people gathered there. But when praise and worship started, he moved to the front row. Charley stood with the rest, recognizing the song as one they'd sung at the joint service.

It started slow, with a solo, but when the other members of the praise team joined in and the tempo kicked up, the church started rocking with praise. Charley clapped her hands, loving the energy, especially from the band. She glanced now and then at the bass player, who was strumming, head bobbing, eyes shut. She was sure if no one else were present, he'd still be in his own praise world.

The next song she didn't know, but she knew the person who led it—Trina. It was slow as well, and remained so, simply and power-fully affirming love for the Lord. Each song in the set spoke to her, maybe because of the subtle changes happening in her life and heart. Worship was exactly what she needed, a singular focus.

After the last song, they sat for announcements, and Marcus leaned over.

"They're about to ask visitors to stand," he said.

She whispered back, "I'm not standing."

"You should."

"No. And technically, since I was at the joint service where Pastor Travis was preaching, I'm not a visitor."

A woman read several announcements—meetings, rehearsals, food and school supply drives—then said, "We want to welcome all first-time visitors to New Jerusalem. We know some of you came to the joint service last weekend and decided to visit again today, and we're so thankful." She adjusted her glasses. "But if this is your first time specifically at New Jerusalem Church . . ."

Marcus elbowed her. Charley elbowed back.

". . . we'd like you to stand and give your name and where you're from."

Charley was surprised to see several people rise. When she felt an elbow jab from the other side—Stephanie's—she came to her feet.

"My name is Darryl Long, and this is my wife, Cathy. We're from Jacksonville, Alabama, in town visiting family. We bring you greetings from King of Kings Missionary Baptist Church."

"Welcome, welcome," the announcer said. She nodded to the next.

"Praise the Lord and good morning." The woman's smile was bright. "I'm Bonita Rogers from Newport News, Virginia, here visiting my Auntie May." She smiled down at the older woman beside her. "Happy to bring greetings from Greater Mount Carmel where the Reverend Timothy T. Raymond is pastor."

Next was a young man. "I'm not good at this stuff," he said, "but I heard about y'all in the paper last week." He shrugged. "Thought I'd come check it out."

The announcer smiled. "And what's your name?"

"Oh. Cornell Freeman."

"We're glad to have you, Cornell," she said. "Make sure you stay after and meet Pastor Brooks."

Two more spoke, then she nodded at Charley, one of three still standing.

She took a breath. "I'm Charley Willoughby. And you can probably see I'm . . . a little different from the others who stood." She paused. "I'm the only one whose hands are shaking."

Cornell raised a hand and made it shake. "Mine were too, Sister Charley."

Charley smiled, and laughter rippled through the congregation.

"Well, Sister Charley . . ." The announcer was smiling. "Tell us where you're from."

"From Hope Springs," Charley said. "Born and raised, but have never been to New Jerusalem. Decided to change that this morning."

She sat back down, surprised to hear some applause.

"We're glad to have you too, Sister Charley," the announcer said. "I encourage you to stay after and meet Pastor Brooks if you don't know him."

When the next two had introduced themselves, she said, "We have one more announcement, and that'll be given from our pastor."

Travis came up to the podium. In a suit he had a different aura, more serious. Or maybe it wasn't the suit at all, but the nature of what he was about to say. Everyone seemed to come to attention.

"This might be the first time I've stood to give an announcement during this portion of the program," he said, "but I wanted to be the one to tell you, if you haven't already heard, that the joint worship services with Calvary Church have ended."

Enough whispering ensued that it started to get loud.

Travis held up his hands to regain their attention. "That's the extent of that announcement," he said, "but I want to take this time to address something else. You all saw the article in the paper last week. It dealt primarily with members of Calvary and their problems with the service. One might conclude that for the most part, New Jerusalem members only quibbled with things like worship music or preaching styles." He paused. "But I know better."

Travis took his time, moving his gaze around the congregation. "I received enough e-mails, office visits, and casual comments about the joint service to give me an indication of an underlying spiritual temperature that exists in this church. And the temperature reading is this: I don't see a fervor for what Jesus tells us are the two greatest commandments, to love the Lord your God with all your heart, soul, mind, and strength, and to love your neighbor as yourself."

Charley leaned closer to Marcus. "Does he always hit things hard like this?"

"Pretty much," Marcus said. "On one hand, he's known as this hip, cool pastor who can identify with people, and on the other hand, he's known for speaking straight truth."

Travis continued, "As the shepherd of this congregation, I would be remiss if I discerned this and did nothing about it. Amen?"

A few "Amens" sounded. Most people were quiet, listening for his next words.

"So I have another announcement," he said. "Beginning today, we're starting a sermon series called 'Love Reigns,' which we'll also touch on during Wednesday Bible studies. It's my prayer that we'll all grow in giving love for God and love for others its proper place—a preeminent place—in our hearts."

Travis sat down, and the choir prepared to sing. Charley pondered his words. Loving God and loving others seemed simple in the abstract, but she had a feeling the action element ran deep. And wasn't easy. Still, something about it registered with her. She'd be coming to New Jerusalem several more weeks at least.

CHAPTER SEVENTEEN

Monday, August 9

Stephanie arrived at Hope Springs High at seven o'clock in the morning, thirty minutes before classes were to begin. She couldn't remember the last time she'd gotten up so early for work—maybe never—and she was sure she'd be dog-tired. But an energy coursed through her veins, even an excitement. This assignment was temporary, fluid, and unpredictable. But she was praying that however long it lasted, God would use her.

She walked into the building looking every bit the teacher— professional skirt and jacket, sling-back heeled sandals. But as she watched a sea of students returning from summer, hugging, yelling down the hall, she felt like a student herself—a new one. She needed to learn the ropes of this place or they'd run all over her.

On the way to the main office, she saw Marcus in the hallway meeting and greeting students. She'd almost forgotten he was new to this school too, though he looked comfortable. Students would likely find it easy to relate to an assistant principal under thirty.

When he spied her, he held up a finger for her to wait. A couple of minutes later—after shaking every hand he passed—he made it over to her.

"You look raring to go this morning," she said. "You excited about the first day?"

"Always— Hey, sir, good morning to you." He shook a student's hand, then looked back at Stephanie. "Love the energy and the newness." Another good morning and handshake. "How about you? You ready?"

"I am," she said, "believe it or not."

"Let's go to the office and get your teacher packet, then I'll take you to study hall."

She followed him. "I still think this assignment is hilarious." She'd gotten the news on Friday. "You totally knew I didn't need to be engaged in any content subjects."

"Don't get excited," he said. "If a need arises, you could be in calculus tomorrow."

Marcus walked to the first office desk, where a black woman with short pepper-and-gray hair was typing on the computer.

"Stephanie, this is Mrs. Walters, the head office administrator. If you have a question about anything, and I mean *anything*, go to her, not me. I don't know half of what she knows about this place." He gestured the other way. "And Mrs. Walters, this is Stephanie London."

The phone rang before the woman could speak. She scooped it up.

"Hope Springs High, please hold." Mrs. Walters's eyes were kind. "Very nice to meet you, Mrs. London. I've got your packet of materials right here. Mr. Maxwell is right, I'll be glad to help if you need anything."

"Thank you, Mrs. Walters."

She returned to the call as Marcus led Stephanie back out. The building was more crowded now as bodies filled the halls, lockers slamming all around. Marcus didn't shake as many hands, moving more quickly now because of time. He led Stephanie down a long hall, the opposite way of the gym.

"Does every student take study hall?" she asked.

"No. Our freshmen's schedules are filled with classes only— Good morning, Miss Hunt." They rounded a corner. "Our upperclassmen have the option to take study hall, where they can do homework, projects, study for tests, that kind of thing— Hey, it's a little early for foolishness, don't you think?"

Some boys had surrounded another boy, play-punching him. They broke it up.

Marcus stepped into the cafeteria. A handful of students were there, talking at a table.

"Welcome to study hall," he said.

Stephanie looked curiously at him. "I thought it was in a classroom."

"We're hoping one day to have a classroom big enough to dedicate to it," he said. "A computer lab would be even better. But this is only our second year doing this, and for now, this is where it happens."

Stephanie lifted her packet. "And this tells me everything I need to know?"

"It has your schedule, student rosters, study hall protocol, fun stuff like emergency evacuation procedures . . . But everything?" He smiled. "No. You'll learn a lot as you go."

Those same boys entered the cafeteria, loudly, and commandeered a table, no books in sight.

Stephanie eyed Marcus. "Yeah, like how to babysit teenagers."

Seemed like a steady stream of them were coming in now. She wondered how many were in this first period.

Marcus glanced at his watch. "I've got a million things I need to do, but remember, call Mrs. Walters if you need anything. Her number's in the packet. You can text me as well. Oh, and the number for security is in the packet too, if you need them."

"Security?"

He was backing out of the cafeteria. "Gotta run."

She sucked in a breath, looking around. Kids were leaning back in chairs, sitting on tables, bobbing heads to music in earbuds, calling to one another from across the room . . . *At seven twenty in the morning.* Weren't they supposed to be barely awake? What would the later periods be like?

Stephanie put her things down on the table closest to her and began skimming her packet, aware of the eyes that were on her. She used to do that herself, size up the substitute. She wondered how they pegged her.

An influx of students came right at the bell. Stephanie waited for them to find their seats, then saw she needed to help them along.

"Good morning," she said. "I need everyone to please find a seat and get quiet."

She immediately recognized she was at a disadvantage. In a classroom, her voice would have a greater impact. There were fifty-four students, and they were all spread out.

She continued, though there were still pockets of conversation. "My name is Mrs. London, and I'm filling in as your study hall teacher today." Walking forward, she scanned faces. "I want to welcome you to a new school year. I'm sure you're excited to—"

A guy's hand shot up.

"Yes?" Stephanie said.

"Mrs. London, I know you're new and all, but we don't need a lecture. This is study hall."

The guy next to him slapped him on the back, laughing, which got the whole table going.

Stephanie got her class roster. "And your name is?"

He sat back, folded his arms. "Roger Everett."

"Roger, yes, I'm new, and I've never been in charge of study hall a day in my life. But the fact remains, I'm in charge." She walked closer to his table. "If I need your input, I'll ask for it. 'K?"

"Ooooh," his table chided him.

"As I was saying," Stephanie said, "I'm sure you all are excited to be back and to catch up with your friends. *But* . . ." She looked around. "Please remember that study hall is not play time. You're expected to do something productive with your—"

Another hand went up, the guy who had slapped Roger's back.

"Your name, please?" Stephanie said.

"Ben Willoughby. It's the first day of school, first period. There's nothing productive to do yet. This is the only time of year we have *to* play."

Snickers sounded around the room.

"I understand your plight, Ben." She injected sympathy. "I take it you finished all your required reading from summer? And any other assignments you were to complete prior to the first day of school?"

"Look, I didn't have time for all that." He leaned close to the girl next to him. "Football practice keeps me busy."

"Totally understandable," she said. "That's the benefit of study hall, isn't it? You can catch up on your work and do your *playing* on the field."

This time the "Ooooh . . ." came from several tables. She knew it would be next to impossible to keep them all from talking and even playing around a little. Some of them probably *had* finished their assignments. But she wanted to convey the expectation.

"Okay, listen," she said. "While I take attendance, I want you all to dig around in your backpacks, find something to work on, and get to it."

She called out each name, looking for a hand or vocal response as she moved around the cafeteria. When she said, "Samara Johnston," she saw a hand go up to her far left. Stephanie looked closer. How had she missed her? It was Sam from the joint service.

Stephanie nodded, acknowledging that she'd seen her, and

continued with roll call. But her eyes kept drifting back to Sam. Why was she the only one sitting alone?

When she was done, she took another tour around the tables to see if they had the good sense to at least pretend to work. At Roger and Ben's table, they'd taken out the same novel, presumably for English. Three girls with them at the table were whispering, looking at Stephanie's feet.

She raised a playful brow at them. "Um . . . do I have my shoes on the wrong feet or something?"

"Those are Ferragamo's, aren't they?"

It was the girl next to Ben, Kelsey.

"They are, actually," Stephanie said.

"I told you, Brittany," Kelsey said to the girl on her other side. "Those are the ones we pinned on Pinterest." She looked at Stephanie. "Love those. Really cool."

"Why, thank you," Stephanie said.

"And I saw that skirt in the Nordstrom catalog," the third girl said. "You could be a model for them."

Stephanie was amused. "Not sure about that, but I appreciate the comment." She noticed all three had on similar skinny jeans, cute tops, chunky wedge sandals, and fully made-up faces. "Are y'all planning to work in fashion design or something?"

"No," Kelsey said. "We're just a little clothes crazy."

Stephanie smiled. "I was too in high school. Okay, maybe still."

"Well, you get the most fashionable substitute ever award," Brittany said.

Stephanie did a slight bow. "Ever so grateful. Now get to work." She smiled at them, continuing on.

The rest of the period moved surprisingly quickly. Never got completely quiet, but thankfully there were no major fires to put out. It occurred to Stephanie about two-thirds through that since she wasn't actively teaching anything, she could use the time to pray for these students. So she did, mostly praying over them collectively. But Roger and Ben got individual prayers, and the fashion girls. And Samara.

The students scurried at the sound of the bell. Stephanie stood, positioned near an exit door as they left. She saw Sam coming toward her, wearing the same jeans she'd had on at the joint service, with an Old Navy shirt dated 2006, and flip-flops. Her big, thick ringlets of ponytailed curls commanded all the attention.

Sam threw up a hand as she left. "Bye, Mrs. London."

"How are you, Sam?" Stephanie said.

The girl kept moving, backpack bunched on her shoulder. "Fine."

Two more study hall periods passed, each with its own set of unique personalities, and the cafeteria converted back to its main function. According to her schedule, Stephanie could take her break in the teachers' lounge. She'd brought a turkey sandwich, baked chips, an apple, and water from home. Sounded like a plan to meet some of the teachers, eat, and relax.

The decibel level soared as students poured in for lunch, some heading straight for the line, others commandeering tables and saving seats for their friends. Stephanie stuffed her things in her tote bag and was on the way out when she spotted Sam entering the cafeteria. Curious, she watched as Sam went to a far side of the cafeteria and sat at an empty table. She took a brown lunch bag and a book from her backpack, and began emptying the contents of her lunch.

Stephanie felt compelled to join her. If teachers weren't allowed to eat with students, someone would have to come break the news. She made her way across the lunchroom, but before she got to Sam's table, she heard, "Hey, Mrs. London!"

She turned to see Kelsey, Brittany, and a few others at a table. Stephanie smiled. "Hey, girls."

Sam had a sandwich in one hand and a book in the other when Stephanie pulled out the chair next to her. "Hi," Stephanie said. "You mind?"

Sam glanced up at her. "No."

Stephanie sat and began taking out her lunch as well.

"You don't have to feel sorry for me, you know."

Stephanie looked at her. "Why do you say that?"

"You're not the first teacher to sit with me," Sam said. "People feel sorry because I'm by myself. But I'm fine."

Stephanie opened her chips and ate one. "So you prefer being by yourself?"

Sam shrugged. "Beats the alternative."

"What's the alternative?"

She took a bite of her sandwich. Looked like peanut butter and jelly.

"Sitting with a bunch of girls who talk to each other about guys or who's wearing what or who did what over the weekend." She shrugged again. "They never include me in the conversation. I mean, why would they? So I might as well be by myself . . . I mean, I'm not *always* by myself. I talk to kids in some of my classes. But like I said, it's fine."

Stephanie tried to mask her heart's reaction. She ate some of her sandwich and took a sip of water. "So, sounds like you're not into guys or gossip—which is a good thing, if you ask me. What sort of things do you like to do?"

Sam held up her book. "Reading, for one."

"What do you like to read?"

"Weird stuff," she said, "like *Pride and Prejudice* and *The Iliad.*"

"Why is that weird?" Stephanie offered her a chip, but she declined.

"It's just not what kids read, unless it's assigned. Even then, they get the CliffsNotes . . . or they'll ask me what it's about."

"You mean people who might not otherwise talk to you will ask you for help with assignments? And you give it?"

She shrugged. "Yeah."

"You have a kind heart, Sam," Stephanie said. "When I was in high school, if someone never spoke to me but had the nerve to ask for my help with something, I'd tell them to jump in a lake."

Sam's eyes got a little wide. "Really? I can't see you doing that."

"Trust me," Stephanie said. "That and a lot more. No one accused me of being nice in high school." Stephanie took another bite of her sandwich. "I wish I'd been more like you."

Sam's little nose wrinkled. *"Why?"*

"You're a nice girl," Stephanie said, "obviously focused on doing well in school—which I wasn't. And you don't seem to be into looking like everybody else or trying to be like everybody else, which is great."

"Well." Sam glanced downward. "I can't, so . . ."

"Can't what?"

"Be like everybody else." She stared at her half-eaten sandwich. "We don't have much money, so my clothes are ratty and . . . I think that's why they don't want to be my friend." She paused. "But it's fine."

Stephanie felt the sting of tears in her eyes, but she fought them. *What to say, what to say?* "Can I be your friend?" she said, which had to be the *dumbest* thing to say. Right. Friends. Teacher and student, buddy-buddy. It was probably illegal.

Sam's brows bunched. "I don't really see how . . ."

"To be honest, Sam, I don't see how either. I just know I want to. I'll leave the rest up to God."

Oh shoot. She wasn't supposed to mention God in school, was she? Or could she? Marcus would probably be firing her by the end of the day.

Sam looked warily at her. "Why do you want to?"

The question took Stephanie aback. "Because . . . I think you're a unique girl. You're special."

Sam put her eyes back to the page, her hand shaking slightly.

"Sam? Is something wrong?"

"No. It's just . . ." She shrugged. "Only one other person's ever told me that."

CHAPTER EIGHTEEN

Wednesday, August 11

J anelle took a pad full of notes to Travis's office, poking her head in the door. Seeing him with a phone to his ear, she thought to come back, but he waved her in. She took a seat across from him. Every time she'd ventured into his office this week, her eyes went to one place—past the stacks of books, random piles of paper, and scattered sticky notes to a single framed photo.

It was taken in the late eighties in Grandma Geri's backyard, four ten-year-olds making silly faces at the camera—Travis, Libby, Janelle, and Todd, in that order. When she'd first noticed it, it jogged the memory that Travis was always bugging Libby, always teasing Libby, always pulling pranks on Libby—always *near* Libby. And that was only the times Janelle was there to see it, when she was visiting during summers, Christmas, and Easter. But given that Libby grew up nearby, she saw Travis much more than that.

The picture had been Todd's, who'd mentioned finding it when he packed to move back to Hope Springs several months ago. Janelle and Travis had asked for a copy. But Janelle was surprised to see that Travis had had a notion to frame his and display it on his desk.

He ended his call, looking hopefully at her. "Good news?"

She affirmed with a single nod. "Lots. First this fun part." She turned to a page of notes. "Did some Googling and found instructions for how to upload your sermons to iTunes so people can download them for free. I'm going to get on that right away."

"Such a great idea, Janelle," Travis said. "I thought we were doing something when we started recording sermons and selling the CDs at cost. But iTunes is where our younger members live. They'll be able to listen wherever."

"And not just members. People can recommend particular sermons to friends and family, and they'll be able to download them in seconds. It's a great way to reach people far and wide. And, of course, so is a website." She turned to another page. "The web guy from my old church got back to me. He can redesign New Jerusalem's site for a fraction of the other two quotes you got. And he's good." She laid the page of notes comparing price quotes in front of him.

"What?" Travis picked it up to see better. "If I hadn't seen the sites he's already done, I'd be skeptical about the quality. Why so much lower?"

"It's not his main job," Janelle said. "He does it for the love, says he gets to work a different side of his brain. But since it's not his main job, he only does it by word of mouth, as he has time. Plus, he's a bit of a perfectionist, so oftentimes it takes *him* longer to be happy with the look than the client. The upside is he doesn't charge an arm and a leg." Janelle added, "But if you're in a rush, he's not your guy."

Travis turned to his computer, where he'd pulled up the New Jerusalem website. "I've waited this long. I don't mind waiting a little longer to get a quality site for a good price. It's a go. I'm looking forward to hearing his ideas."

"Cool. I'll let him know and put you two in touch." She flipped the page. "Last piece of business I came in here for . . ." A smile spread over her face. "Kory and I have a date. That is, if it fits with your schedule."

He looked confused. "What does my schedule have to do with it?"

She narrowed her eyes at him. "Like Grandma Geri used to tell you, 'Don't play with me, boy.'"

He laughed. "I can hear her now. And you know I'd marry you and Kory even if you *didn't* want me to. What date are you looking at?"

She crossed her legs. "Since it's a second wedding for both of us, we want to keep it small—"

"How small?"

"Maybe just Kory, me, and the kids."

"Uh-huh. You'll never pull that off. Go on."

"We can dream, can't we?" she said. "Anyway, however small it is, it won't take much planning. And we don't see the point of a long engagement. So we're thinking the first weekend in October."

He checked his calendar and made a notation. "All clear on this end. We need to schedule premarital sessions too. I'll check with Kory—"

The church phone rang.

"I'll get that," Janelle said. She reached over and picked up. "Good afternoon, New Jerusalem Church."

"Hi . . . Janelle? This is Charley."

"Hey, Charley, why didn't you call my cell?"

"Actually, I was calling for Pastor Travis. I knew I'd see you later." She had a smile in her voice. "Is he available?"

"Let me check. One moment." She put the call on hold. "Charley wants to speak with you."

"I'll take it," he said. "Wait right here." He answered, "Charley, hello, what can I do for you? . . . Membership? . . . I don't understand."

Janelle wished she could hear Charley's side of the conversation.

"Sure," he said. "Friday at four will work. See you then."

He hung up the phone slowly.

"Charley's doing it, isn't she? Taking steps to become a member?"

"You knew about this?" Travis said.

"She's been talking about it all week," Janelle said. "But it's not like it's out of the blue. She was here on Sunday."

"Which was also a problem."

Janelle moved forward in her chair. "A problem?"

"When Skip found out, he told Todd it was an unfortunate byproduct of the joint service. When they find out she wants to join . . ." He stared off, thinking.

She looked at him. "I can tell you're still disappointed about the joint service."

"How can I not be?" He sat back, let out a sigh. "You were there, Jan, when Todd and I realized we felt God called us back to Hope Springs to do a new thing, as Isaiah 43 says. That's when it hit us that we needed to pray together. And what we kept hearing was unity between the churches. Everything pointed toward the combined service." He paused several seconds. "I feel like we took a giant step forward, focused on God. But when the focus shifted to reaction and opinion, we took several steps back."

Janelle pondered that. "But like Todd said, you have elders to answer to, and a church membership. You're not islands unto yourselves."

"Yeah, I know," he said. "I just think we gave up the fight too easily." His gaze shifted to the photo. "And the hardest part is I don't feel I can tell Todd exactly what's on my heart and mind. I have to tread lightly because I don't want to get between him and his elder board."

"That discussion last week was treading lightly?"

"You know me. I tried. But now, thanks to Charley, I've got *another* issue that's related to Todd's elder board, literally."

"So you're focused on reaction and opinion?" Janelle smiled.

"From what I can see, Charley's experiencing a 'new thing' in her life as well. She wouldn't be doing this if God wasn't moving in her heart."

Travis eyed Janelle, steepling his fingers. "You just earned your paycheck for the week." He nodded to himself. "I've been duly checked. I've got to keep my focus on God."

"You sure do," Janelle said. "By the sound of it, things may get worse before they get better."

CHAPTER NINETEEN

Charley walked into New Jerusalem for Wednesday night Bible study, late and looking for Stephanie. With Lindell in Haiti this week, they'd had lots of girl time—dinner, an evening walk, even a board game. That they were now attending the same church was icing on the cake. Stephanie had quickly become a treasured friend.

Charley spotted her midway up the aisle and scooted past a few people to join her.

"Thought you were on your way fifteen minutes ago," Stephanie said.

"You won't believe this," Charley said, whispering, "but my grandpa was at the house and flat-out told me I needed to be going to Calvary's Bible study tonight, not New Jerusalem's. I've never seen him so agitated. Like I was hurting *him*."

"He's been a Calvary elder a long time. It's in his blood. Maybe he can't fathom that you'd even *want* to go anyplace else."

"It's good to see everybody tonight," Pastor Travis said.

Charley hadn't seen him walk up front. She glanced around

the sanctuary, which was nowhere near as crowded as Sunday, but the pews were still half full. Charley saw Trina and two other Soul Sisters near the back. And as the door opened and a handful more entered, she saw Marcus. She turned back around.

Travis stood between the front pews, talking into a wireless mic. "Are you all ready for this deep discussion we're about to have about love? I see y'all out there, all dreamy-eyed."

People smiled back at him.

"I'm gonna let you all in on a secret," Travis said. "I'm not married." He smiled. "Okay, that's not the secret. This is . . . It might be because for a long time I had the wrong view of love. I thought it was something that just happened. I would meet someone, fire-crackers would start popping, Cupid's arrow would fire, and I'd be knocked silly off my feet." He paused. "I guess y'all can see why I'm not married."

"That's all right, Pastor, I got a few people I can introduce you to," an older woman said.

"You can leave their résumés," Pastor Travis said, "but only if they include gourmet cooking skills."

"Gotcha covered," she said.

When the laughter subsided, he continued, "But seriously, love is not the dreamy, mysterious thing we make it out to be. Love is *real*. It means action. It means risk. It means decision." He walked to the other side of the church, surveying faces. "Did you know you can *decide* to love? You don't check your minds at the door where love is concerned. Sometimes you have to say, 'I don't care if so-and-so doesn't show me love, I'll love because God commands me to.' That's a decision."

Charley turned as he walked down the aisle.

"You might have to *decide* you're going to love someone despite what people will think or say—despite what it will mean for your life. Love reigns above people's opinions. It reigns above the status quo.

It reigns above all. One of the most important decisions you'll ever make is to set your heart and mind on loving God with everything in you." He let that settle as he walked back to the front. "That's what we're focusing on tonight."

Bible study had ended several minutes before, but many remained, talking to the pastor, mingling. Some of the Soul Sisters had formed an impromptu circle and were chatting.

Charley saw Marcus in her peripheral vision, talking to a few guys. She'd barely seen him at school this week, and the void was glaring. She couldn't understand it. They hadn't spent *that* much time together. Shouldn't it be easy to erase?

Stephanie turned to Charley and Trina. "Ready? We can walk out together."

"You two go ahead," Trina said. "I'm waiting to talk to Travis."

Charley and Stephanie headed out.

"I'm parked right over there," Stephanie said when they got outside. "Where are you?"

"Around the corner," Charley said. "See you at school tomorrow. Meant to tell you I love that you're eating with Sam."

Stephanie put a hand to her heart. "Love that girl. Can't even explain it."

"You don't have to," Charley said. "I know exactly."

She rounded the corner and in the darkness made out Marcus farther down the sidewalk, talking to someone. Charley squinted. Was that . . . ? It was. The young woman who'd been rude on Sunday. Why was he talking to her? Worse, why did it bother her? She hated she had to walk past them.

When she got within a couple of yards of them, she saw Marcus backing away from the woman, who then crossed the street and got in her car. Marcus seemed to notice Charley just then and closed the distance between them.

"I can't believe that," he said.

"What?"

He aimed a thumb at the car driving off. "That was the woman who made the 'blond chick' comment Sunday. Telling me she wanted to apologize." He shook his head. "Can you believe she thought maybe we could go out one day?"

"What's wrong with that?"

"Are you kidding? She's nowhere near my type."

"Really? She looks like your type to me."

Took him a split second. "Touché, Coach Willoughby." He eyed her. "That was quite a message tonight, wasn't it?"

"Changing the subject?"

"I'm totally *on* the subject," he said. "Both Sunday and today, Travis has been in my head about this whole relationship thing. Actually, I'm getting a full assault because he and I have been talking about it at home too." He paused a moment. "I told him about the conversation you overheard, to get his opinion."

"What did he say?"

"A lot." Marcus seemed reflective. "Between him and Stephanie, I've been challenged."

Charley frowned. "Stephanie?"

"She didn't tell you?" Marcus said. "When she got an opportunity later that week, she let me have it. Said I was in denial and didn't want to admit . . . that I was drawn to you."

Charley didn't know how to respond. "She said that?"

"She said that."

Several seconds elapsed.

He looked at her. "And she was right."

Charley half frowned. "I'm not following."

He sighed, watching a car as it passed. "I've been saying I'm finally ready to have a real relationship, that there are no single women around here—and boom. Here comes Charley. The vibe is there, fun to be around, can talk about anything, *loves the Lord . . .*" His eyes were focused on her. "I felt myself wanting to be near you, forsaking sleep when I knew I had to be up at six for a ball game to be near you. Yet the thoughts kept coming to me . . . *But she's white . . . That's not you . . . What would people say? . . . It wouldn't work . . .*"

Charley waited, mostly because her heart was beating so fast she didn't know what to say.

"But listening to Travis," he said, "I'm wondering." He seemed to be thinking it through even now. "It's like, 'Dude, really? You find a woman with all that on the inside, and you're worried about the outside?'" He quickly added, "I know I sound really stupid right now, like I'm assuming that means you and I—" He waved his hands. "Not at all. I'm just telling you what God's been doing in my heart since that night, though you probably couldn't care less." He shook his head. "I think I just shared way too much and made a fool of myself."

Charley stared at him, working up the nerve to be honest. "So . . . you really didn't understand why I reacted the way I did?"

Now it was his turn to wait.

"Stephanie called it right, Marcus. There was a 'teeny little something there' . . . on my part."

He didn't say anything. Then, "I don't think I've ever had a moment like this. Like there's this line, and God drew it, and I know He wants me to cross it. But I'll be walking completely by faith, no idea what to expect. And *yet*, feeling a complete rush because there's no doubt that it's utterly and totally of Him." He blew out a breath. "Or I can stay where I am."

"Wow. You're really deep tonight," she said. "Not sure what it says about me that I totally understand."

He smiled slightly. "I don't know what's gotten into me. I just feel like . . . I want to cross that line. I want us to get to know one another . . . if that's still what you want to do."

"What are you saying?" Charley said. "What would that look like?"

"For starters, I'd hopefully see more of the *other* Charley, not the one that's been cold to me."

"I haven't been cold."

"You've been cold."

He let their gaze linger. "But honestly, I don't know what it would look like. I told you, I'd be walking by faith. All I can tell you is we'd be looking to God, trusting Him to take us wherever He wants to take us."

Charley's heart fluttered at that. "I like that. I'm willing to trust God with . . . us."

CHAPTER TWENTY
Thursday, August 12

Stephanie threaded her way through the end-of-day chaos in the halls. Her fourth day, and she was still amazed by the phenomenon. The moment the bell rang, it was as if every ounce of pent-up energy got the signal *Go!* Students shot out of classrooms, staging mini-celebrations of freedom with actual roars—at least, it sounded like it—all through the building. The first three days she had a mind to wait until the bedlam had moved outdoors and onto yellow buses before leaving the cafeteria. But volleyball tryouts were being held today, and Sam let Stephanie know she was going. Stephanie had to get to the gym to ask Charley if she had a chance.

As she walked, she saw a cluster of students gathered by a section of lockers. Nothing unusual about it, except Ben Willoughby was among them. If she'd learned anything this week, it was that Ben had no problem finding himself in the middle of something— and it was seldom positive. This time he had a girl against the locker, kissing her neck, and it wasn't Kelsey.

Stephanie came to the main entryway, moving toward the gym,

when Marcus flagged her down. She stopped and waited for him to finish a conversation with a student.

"Steph, I wanted you to know we've got a permanent teacher for study hall, and she's starting tomorrow."

"Oh. Okay." Her first thought was she'd miss lunch with Sam. "You don't need me for anything else, then?"

"Not right now," he said, "but that could change any moment. You'll get a call if there's a need." He heard his name and turned. "Be right there," he shouted, then to Stephanie, "You've been great this week. Thank you."

Marcus was off, and Stephanie continued on, finding Charley in the gym.

"Welcome to my side of the world." She looked gym official with her ponytail and sweat suit. "I don't know why you haven't come over here more often."

"Girl, I was trying *not* to get caught over here. You might've made me run a lap or something."

"You know, that's a great idea," Charley said. "You'd be perfect next time we need a substitute."

Stephanie blank-stared her. "*Anyway,* did you know Sam was trying out for volleyball today?"

"I thought she might." Charley sighed a little. "She's been practicing after school."

"Please tell me she's got a shot," Stephanie said. "I've been praying for God to really bless her and encourage her in a special way. When she told me she was trying out, I said, 'Lord, please don't let this girl be disappointed.'"

Charley gave a hard sigh this time. "It really depends on the overall skill level of the girls who show up, and on how Sam does during tryouts. If she really brings it today and tomorrow, she's got a shot at making J V."

"Today *and* tomorrow. I don't know if I can take it. I'm too nervous." She eyed Charley. "Can I give you some money right now, and we can make it happen?"

Charley put her hands on Stephanie's shoulders and turned her around. "What you can do is sit on the bleachers and watch the tryouts if you want."

Stephanie looked back. "Ooh, really, I can watch? I could be praying for her during the tryouts."

"Just so you know, though, it's two hours."

"Two hours? After being here since seven? Might have to pray from home." She walked toward the bleachers, calling over her shoulder, "Just kidding!"

The girls began to trickle in from the locker room—many in volleyball shorts, some in general athletic shorts—and started warming up. A few started passing the ball back and forth between them. Some practiced the skill by bumping it against the wall. Others simply sat on the floor and stretched.

Stephanie perked up when Sam entered. She got a ball and joined the others at the wall. Her ball control wasn't as steady, but it was respectable. At least it looked so to Stephanie.

Over the next few minutes, more and more girls came onto the court, including Kelsey and Tia, a black girl she was sometimes seen with. It was clear they were the stars. Many flocked to say hello. Others stared, seemingly wishing they knew them well enough to enter the circle. Sam stayed at the wall.

Stephanie could count on one hand the number of volleyball matches she'd watched. She barely knew the skills and techniques. But when Kelsey and Tia began passing the ball to one another and demonstrating other drills, there was no doubt they were showing how it was done.

Charley dashed over to Stephanie. "A lot more girls showed up than anticipated. Pour on those prayers."

Stephanie did. Amid the noise in the gym, she sent up one

prayer after another for Sam to do her best, to show confidence, and ultimately, to make the team. When the whistle blew and Charley and her assistant started giving instructions, Stephanie was sure her blood pressure was going up. *Calm down. You're not the girl's momma.* She could only imagine what it would be like when she had her own kids.

Several girls suddenly came toward Stephanie, taking spots on the bench. Looked like the coaches had separated the girls into two groups, and the group on the floor—which included Sam—would go through some drills first. Kelsey, Tia, and others were waiting their turn.

Stephanie couldn't hear everything Charley was saying to the girls, but when she blew her whistle, they took off in sprints from one end of the court to the other. Then a fast-walk with knee raises. Then another sprint. And something where they ran and touched a line.

"Look at Sam," Kelsey said. "Last in every drill."

"Girl, what else is new?" Tia said.

Stephanie's heart dropped. *Show 'em, Sam. You can do it.*

The whistle blew again, and the girls dropped to do sit-ups. Charley had a timer in her hand, walking between the girls, shouting encouragement.

Sam did okay with the first few, then got progressively slower. A lot of other girls did too, though, so she wasn't alone. When the whistle blew again, they switched to push-ups. Stephanie was worn out just watching. If her life depended on it, she probably couldn't do three. But they had to keep moving, keep pushing.

Except . . . Sam had stalled. She was flat on the ground, arms in position to push up, but she hadn't moved.

Charley bent down next to her while the other girls continued. Seconds later Sam sat up, wiping tears from her eyes.

Charley blew the whistle for the others to stop, then put an arm around Sam.

"Why is Coach Willoughby always babying her?" Tia said. "She did it all summer."

"You know why," Kelsey said. "She feels sorry for her. The girl's, like, a charity case. Same ol' jeans every other day." She hit Tia's arm. "Heck, *I* feel sorry for her. You should to."

Tia watched her get up and head for the locker room. "Yeah, she's sorry all right."

Stephanie left the bleachers and followed Sam into the locker room. The girl was curled on a bench, chest heaving with sobs.

Stephanie sat next to Sam and put an arm around her. "What happened out there, sweetheart?"

"I . . . was too nervous to . . . eat before tryouts." She sniffed and wiped her face with both hands. "And I just got . . . weak. I didn't even get to the . . . main *part*."

Lord, why? All that praying and it ends like that?

Stephanie stood. "Come on, Sam, let's get your things."

"Where are we going?"

"Not sure yet. But I can't think of a more perfect time to get to know my new friend."

⁂

Stephanie poured Sam another glass of fresh lemonade. "Do you want some more chicken?" Stephanie asked.

Sam looked up from her near-empty plate. "Um . . . no, that's okay."

"Sam." Stephanie put a hand on her hip. "If you're trying to be polite, you need to know that our grandma taught us to always make enough for seconds and for guests. And all you ate was a little chicken wing and some brown rice." She looked at her. "Aren't you still hungry?"

Sam allowed a smile. "Yes, ma'am."

"Awesome," Stephanie said. "Go on over there and get a real piece of chicken. And eat those vegetables on your plate. Don't you like brussels sprouts?"

Sam wrinkled up her nose as she got up. "No, ma'am."

Stephanie chuckled. "Me neither. Janelle's the one who made 'em, but they're good for you, so eat." She smiled as Sam got a chicken breast. "So what are your favorite foods? What do you normally eat for dinner?"

Sam returned to the table. "Hot dogs, potpies, stuff like that."

Stephanie almost said her mother never let her eat that sort of thing regularly, though she wanted to. "So . . . your mom doesn't cook much?"

"No." Sam tore off a piece of baked chicken. "She's gone a lot, either working or with her boyfriend. And when she's home, she says she's too tired to cook." She tucked the chicken into her mouth.

Stephanie nodded. "I remember you said you're an only child. What do you do when you're home alone?"

"Homework, read books." She shrugged. "It's not a big deal." Sam cut off a sliver of a brussels sprout and tasted it, her face contorting. "Eww."

Stephanie laughed. "It's definitely an acquired taste." She sipped her lemonade. "What about family to hang out with? Anyone nearby?"

Sam shook her head. "My great-grandma died when I was little. We live in her old house. I don't really have anyone else around here." Her face lit up a little. "I loved my Grammie. She spent a lot of time with me. She's the one who gave me my name."

"Really? Tell me about it."

"Not much to it," she said. "I just remember she used to tell me Samara was a special name, and she picked it for me from the Bible."

Stephanie leaned in, intrigued. "Have you ever looked it up?"

"I've got a Bible Grammie gave me as a baby. But I've never read it."

"Let's find out about your name." She got up and took the Bible from a shelf. "Hey, Janelle! Can you come here?"

Janelle had been helping Daniel with his homework in the dining room, and she came right in. "What's up?"

Stephanie was thumbing through the Bible. "Who's named Samara in the Bible? Where is that?"

Janelle quirked her brow. "I can't think of anyone." She grabbed her purse. "Let me do a quick search on the Bible app on my phone."

Stephanie looked over her shoulder. "I need to download one of those."

"See," Janelle said, "no results." She started typing again. "Let me try Samaria . . . Yep. I bet it's meant to be a variation of Samaria, which was a place in the Bible."

Stephanie sat back down, laying the phone with the search results next to her Bible. "Okay, so Sam's grandmother picked her name 'specially for her." She looked up at Janelle. "Why would she choose the name of this place?"

Janelle joined them at the table. "Well. Remember the parable Jesus told about the man from Samaria? We call him the Good Samaritan. The parable was strange to Jewish ears because it was the Samaritan who was the good neighbor who stopped to help the man who'd been robbed and beaten, while the Jewish leaders passed him by."

"Why was that strange?" Sam asked.

"Because the Samaritans were a mixed race," Janelle said. "Jews of that day looked down on them and wouldn't even speak to them. Jesus knew exactly what He was doing when He made the Samaritan the good guy."

"Oh my goodness! I am such an idiot." Excited, Stephanie started turning pages. "I can't believe I didn't think of this. Where is it . . . ?" She flipped back and forth until she found it. "Sam, I think this is it right here."

Sam rose up on her elbows so she could see the page. "What does it say?"

"The woman at the well," Stephanie said. "Okay, Jesus was traveling on foot, and He decides to go *through* Samaria—and like Janelle said, Jewish people didn't roll like that; they avoided Samaria like the plague." Stephanie skimmed the verses. "So He meets this Samaritan woman at the well, and they go back and forth to where Jesus lets her know *all* her business, and she's, like, 'How you know *my* business?'"

Stephanie acted it out, and Sam smiled.

"And then it just clicks," Stephanie said. "And she realizes, 'This man ain't just a Jew or a prophet or nothing like that. This is the Messiah.' *Blew her mind.* Homegirl went and testified to *everybody* in Samaria about Jesus."

Sam sat back, taking it all in. "But what does that have to do with me?"

"Like Janelle said, the Samaritans were mixed-race people, biracial," Stephanie said. "You're biracial. This woman had to deal with people who treated her differently because of that, just like you. But Jesus Himself made time for a one-on-one conversation with her."

"Don't you love it?" Janelle said. "She was special to Jesus. And that conversation with Him changed her forever." She smiled at Sam. "I think in giving you that name, your grandmother wanted you to know that *you* are special, to the most important Person in the universe."

Sam was quiet a few moments. "I don't even know a lot about Jesus. I wish they hadn't canceled that joint service, because I felt like I learned something there."

"But you can still go to Calvary or New Jerusalem, Sam," Janelle said.

"My mom said she's never stepping foot in either of those churches, so I don't think I'd better either."

"Well, how about this?" Stephanie said. "The Soul Sisters Bible study starts in an hour. Your mother hasn't said anything about that, has she?"

CHAPTER TWENTY-ONE

S am waved bye to Miss Stephanie as she drove off, then unlocked her front door. It was dark inside. She turned on a lamp and picked up a bowl with tomato soup stains from the coffee table. Her mom must have come home for lunch.

Carrying it into the kitchen, she sighed at the sink full of dirty dishes. With volleyball tryouts looming, she'd let them pile up the last few days, too tired to deal with them after all the extra practice. Lot of good that did.

She squirted dishwashing liquid into the sink and filled it with hot water, washing the glasses, plates, and bowls. She dried them and put them away, then wiped down the counter and swept the floor. Her mom would be pleased with a spotless kitchen when she got home . . . whenever that would be.

Sam went into the bathroom next—*yuck . . . need to clean this too*—and took a quick shower. Snug in her pj's under the covers, she curled up with her journal, pen in hand. It was the one place she could truly bare her soul.

I didn't make the team. Coach Willoughby said today she was focusing on endurance, tomorrow skills. Couldn't even show her I finally got my overhand serve down. Figures. That's always been the question, hasn't it? Whether I can endure . . .

There was a bright spot, though. Miss Stephanie came to tryouts and saw what happened. She took me to her house, and I got to have dinner there. A real dinner at a table. She and her cousin Janelle were nice to me, like they really wanted me there. And then they took me with them to the diner for a Bible study.

I was the youngest one there, and I thought they'd be super serious and talking about things I had no clue about. But they were laughing and having a good time talking about patience, or lack of it—and I actually enjoyed it. They asked me to come back next week. I might.

Sam chewed on her pen, thinking about the part she'd saved for last.

One more thing . . . Miss Stephanie showed me where my name comes from. A woman in the Bible who's mixed race like me. But it was her native people that were mixed. I bet her mom and dad were the same, not one from one race and one from another. I bet her mom and dad were married too.

Miss Stephanie and Miss Janelle said it was a big deal that Jesus talked to this woman and told her who He was, while other people treated her like she was nothing. She was special to Jesus, and I guess Grammie wanted me to know I was special to Him too.

I know that's supposed to be a good thing, but all I could think was I wish I was special to Mom. Maybe if she didn't have to work two jobs. Or if Hank hadn't said he'd marry her if he didn't have to take me as an added burden. Maybe then I'd be special.

I think I'm just not a special kind of girl. That's why I

didn't have what it took to push through tryouts, let alone make the team. That's why I don't have any friends. As nice as Miss Stephanie is, it's not like we can be *real* friends. She's at least ten years older. She's got her own adult life.

A single tear rolled past Sam's nose.

I'm still sure of one thing—it would've been better if I'd never been born.

CHAPTER TWENTY-TWO
Saturday, August 14

Libby took the exit off the New Jersey Turnpike that led to Neptune, relieved the journey was almost at an end. She wasn't good at driving long distances alone, and after eight hours, she'd run through her keep-awake stash of Starbursts, gum, pretzels, and popcorn. Right now a supply of CDs playing extra loud was keeping her alert—that plus a surge of excitement when she thought of the visit that awaited her.

She glanced at the directions on the console. *Keep right, merge onto another toll road for a few miles.* After that she was good as there.

It still boggled her mind that Aunt Gwynn had even invited her. She'd been such an enigma for so long that there was no expectation of even a Christmas card, certainly not a relationship. Not that this visit meant they'd now *have* a relationship. But who knew? Libby had no idea what to expect. She just felt she had to come.

She merged onto the toll road, stopping at the booth. It had been years since she'd come to New Jersey as a girl with her parents, but for some reason she remembered the tolls. She'd bagged up all the loose coins she could find around her apartment for the trip.

Her cell phone rang and she glanced at it, ready to ignore it if it was Janelle. She'd called once today already, following at least two voice mails during the week. It's not that Libby was avoiding her cousin. She was simply in a weird space. She'd been feeling alone when contact with Travis and Omar was cut off. But now it was as if she *needed* to be alone, needed time to think, time to assess her life.

Libby smiled when she saw it was Keisha.

"I'm almost there," Libby said. "My directions haven't let me down yet."

"Yay!" Keisha said. "We're all at Mom's, excited to see you. Holler if you run into any problems."

Libby knew her parents, Janelle, and everyone else would be shocked to know where she was. But even this she wanted to keep to herself for now.

The remaining miles passed quickly. Libby made her final turn and pulled up to the house on the corner. That was what she remembered most, that it was on the corner. Looked smaller—because *she* was bigger—and quaint, with pretty flower beds and nice, manicured shrubbery.

She got out and stretched, enjoying the cooler breeze here up north, taking in the surroundings. Keisha and her family lived on the same block, but she wasn't sure which house.

Libby heard voices and looked in the direction of the house. The whole gang was coming toward her—Aunt Gwynn, Great-aunt Floretta, Keisha, and her husband and son.

Libby left her things in the car and went to greet them. It shouldn't have thrown her to see Aunt Gwynn with an easy smile, but it did. Months before in Hope Springs, she'd looked so pained and uncomfortable, her jaw firmly set.

"Welcome to Neptune." Youngest of her siblings, Aunt Gwynn was in her fifties but looked like she kept herself in shape. She hugged Libby and stepped back, looking her in the eye. "I'm so glad you came."

"Me too," Libby said. "I'm really glad to be here."

Libby walked a few feet to meet Aunt Floretta, who was lagging behind the rest. Grandma Geri's little sister was in her early eighties now. It had felt good to see the two of them visit with each other at Grandma Geri's birthday party.

"Aunt Floretta, it's good to see you again." Libby hugged her.

"Third time this year," Aunt Floretta said, counting the funeral. "It's really something, isn't it?" She winked at her. "I'd say God is up to something."

"I'll say amen to that," Keisha said. "Give me a hug, cousin."

Libby was struck once again by how much Keisha's facial features reminded her of Todd—the eyes and eyebrows, in particular. Her café au lait skin was a definite blend of her parents, her hair dark, wavy, and layered short like her mom's.

Keisha turned to her husband next. "You remember Wayne from the funeral . . ."

"Absolutely. Nice to see you again." Libby smiled as they exchanged a quick hug, then focused on the boy in his arms. "And I definitely remember this little cutie pie." She held out her hands. "Can I have a hug, Jason?"

He turned into his father's chest.

"Jason, I thought you were a big boy," Keisha said. "You told me you were almost four and old enough to go on that ride down on the boardwalk. But if you can't hug your cousin, I don't know . . ."

He reached out his arms and wrapped them around Libby's neck, and she laughed, bear-hugging him back. "Thank you, little sweetie," she said.

The women and Jason headed to the house while Wayne got Libby's things from the car. Soon as they walked inside, she smelled a feast in the making. "Okay, who's the cook around here?"

"Used to be me and Gwynn." Aunt Floretta headed for a seat at the kitchen table. "But my knees hurt so bad she does the lion's share now."

"Mom doesn't mind." Keisha helped Jason to a banana he was reaching for. "She's always cooking up something."

"I guess some things run in the family," Libby said. "You're just like your sisters, Aunt Gwynn." She added, "But for some reason the cooking gene skipped me."

"You too?" Keisha said. "I can make a few things, but thankfully, Wayne's our resident gourmet."

Aunt Gwynn was checking something in the oven. "I'm more than willing to hold a cooking clinic this evening," she said, amusement in her voice. "You girls aren't too old to learn."

Libby sat down at the table. "Aunt Gwynn, my mother has tried every kind of clinic and gifted every kind of cookbook. It's hopeless."

"Maybe you just haven't had the right motivation."

"Hmm." Keisha wagged her eyebrows at Libby. "I think there was some hidden meaning in there."

Libby crossed her legs. "And I'm letting it stay hidden."

They all laughed.

"Libby, there're a couple of trays on the table with things to nibble on till dinner," Aunt Gwynn said. "What can I get you to drink?"

"Water will be great."

Wayne stepped into the kitchen doorway. "I put Libby's bag in the guest room," he said. "No offense, but I think I'll let you ladies have your time alone to chat. I hear ESPN calling me."

Jason ran to his side and announced, "I'm going with Daddy."

Keisha stood with her arms slumped, looking dejected. "Okay." Then she winked at him. "You'll be back when dinner's ready?"

Jason nodded. "Yep."

"Aww." Libby watched them walk off hand in hand. "That's so cute. Says a lot about Wayne."

"He's a great dad," Keisha said, making herself comfortable at the table. "By the way," she said, "I got a chance to watch the family reunion DVD you sent Mom. Made me wish I'd come this year."

Libby tossed her a look. "How many texts did I send to try to convince you?"

"I know, I know. I admit I was thinking about myself and not wanting to deal with all the questions." She grabbed a raw carrot from a vegetable tray. "But when I saw all the kids on the video, I thought of Jason. He met some of his little cousins at Grandma Geri's funeral, and it'd be nice if he could get to know them and grow up with them."

Aunt Gwynn joined them. "I thought about that when I watched the video too," she said. "Not about Jason, but about you, Keesh. You could've been running around with Libby and Janelle at the reunions when you were younger." Her eyes showed a measure of regret. "I guess I was trying to exact my own personal revenge—wanting Momma to hurt as much as she hurt me."

"And what have I always told you?" Aunt Floretta was calm but assertive. "She wasn't *trying* to hurt you. I'm not saying she was right, but she was trying to protect you. I think you forget how crazy the times were down there back then."

"That reminds me." Libby dug in her purse. "I thought you might want to see this." She pulled out the newspaper clipping about the churches and passed it to Aunt Gwynn.

Aunt Gwynn put on her reading glasses to examine it. When she'd finished reading, she sat back but didn't speak for several seconds.

"I can't believe how my heart is racing from reading that," she said finally. "Took me back." She passed the clipping to Keisha.

"How so, Mom?"

"That name—Skip Willoughby."

Libby was surprised. "You know him?" Libby added, "I mean, everybody knows just about everybody in Hope Springs, but the way you said it . . . I'm curious because his granddaughter was hanging with us at the reunion."

Aunt Gwynn looked as if she must've heard her wrong. "Skip Willoughby's granddaughter was at the Sanders family reunion?"

"Okay, Mom, what's up?"

"If it weren't for that man and his father, I really believe Jim and I might've had a chance." Aunt Gwynn's gaze moved back in time. "Our parents knew I was pregnant, and they were trying to figure out what to do. They said it would never work for us to be together. But Jim and I kept saying we loved each other and wanted to be together. It seemed like they were listening to us, at least a little . . . enough to give us hope, anyway."

Libby was riveted. She wished Todd were here to hear more of what his dad was going through at that time.

"And what happened, Mom?" Keisha said.

"What happened was Skip Willoughby drove up to Jim's house." Aunt Gwynn's tone changed just thinking about it. "Now keep in mind, Jim's dad, Jerry, was pastor of Calvary at the time. And Skip was an elder even then. A lot younger, but because of his dad, he had power in town."

"The article says he was outspoken against school integration. Do you remember that?"

"Aunt Floretta is right. Those were crazy times." Aunt Gwynn shook her head. "They shut down the all-black high schools right before I was supposed to go. And there was all this drama surrounding the new high school that was opening for *all* students. Whenever we heard about opposition to it, the Willoughby name was in the mix—either Skip's or his father's. They were very vocal, some said even intimidating." She uttered an empty laugh. "Yeah, I'd say that article is right."

"All right," Aunt Floretta said. "I'm back at Jim's house when Skip drove up. I never heard this before. What happened?"

"Jim and I saw him drive up, and we just had a feeling it had to do with us." Aunt Gwynn took a sip of water, her hand shaking slightly. "Skip told Jerry people had seen Jim and me together, hugged up. He said it was obvious Jerry wasn't conducting himself as a pastor ought, because he couldn't manage his household or keep his son under control. He said . . ." She took a breath. "He said, 'You better get your house in order before Jim gets that girl pregnant'—only that's not how he referred to me—'because you *will* lose your job and your reputation if that happens. Dad and I have met with the elder board, and we're all in agreement.'" Tears rolled down Aunt Gwynn's face. "And I was already pregnant . . ."

For Libby, hearing the story like this, from her aunt's own mouth, was like hearing it for the first time.

The table was silent.

Aunt Gwynn took a moment and dried her tears. "Despite Skip's horrible comments, our parents were the ones we were upset with because we wanted them to support us, not bow to the pressure. But I knew it was hard." She glanced at the article. "By the looks of things, it's still hard."

"It's hard to wrap my brain around the fact that the latest Calvary pastor is my brother," Keisha said. "There's so much history there. And I can't believe I talked to Todd last week and he didn't mention the article or the boycott."

"He's feeling pretty burdened by it all," Libby said. "Janelle left me a voice mail saying he decided to cancel the joint services."

"That's too bad," Aunt Gwynn said. "I was heartened to read what they were trying to do."

"What's Travis say about it?" Keisha asked.

Libby shrugged. "I don't know. I don't go to New Jerusalem."

"Oh, for some reason I thought you did."

Aunt Floretta looked at her. "What's your church home, Libby?"

"I don't really have one," Libby said. "I grew up in a church in Raleigh, but I haven't gone regularly since high school."

"Really?" Keisha said. "I don't know why I assumed otherwise."

Libby gave a wry smile. "You had me confused with Janelle."

"So, okay, let's talk." Keisha perked up. "I find this interesting because I wasn't raised in church, but Wayne and I started going four years ago. Literally changed my life." Her hands were animated. "I started praying for Mom and talking to her. Took a *long* time"—she smiled at her mother—"but this summer she started coming with us." She turned back to Libby. "So I know what it's like to be the skeptic who's never belonged to a church. But you grew up in one. What happened?"

"I've asked myself that same question," Libby said. "I grew up in church but was never really committed to what was being taught. Guess I was a rebel at heart, and when I went to college—and even in high school—I did my own thing." She paused. "I had a relationship in college that left me heartbroken. After that I had all the reasons I needed to avoid committing to anyone, including God. If I don't take a risk, I don't have to worry about getting hurt."

"But that doesn't make sense," Keisha said.

"Why not?"

"Don't you think you're taking a bigger risk by not committing to God?" Keisha had moved forward in her chair. "You're staking your eternal future on a belief that you're fine without Him."

Libby blank-stared Aunt Gwynn.

Aunt Gwynn nodded in sympathy. "Didn't I tell you she stayed on me? This is what I was talking about."

Libby turned back to Keisha. "Well. Still. I think deep down I'm afraid to hope in God. Afraid of taking a step beyond what I know and giving up control, because who knows what will happen? You're worse off if you try to hope and it only leads to disappointment."

Keisha nodded as if considering. "I hear you. You're afraid to hope in God. But the Bible says there's no hope without Him. So you can either stay where you are, with zero hope. Or you can put your hope—you don't have to 'try'—in Jesus and receive a promise . . . that that hope won't disappoint."

"Seriously," Libby said, "I want to know who turned on your switch. How did you get so passionate about this?"

"Girl, I just look at my life and how it's changed so much because of the Lord. I had a lot of baggage because of what happened with Mom." She sighed. "And frankly, after hearing that story Mom just told, I need to pray I don't get an attitude all over again." She leaned in. "But back to you . . ."

Libby rolled her eyes playfully. "Great."

"Have you ever drawn near to God?" Keisha said. "Have you ever said, 'I'm going to see for myself what His Word is about'?"

Libby thought a moment, though she didn't need to. "No,"

"I'm challenging you to do that." Keisha sat back, arms folded. "And then you tell me if you're disappointed."

Libby turned back to Aunt Gwynn. "You should've warned me what I was getting myself into when I decided to come."

The look in Aunt Gwynn's eyes said she knew exactly what she'd gotten Libby into. But more than that, her eyes were warm. "You sent a DVD that got me thinking about my family again and moved me to reach out," Aunt Gwynn said. "Maybe I was meant to return a greater favor . . . to invite you here so you'd think about God again and be moved to reach out to Him."

Her words and Keisha's stayed with Libby all night.

CHAPTER TWENTY-THREE
Sunday, August 15

Charley didn't know which was pounding more—her head or her heart—as Marcus assembled everyone in the living room at Janelle and Stephanie's house. They'd gone to New Jerusalem together this morning and had a meal here afterward, and amid obvious stares and whispers decided to get everything on the table. Marcus's mom was there, so there was sure to be an objection, and that was the part that was making Charley's head hurt.

"Marcus, what's this about?" Aunt Gladys took a seat in the recliner. "Is somebody sick? This reminds me of when we all found out Momma had cancer."

Marcus was still standing, waiting for everyone. "Nothing like that, Mom, trust me. Just a quick little impromptu meeting."

Charley sat on the sofa with Stephanie and Lindell, who'd returned from Haiti late last night. Kory came in and plopped down on the love seat.

"Where's your lovely fiancée?" Marcus asked.

"She took Dee and Tiffany next door to play with Claire, then drove Daniel around the corner to a friend's house," Kory said. "She should be back any second."

"I haven't heard much about any wedding plans," Aunt Gladys said. "Have you two set a date yet?"

Janelle opened the front door just then and entered the family room.

"Right on time." Kory sat back, crossed a leg over a knee. "I'll let Janelle answer that."

She joined him on the love seat. "Answer what?"

"I asked if you two had set a wedding date," Aunt Gladys said.

"Oh." Janelle looked at Kory, then back to her aunt. "We sort of have, but we're not making it public yet. We're deciding how we're going to handle things. Might be just us and the kids at the ceremony."

"And not invite the rest of your family?" Aunt Gladys said. "You know—"

"Uh, excuse me." Marcus looked from side to side at them. "You all can call a separate meeting to discuss Janelle and Kory's wedding plans. This is our meeting."

His mother frowned. "'Our' who?"

"Me and Charley."

Eyebrows went up around the room.

Marcus sat beside her on the sofa. "This really isn't meant to be a big deal," he said. "Charley and I simply wanted to let you know that we're dating."

"And that . . . requires an announcement?" Stephanie looked confused. "Just askin'."

"Good question," Marcus said. "If we were living anywhere but Hope Springs, with family, church, and other dynamics in the mix, maybe not. But can we be real?" He lifted his hands. "I'm black. Charley's white. We've already seen stares and whispers. So we wanted to get it out there, especially with the family."

"I'm sure you saw me staring," Stephanie said. "'Cause I was thinking, *It's about time*." She smiled. "But I can't see anybody in our family having an issue with the color aspect."

"As a matter of fact," Aunt Gladys said, "I've got an issue with it."

"Okaay . . . this is awkward." Stephanie sat back.

Charley's stomach clenched.

Marcus cleared his throat. "I, uh, thought you might, Mom. That's why we wanted to talk about it."

"Well, I'm not talking about it here," Aunt Gladys said. "You're my son. What I have to say, I can say to you privately."

"But that's exactly what I don't want," Marcus said. "I don't want any behind-closed-doors type discussions. If this weren't important to me, there wouldn't be *any* discussion. I'd just kick it with Charley for a while, then move on to the next person, like usual." He took her hand. "But this isn't usual for me. I want to build something meaningful with Charley. I want to see where God takes it. And if there's an issue based on something we can't control, like the color of our skin, I want us both to hear that and address it." He spoke earnestly but evenly. "That's where I am, Mom."

"I can respect that, son," Aunt Gladys said, "and I don't have a problem with Charley personally." She looked at her. "From what I've seen, you're a very nice young lady." Her attention shifted back to Marcus. "But I told you not to date white girls for a reason. Life is complicated enough without you *making* it complicated for you and your future children. There was a time in this very town when you couldn't have looked at this girl without suffering some kind of consequence."

"Mom, really? You're going back fifty years?"

"Sometimes you need to be reminded." Aunt Gladys had him fixed firmly in her gaze. "And do you know *why* you couldn't look at her? Because white women were considered superior—especially blond-haired, blue-eyed white women."

Charley cast her own eyes downward.

"And black women?" Aunt Gladys continued. "Inferior. That's the history. And whenever I see a black man with a white woman, all I can think is he must think the same way—a black woman isn't good enough." She paused. "The last thing I wanted was for my son to think that way."

"Mom, I *don't* think that way." Marcus looked incredulous. "If I were focused on skin color, I wouldn't even be with Charley. It's not about that. I'm looking at her heart."

"Aunt Gladys," Janelle said, "even back in the day, *everyone* wasn't focused on skin color. Jim Dillon fell in love with your little sister, a black woman, and she fell in love with him."

"Mm-hm," Aunt Gladys said, "and you see where that got them. Just like I said, she suffered consequences, to this very day."

Stephanie peered over at Janelle. "That might not have been the best example. I'm just sayin'."

"The point is the same," Janelle said, "and I'm sticking to it. Nobody's road is trouble-free when it comes to relationships. Look at mine and David's. Look at Kory's." She gestured toward Marcus and Charley. "But if you've got two people who love Jesus and put Him first—I don't care if one is striped and the other polka dot—there's no better foundation."

It got quiet, and Charley wondered what everyone was thinking.

"I've got one request," Aunt Gladys said. "I want you two to make this same announcement over at the Willoughby house, with Skip Willoughby present."

Charley looked at Marcus. "I don't mind if we go there next."

Gladys pushed back in the recliner and put her feet up. "Then I've got nothing to worry about."

Charley and Marcus stepped into the foyer of her home. She had called ahead, telling her mom she wanted to talk to her about something and asking if she'd make sure Grandpa Skip was there too. Of course her mother wanted to know then and there what was wrong. Charley assured her that actually, for the first time in a long time, something was very right.

"Mom," Charley called.

"We're in here," her mom said.

Charley led Marcus into her family room. Her mom and Grandpa Skip rose from their seats, eyes on Marcus.

"Mom, Grandpa, I'd like to introduce you to Marcus Maxwell." She turned. "Marcus, my mom, Dottie Willoughby, and my grandpa, Skip Willoughby."

Marcus shook her mom's hand first. "Very nice to meet you, Mrs. Willoughby."

Charley's grandfather eyed him, then shook his hand.

"Nice to meet you, sir," Marcus said.

Skip looked at his granddaughter. "What's this about, Charley?"

Charley smiled. "Marcus and I are friends. I wanted to introduce you because . . . well, we're dating."

"You're dating?" her mom said. "But . . . we've never even met him."

"That's why I wanted to introduce you."

Skip returned to his armchair. "Tell us about yourself, Mr. Maxwell."

Her mother sat again as well, and Charley directed Marcus to the vacant love seat.

Marcus sat. "Well, I'm the assistant principal at Hope Springs High—"

"Ah, now it makes sense," Dottie said.

"—and a member of New Jerusalem Church—"

"That makes sense now too," Skip said.

"I grew up in Raleigh, but my family goes back a couple generations in Hope Springs."

"Who's your family?" Skip asked.

"My dad is Warren Maxwell—and my mom, Gladys, is a Sanders."

"I remember your family," Dottie said. "Your mom was a few years ahead of me in school."

An awkward silence descended. Charley was finding this a little harder than she thought.

"Marcus, I want to give you some Willoughby family history," Skip said. "We value family very highly. My wife and I raised Charley's dad in such a way that he respected our opinion, sought our counsel, and even sought our input on whom he should date." Skip gestured toward Charley's mom. "Dottie was a natural choice because we knew her parents. They were good friends, rest their souls."

Her mom nodded reverently.

"Charley was raised that same way," Skip continued. "We were longtime friends with the parents of the young man she was engaged to. And although that didn't work out—scoundrel that he turned out to be—we still intend to play a part in helping Charley choose whom she will bring into this family, which of necessity starts with whom she will date."

Skip paused, but it was clear he wasn't done.

"I respect that you seem to be a hardworking, churchgoing young man," Skip said, "but the fact is, we don't know you or your family."

"What?" Charley was incredulous. "Mom just said she knows his mother and the rest of his family."

"Charley, that was eons ago," Dottie said. "I haven't seen them in years."

"Well, I can't give my blessing to this," Skip said. "Frankly, you scared me when you first walked in. I thought you were about to announce an engagement."

Charley felt an incredible letdown. "What about you, Mom?" She looked at her. "Are you supportive?"

"Did you two talk to Marcus's parents?" Dottie asked. "I'm curious as to what they said, Marcus."

Marcus glanced at Charley. "My dad wasn't there, but we talked to my mom. She had her reservations."

"See, that's interesting," Dottie said. "I admit I have my reservations as well. Maybe it's our generation. Maybe we're a little wiser from all we've seen in this town." She sighed. "I'm sorry, but it's hard to be supportive of this. I have to agree with your grandfather."

Charley stood, reaching for Marcus's hand. He stood with her.

"It makes me sad that I don't have your support," she said. "I don't know if Marcus and I will last a week, a month, or a lifetime. I just know we've decided God's opinion matters most. And we can't think of anything He doesn't approve about our relationship."

They walked out of the room, her family following.

Charley turned. "I'm glad we talked to our families at this early stage, so we'd know where we stand. I just ask that you'd be willing to pray about this and see if your heart is God's heart."

Skip folded his arms. "Charley, as the head of this family, I have to tell you that this isn't over. I have to look out for your best interests."

Charley and Marcus walked out the door.

CHAPTER TWENTY-FOUR
Tuesday, August 17

Stephanie and Sam entered the side door, shopping bags in hand. They lugged them into the kitchen, but no one was there.

"Hey, Janelle, where are you?" Stephanie called.

"You're back?" Janelle said. "I'm in the bedroom. Come in here."

Sam was excited. "Wait till she sees," she said.

They passed Daniel and Tiffany's room, where Daniel was at a desk doing homework.

Stephanie looked over her shoulder at Sam. "That's probably what you needed to be doing tonight instead of shopping. I should've asked you."

"No worries," Sam said. "I didn't have a lot of homework today. Plus, I get a lot done in study hall."

Janelle was ironing the kids' clothes, with Tiffany spread across the bed doing a worksheet.

Sam dropped her bags on the floor, looking at Tiffany. "You've got homework in kindergarten?"

Tiffany sighed, head propped on her elbow. "I finished that as soon as I got home. This is *Mommy's* work."

Janelle chimed in, "The class is learning the alphabet, but Tiff was already working on reading and writing, so I make sure she keeps moving from where she was."

Sam took a closer look. "Nice penmanship," she said. "And I like the way you drew that cat next to the word."

Tiffany beamed. "Thanks." She looked at her mother. "Mommy, can I take a break and play with Sam?"

"Y'all love playing with Sam," Stephanie said. "What's up with that?"

Sam had come over on Saturday and stayed much longer than she'd planned because Tiffany, Claire, and Dee were having such a good time with her.

Janelle laid aside a shirt she'd ironed and picked up another from a pile. "You're almost done, and anyway, Sam's about to show me what she got. You can play with her in a minute . . . if she's up for it."

"If *I'm* up for it?" Sam said. "Question is whether Tiffany's up for it. I think the piggyback rides were too much for her last time."

"No, they weren't." Tiffany sat up, shaking her head. "It was fun! Can we do it again? We can go get Claire too."

Sam had a tentative look. "Well, only if you think you can take it. I'm going super fast this time."

Tiffany's eyes got wide. "This is gonna be so wild." She hunkered back down. "Okay, let me hurry up and finish."

"Do it neatly, Tiff."

She didn't look up. "Yes, Mommy."

Janelle set the iron down and smiled at Sam. "So show me the goods. Looks like the outing was fruitful."

"Miss Stephanie went kind of crazy," Sam said.

"Did not." Stephanie pushed her two shopping bags behind her legs. "There was just a super abundance of cute things—plus a super *sale*—so it only made sense to take advantage of it."

Sam nodded with excitement. "Yeah. Turns out they reduce the prices even more *after* the back-to-school sales. I told Miss Stephanie she was like an angel. Felt like a thousand Christmases wrapped up in one."

Sam had come over for dinner, and Stephanie gently asked if she'd had a chance to do any school shopping. Sam said no, that her clothes had gotten too small, but her mom couldn't afford to buy anything new. So Stephanie had pulled Lindell aside and asked if she could take her shopping for maybe two pairs of jeans and a couple of shirts. She may have gone a tad beyond that.

Sam was digging in one of the shopping bags. "Check this out, Miss Janelle." She held them up. "I've never had capris before, and I got *three* pair. Aren't these olive green ones pretty?"

"I love that color," Janelle said. "Try 'em on so I can see."

Sam's eyes lit up. "Really?"

"Yeah, and put on one of your new shirts with it."

"Ooh, that's the other thing," Sam said. "They had graphic tees on sale—"

"Girl, *five dollars* each," Stephanie told Janelle. "Crazy."

Sam was laughing. "And Miss Stephanie was grabbing tees she liked, and then she stopped and said, 'Oh. I guess I should ask if *you* like this.'" She extended her arms like it was a no-brainer. "I was like, are you kidding?" She rummaged around in the bag. "There's a really cute one that says *Peace*, one that has *Hope*, and another one that has *Love*." She rummaged around in the bag. "I'll try the *Love* one on with the capris."

She started changing, and Stephanie and Janelle exchanged glances. They'd already marveled about it on Saturday, how Sam was coming out of her shell around them, talking more, laughing. It warmed Stephanie's heart. She'd never had a relationship like this, where she was pouring into someone else—where she *wanted* to.

"Ta-da!"

Janelle turned. "Sam, you look so cute! Those colors really look good on you."

Tiffany jumped off the bed to take a good look. "Kinda matches your eyes. They're so pretty."

"Really?" Sam said. "Thanks, Tiff." She went and dug in the bag, holding up another shirt. "This red one is my favorite."

"Yeah, learned something new about Miss Sam," Stephanie said. "Girl loves red."

"I'm not surprised," Janelle said. "It's bright and pretty, just like Sam."

"Can we go get Claire to play piggyback now?" Tiffany said.

"Sam's still showing us her clothes," Janelle said.

"I can finish that when we're done playing, if that's okay," Sam said.

Janelle smiled. "Of course. I appreciate your willingness to play with the girls."

Sam shrugged. "I love it. They take you as you are." She looked at Tiffany. "Let me change out of these clothes, and I'll be ready."

The doorbell rang then, and Stephanie and Janelle glanced at each other.

"Wonder who that is," Stephanie said. Almost everyone simply walked into the Sanders house.

They both went to see, leaving Tiffany and Sam.

Janelle opened the door. "It's Trina. Hey, girl, come on in."

Trina walked in. "Hey, glad I caught you both home."

Stephanie hugged her. "Come on in. Can I get you something to drink?" She eyed her. "See, I'm still practicing my hospitality."

Trina laughed. "I don't need anything, but I'm proud of you. I'm not doing too good with patience this week."

"We won't even go there," Stephanie said.

Janelle ushered her into the family room.

"Okay, what am I forgetting?" Stephanie sat on the sofa.

"Wednesday night is Bible study, Thursday is Soul Sisters. What brings you to Hope Springs on a Tuesday?"

Trina's smile was bright. "I was helping Travis and Marcus clean up over there."

Stephanie didn't look at Janelle, only because she was dying to.

"They're hilarious," Janelle said. "We told them we wouldn't help because they needed to learn to do it themselves. And they went and got help anyway."

"Sorry. If I had known, I would've surely held the party line." Trina took a seat. "Travis and I are about to grab dinner, but he had to make some calls first. So I thought I'd duck in and say hey."

The sound of heavy feet and loud screams came at them suddenly. Sam came barreling into the family room with Tiffany on her back, ran around the perimeter and back out, zooming down the hall.

Janelle turned to Trina. "This is how we wind down before bed around here."

"Ah, I'll have to remember that for when I have my own kids." Trina smiled when they heard another stampede in a different part of the house. "You know, I'm sure I've heard you two mention it, but I didn't realize until today that your family grew up right next to Pastor Todd's family, and Travis was right up the street. There's so much history."

Stephanie nodded. "There really is. I missed a lot, living so far away in St. Louis. But Janelle knows everything about everything when it comes to the Sanders family."

"Not me," Janelle said. "Libby's the one, because she lived down here."

"Oh," Trina said. "Libby probably told you we saw her in Raleigh two Saturdays ago."

This time Stephanie had to glance quickly at Janelle. "Where'd you see Libby?" she asked.

"At Mama Jay's."

"I keep hearing about that place," Stephanie said. "How'd you like it, Trina?"

"It lived up to the hype. I had the catfish, which was so good, and I tasted some of Travis's jerk chicken—it was hot but really good."

A quick knock sounded, and Travis walked in. "How's everybody to—whoa!"

Sam was galloping through again, bellowing, "Hi-yo, Silver! Away!"—her horse a little wobbly as she almost ran Travis over.

"Sorry," Sam yelled, galloping on.

Travis watched them disappear into the next room. "Who was that young lady?"

"She was one of my students in study hall," Stephanie said.

"And she came to Soul Sisters," Trina added. "Really sweet girl."

Trina's phone rang, and she checked it. "Work. I've got to get this." She got up, looking at Travis. "Meet you outside?"

"Okay," he said.

"See you guys tomorrow night." Trina waved bye as she answered her cell and walked out.

Janelle and Stephanie stared at Travis.

"What?"

"Oh, nothing," Janelle sang.

"Spill it."

"I just find it interesting," Janelle said, "that I've been working with you for several days now, and you never mentioned running into Libby at Mama Jay's."

"There was no need. I knew she'd tell you."

Janelle looked up at him. "Actually, she didn't. I haven't talked to her."

"At all?"

"Nope," Janelle said. "She hasn't returned my calls. What about you? Have you talked to her?"

"No. She texted me once I left Mama Jay's and let me have it for bringing my 'girlfriend' to her favorite restaurant."

"I imagine she was hurt, Travis," Janelle said. "Of all the restaurants you could've chosen . . . I think she gets carryout from there every weekend."

"I felt bad," he said. "I wanted to call her when I got home, but it would've only made things worse." He sighed. "I'm resolved that I need to give Libby her space. She can do her thing in her world, and I'll do mine."

Janelle's gaze drifted toward the door. "You know it's not easy for me."

Travis only looked at her and waited.

"Trina's my Soul Sister and a great person, and there are so many reasons to be glad the two of you are connecting." She paused. "But I so want Libby to see the light—I've prayed for that—because I think both of you, deep in your hearts, feel deeply for one another."

"Keep praying for Libby, Janelle." Travis backed toward the door. "I'm committed to doing the same. But I can't dream about what she might hopefully be one day." He opened it. "I have to live my life in the now."

CHAPTER TWENTY-FIVE
Friday, August 20

The door buzzer startled Libby from her work early Friday evening. She wasn't expecting anyone and was inclined to ignore it—probably the boy from several units over selling something again—but then she heard, "Libby, you in there? Open up."

Omar. He'd gone a week and a half without calling. Then Wednesday he'd left a voice mail, and again this morning, plus a handful of texts.

He knocked hard this time. "Libby, if you're in there, open the door. I'm worried about you."

She sighed, rising from the dining room table. In her duplex-style apartment, she had only two other neighbors close enough to hear, but they paid attention to everything. If she didn't answer, they'd start calling and stopping by to make sure she was okay.

She opened the door and stood aside so he could enter. Might've been because she hadn't seen him, but he looked more handsome than normal in beige walking shorts and a black polo shirt. She felt the adrenaline surge she always felt around him. There was never a doubt about that—she was attracted to him.

He stood within inches after she closed the door. "You don't return my calls. I had to bang on the door to get you to answer. Is that where we are now?"

Libby frowned at him. "Excuse me? You're the one who left the reunion with an attitude, acting like you didn't want anything more to do with me."

"You were wrong, Libby." He was matter-of-fact. "You invited me to come, but only as a pawn in some game you were playing with Travis."

"I wasn't playing a game," Libby said. "I was just . . . I don't know what I was doing." She looked at him. "You're right. I shouldn't have done that. I apologize."

A brow went up. "I wasn't expecting that," he said.

"What *were* you expecting? Why did you come?"

"Like I said, I was worried." His voice was tender. "And you know I couldn't stay mad at you." He caressed her face. "I missed you."

She moved around him, from the entryway to the dining area, her heart palpitating. This was the Friday night norm she'd been missing the last two weeks, she and Omar spending time together . . . spending the night together.

"Did you eat already?" he asked. "I almost brought some carry-out, but I didn't know if you'd be here. I can go back out and get us something."

"I'm fine," she said. "I have leftovers from last night."

"From where?"

"From here. I cooked."

"You cooked?" His voice was full of doubt. He went straight to the kitchen and opened the refrigerator. "This here?" He pulled out a covered dish, put it on the counter, and took the top off. "It looks good. What is it?"

She felt proud. "A chicken and linguine casserole my aunt taught me how to make." She smiled. "Turned out pretty good too."

He smiled back. "Are you game for me to try it? I *am* starving, by the way."

"Then how can I refuse?"

They prepared two plates, warmed them in the microwave, and took them to the dining room table. She let him take the first bite as she watched.

He pointed at the plate with his fork. "So you said your aunt made this?"

"I said I made it."

"I don't believe you."

"Is that a compliment?"

He scooped another forkful. "It's delicious, whether you made it or not. But if you really made it, I'm big impressed."

Her head did a slight bow. "Thank you."

Inside she was thrilled. Couldn't wait to call Aunt Gwynn and tell her that her step-by-step directions—which for Libby were broken down to half-step by half-step—had actually worked. Beautifully.

They continued with the meal over small talk. Libby even mentioned her trip to New Jersey to see family, but without going into detail.

Omar gestured toward the other end of the table. "So what were you working on before I got here? You've got a lot of books over there."

"Yeah. Bible, concordance, word study dictionary . . . I'm doing some digging. Learning about God, me, life . . ."

"What brought that on?"

"I think a lot of things jump-started it." Libby had asked herself that question and didn't know where to begin. "But the culmination came on that trip to Jersey. Long talks with my family, visiting their church . . . I feel like I'm on this expedition, trying to see what I find."

"I think it's cool to tap into your spiritual side." He picked up their plates and carried them into the kitchen. "Maybe some of it'll rub off on me."

When he returned, he lifted her by the hand and looked into her eyes. "Why don't I get us a glass of wine and we can relax in the bedroom, maybe watch a movie." He pulled her closer, his arm around her waist. "And after the movie, I'll let you know my other ideas for the night."

Her skin tingled with a yes. She'd missed him. Maybe her feelings for him were more than she thought.

He kissed her, and she was intoxicated with the feeling it gave her . . . until her mind carried it through to her bedroom and waking up beside him tomorrow morning, and how *that* would make her feel. That wasn't what she wanted, a momentary thrill that ultimately meant nothing. She couldn't explain why. It just wasn't. Not anymore.

"Omar, I can't."

He kissed the side of her lips. "Can't what?"

She took a step back. "I'm not in the mood tonight."

"I understand if you're tired." He held her fingertips. "But you've still got to relax. What if we at least start the movie? If you fall asleep, you fall asleep."

His words and his touch pulled her in again. She didn't *want* to be alone. But was this the type of companionship she yearned for?

She took a big breath. If she didn't do it right now, she wouldn't do it.

Libby walked away from him to the door. "Omar, you have to go."

His brow creased. "You're saying I can't even stay with you? I told you, Libby, I understand if you don't want to—" He stopped. "Are you gaming me again? Some other guy is on his way over here?"

"No," Libby said.

He came closer. "Then what's going on? The way you kissed me, I know there's still something there."

"It's this journey I'm on," she said. "I want to be focused. If I let my heart and soul get distracted, I might miss what I'm really after, though I'm not even sure what that is."

"If you want to know the truth, you seem confused."

Libby smiled faintly. "I know. That's my aim, to clear it up." She opened the door.

"Call me when you're done with all your digging."

She nodded. "Bye, Omar."

Libby returned to the table, heaving a heavy sigh. Turning back to where she was, she continued reading in the book of Romans. She'd always been fascinated watching legal arguments on Court TV. Who'd have thought that the apostle Paul making his case for the gospel could be as riveting?

CHAPTER TWENTY-SIX
Friday, September 17

Charley sat lotus style on Marcus and Travis's living room floor, eating pizza and laughing while arguing her point. Marcus had invited her to join the informal Bible study he'd been doing with Travis, and this was their third meeting.

"It is *not* stupid." She pushed Marcus's shoulder. "I can't believe you never heard it."

"Good, better, best . . ." Marcus looked at her. "Wait, say it again."

"No, 'cause you think it's dumb."

"I can't believe you've never heard it either," Travis said. Across from them, his back propped against the sofa, he chugged some of his Coke. "I think I learned that, like, in kindergarten. 'Good, better, best, never let it rest; until your good is better and your better is best.'"

"Oh, now I get it," Marcus said. "You both learned it in school. It's a Hope Springs ditty."

"Are you making *fun?*" Charley sat up straight, fists on her hip. "I'll have you know we learned only the best here in Hope Springs. For example, I know your statement just now was factually incorrect because a 'ditty' is a song. 'Good, better, best' is a maxim. So there."

"All right, my Hope Springs homie." Travis leaned over and gave her a fist bump. "And a fist bump for the point you were making before Marcus interrupted too."

"What?" Marcus raised his hands in defense. "I can't help it if it struck me as funny. And it *could* be a ditty, like this." His head started bopping playfully side to side. "Good, better best, never let it rest, until your good is better and your better is best."

"Hey, that was pretty funky. But you still get a"—she pushed him again—"because you were making fun."

"Okay, class, settle down." Travis chuckled as he looked down at his Bible. "That was good, Charley, because that's what Paul is saying right here. We may be doing 'good' in certain areas, but we could always do better. Right? And we have in our sights before us what's best—the example of Jesus Christ. So when he says of pleasing God that we ought to 'excel still more,' he's saying we should always be moving from the good to the better toward what's best."

Marcus gave a reluctant nod. "Okay, when you put it that way, the *maxim* fits really well." He gave Charley the side-eye. "And I'm curious how you'd apply the good, better, best to the verses that follow."

"I'm not surprised you're curious." Travis gave him the eye. "Isn't it interesting that after Paul speaks generally of 'excelling' in our Christian walk, the first subject he hits is abstaining from sexual immorality?" He looked at Marcus. "You tell me how you can apply it. Give me a scenario that would be good, then how that same scenario could be better, then how you could excel still more in it."

Charley took a bite of her slice of pepperoni, more than interested in what he would say.

Marcus thought a moment. "Okay. If Charley and I brought carryout to the house and you weren't home, and we ate and talked on the sofa and . . . kissed but didn't go further, that would be good."

Travis glanced between them. "Is this theoretical or historical?"

"I plead the fifth," Marcus said. "Better would be if we ate in the kitchen and talked at the table, to avoid possible . . . you know."

"Yes," Travis said. "Definitely moving upward."

"Excel-still-more would be if we realized we didn't need to be alone, so she only came over when our pastor was home, and on top of that we did a Bible study."

"Ding, ding, ding," Travis said. "And we have a winner."

Charley laughed, though she was a little red-faced remembering that moment on the sofa.

"Seriously," Travis said, "you two are going hard after 'excel still more.' You're making tactical decisions that show how serious you are about keeping the Lord at the—"

They all looked toward the entryway when a knock sounded and the door opened.

"What's up, man?" Travis said. "Come on in."

"Hi, Todd," Charley said.

"Hey, Todd, you should join us," Marcus said. "We'd be taking good to better to double best with both of you."

Todd's smile showed his confusion. "What exactly did I walk into?"

"A Friday night Bible study," Travis said. "We're in I Thessalonians 4." He patted the floor. "Have a comfy seat, grab a slice, and jump in." He smiled up at him. "Unless you actually had a reason for stopping by."

"Sure didn't." Todd sank down onto the floor. "Becca and the kids are next door at some girly sleepover party thing."

Charley smiled. "That was Sam's idea. She's over there too."

Todd continued, "Kory rescued Daniel and took him to Rocky Mount. Lindell's in Haiti. So I decided to take a walk on a nice night and hang out with the guys."

"Sorry," Charley said. "You didn't know a gal would be here too."

"No, this is awesome." Todd glanced around. "Place looks a million times better when a gal's here, trust me."

"You're real funny, Todd," Travis said.

"Todd . . . I want to say again I feel bad about leaving Calvary. I really hope you know it was nothing personal."

Todd held up his hand. "Charley, we already talked about it, and you know I'm fine with it." He threw an arm around Travis. "This is my guy. I love how God is using him." He focused on Charley. "I wish more people in town operated like you."

"What do you mean?"

"It would be great if people would visit both churches and pray about which one God wanted them to attend, not just assume, 'I'm white, so I go here,' or 'I'm black, so I go there.'"

"That's what I loved about the joint service," Charley said. "On that Sunday, there was no need to choose. We were all together." She looked at Todd. "Can I be honest with you?"

"Of course you can."

"I'm sure my grandpa pressured you. I wish you hadn't given in."

Todd looked taken aback. "It wasn't that simple, Charley. It's pretty complicated, actually."

"What's the worst that could've happened?" Charley said. "Them firing you? I'm sorry if I'm out of line, but I wish you had stood firm. I feel like my grandpa won and the kingdom lost."

She couldn't read Todd's face, but it was somewhere in the neighborhood of dumbstruck.

"I'm a little surprised at what you're saying, Charley. Like I said, a lot went into the decision. Your grandfather made compelling arguments about the history of Calvary and the importance of maintaining the integrity of the church."

"Just like he made sure I understood Willoughby history and the importance of maintaining the integrity of our family—as a basis for ending my relationship with Marcus." Charley hadn't intended to spill her heart, but here she was. "Todd, my grandfather was against worshiping with New Jerusalem, and he's against my relationship with Marcus. In the sixties, he was adamantly opposed to integrating the schools. What do you think this is really about?" She heard her cell phone ringing, but she ignored it.

Todd stared downward for several seconds, then back at Charley. "Your grandfather is a longtime elder of a church, the church of which I'm a pastor. He was instrumental in my decision to uproot my family from St. Louis and move here. Until I hear hard evidence to the contrary, I feel obliged to think the best of him."

"I can understand that," Charley said. "He's my grandpa, and I love him. I want to think the best too." Her phone had stopped and started ringing again. "Excuse me a minute." She found her phone in the kitchen. "Why are you blowing up my phone, Ben?"

"I need a ride home. I'm at Kelsey's."

"I'm busy at the moment. Can't Kelsey take you home?"

Ben sounded agitated, and loud, like he'd been drinking. "I don't want that lying, cheating slut taking me anywhere. I found out she's been seeing Roger behind my back. My own teammate!"

Charley could hear Kelsey in the background saying he had no right to be snooping in her Facebook messages.

"Didn't you have another girl at the house last weekend?" Charley asked. "Wasn't that behind Kelsey's back?"

"This is my *teammate*, Charley." He spoke to Kelsey again. "You slept with him, didn't you, you slut! Kelsey, you swing at me again, and I'll—"

"Ben!" Charley grabbed her purse. "Don't you dare touch Kelsey. Go outside and wait for me. I'll be there in a minute."

She walked back into the living room. "Ben's got an emergency. I need to run him home real quick."

Marcus jumped up. "You need me to go with you?"

"Thanks, but I'll be okay."

He hesitated, holding her gaze. "You coming back?"

She bit her lip as if unsure. "Only if Travis will still be here."

Travis called over his shoulder, "You'll have two pastors here—excelling beyond excel."

She smiled. "Okay, cool, I'll come back."

Marcus held her hand and walked her to her car. "You sure you don't need me?"

"It's Ben and Kelsey. He's losing it because she cheated on him or something." She stalled by her car. "They're living way beyond where they should. I wish *they* could've heard what we studied tonight."

"I've been praying for Ben like you asked me," Marcus said. "I'll pray for Kelsey too."

"Thanks."

Eyes penetrating in the dark, her heart accelerating, Charley couldn't move. Moments like this, the two of them so close, she wanted to melt into his arms.

"Don't you have an emergency?" he whispered.

"I do."

"This is why we need two pastors."

She forced herself to open the door and smiled her good-bye.

CHAPTER TWENTY-SEVEN
Thursday, September 23

Stephanie couldn't wait to talk to Sam at lunch. She'd gotten a call to substitute for the new study hall teacher and saw an entirely new dynamic in first period. Sam was no longer alone on a far side of the room. There were girls at her table who didn't simply happen to be at her table. They were engaged in conversation with Sam, and Sam with them. Stephanie was so excited she didn't bother to shush them up.

Before lunch she had gone to the front office to ask a question of Mrs. Walters. In the cafeteria now, she looked for Sam at the usual spot, "usual" one month ago, anyway. Sam was indeed there, though Stephanie almost missed her for the four other girls at the round table.

She walked over, wondering if she should find another table and catch Sam later. The others might not think it was cool for a teacher to sit with them. But Sam waved her over.

"I saved you a seat," she said.

Stephanie slid into the chair next to Sam, where conversation was flying about several subjects at once—music; movies; history class, where someone got put out for cussing the teacher; and

Facebook and Twitter statuses, including their own, which they were updating at the table.

Sam didn't have either a Facebook or a Twitter account, so Stephanie leaned over to her while the others talked social media.

"Things have changed a little at school, huh? Are these your new friends?"

"I wouldn't exactly call them *friends*." Sam spoke low. "Whenever I think that, I end up disappointed. But we sit together sometimes, yeah."

"How did that happen?" Stephanie asked.

"You might not believe this, but I think it was the clothes you got me. Seemed like people started noticing me. But also, I wasn't embarrassed about the way I looked anymore, so maybe I didn't stay to myself as much."

Stephanie touched her hand. "You never said you were embarrassed."

Sam glanced downward. "I know."

"Hey, Sam, come here a minute."

Stephanie and Sam both turned. Ben Willoughby had taken a seat at the next table.

Sam pointed at herself. "Me?"

"Of course, you." Ben laughed. "Come here. I want to talk to you."

Stephanie was about to tell her to ignore him, but Sam was already up and walking over. Ben had never spoken to Sam before, as far as Stephanie knew. What was going on?

Ben pulled out his phone and typed something. They said a few more words, then he left and Sam returned.

The other girls at the table leaned in on her. "What did he want?"

Sam shrugged. "Nothing much."

"Oh, come on!" one of them said. "It's Ben Willoughby, senior, football star. He never talks to any of us. What did he say?"

Sam balled up her empty bag of chips. "He wanted my cell number. Said he'd like to get to know me."

"What?" Another girl's eyes widened. "He said that? He's so cute. I'd die if he said that to me."

The bell rang, and everyone scrambled to throw away trash and get to the next class.

Stephanie touched Sam's arm. "Hold on a sec." She waited until the other girls were gone. "Sam, stay far away from Ben Willoughby."

"It was just one conversation," Sam said.

"But you gave him your number, didn't you?"

"Well. Yeah."

"I wish you hadn't. Don't answer if he calls."

"Why not?"

Stephanie got up and walked with her so she wouldn't be late. "How much experience have you had with guys?"

Sam didn't have to think about it. "None."

"That's what I thought," Stephanie said. "We'll have a long talk about guys later. Right now, I'm just saying stay away from him. He's not your type."

"I don't even know what my type is," Sam said.

"That's okay. It's enough to know what it's not."

They needed to part ways. "Soul Sisters tonight?" Stephanie asked.

"Yep. You coming to get me?"

Stephanie started down a different hall, saying, "I'll be there at six fifty."

Stephanie drove slowly up the lone street that led to Sam's house. Her car jerked along on the gravel, and she wondered again why the town hadn't bothered to lay fresh blacktop. Perhaps they felt no need, with only three old homes, one unoccupied, served by a road that led to a dead end. Whenever she came to get Sam, it seemed she'd stumbled onto a section of Hope Springs that hadn't quite kept up with the rest.

She pulled up to the house, situated alone on an unkempt plot of land. A couple of minutes early, she put the car in park and waited, since Sam always said she'd meet her outside. An Oldsmobile was parked in the yard, the car Sam's mom drove. Stephanie had never met her, though she wanted to. If her mom was home when Stephanie came, Sam would say it wasn't a good time.

Stephanie checked the clock on the dash. 6:54. Wasn't like Sam to be late. She called her cell, and no one answered. Two minutes later she cut the engine and walked up to the house.

Seeing no doorbell, she knocked. A woman answered, somewhat petite like Sam but with long, dirty-blond hair and makeup adorning weathered eyes. She held a cigarette in her hand.

"Miss Johnston?"

She eyed Stephanie. "My last name is Schechter."

"I'm sorry. Miss Schechter, my name is Stephanie London. I'm a substitute teacher at the high—"

"I know who you are." She flicked ashes to the left of Stephanie on the front porch. "You're the one's been telling my daughter I'm not good enough."

"Ma'am?"

"That's what it amounts to," she said. "She's always asking why we don't have 'real meals,' why we don't eat at the table, why we don't talk about this or that . . ."

"I certainly didn't mean to cause any conflict," Stephanie said. "You've raised a special girl, and I was just moved to spend time—"

"And what right did you have to buy her all those clothes? Maybe I didn't *want* her looking fancy. Did you think of that?"

"Oh, wow . . ."

Lord, help. How do I respond?

"I truly do apologize," Stephanie said. "I wasn't trying to make her look fancy at all. She said her clothes had gotten too small, so I wanted to help."

Sam's mom took a drag and flicked more ashes. "Well, we don't need your help."

"I understand. It won't happen again."

"Teri, didn't I ask you to get me a sandwich?"

Teri turned to a voice behind her in the living room. Stephanie couldn't see a face.

"Tell whoever that is that you've got to go," the guy said.

"Coming, baby." She turned back to Stephanie. "Guess you heard. I've got to go."

"Actually, I was coming to pick up Sam. Do you know . . . is she ready?"

"That Soul thing?" She took another drag and blew it out. "She ain't going. That's the other thing. I'm sick of her all of a sudden talking to me like I need to find religion. I got enough problems without you filling her head with that junk." *Flick.* "Matter of fact, if you contact Sam again, I'm calling the school board. Probably against the law for you to be taking her to this stuff. Try me and see what happens."

Stephanie felt like she'd been knocked backward.

"Teri! You want me to starve?"

Stephanie needed to get out of there before she went off on both of them.

She looked Sam's mother in the eye. "Appreciate your time."

❧

Sam couldn't stop crying. From the window, she watched Miss Stephanie walk back to her car. She'd heard every word, and she wanted so badly to run out there, defy her mother, and go to Soul Sisters anyway. But she'd only feel bad when she got back home. She hated when her mother was mad at her.

Miss Stephanie turned her car around and took off up the road. Sam watched until she was out of sight, then lay across her bed. That's where she'd be all night, with Hank in the house. She hated that too, when they hung out here instead of at his home. Her mom paid her even less attention when he was here, which Sam had hoped would work to her advantage tonight.

But her mother got an attitude when Hank told Sam she looked cute when she walked in from school. It went downhill from there, and later, when Sam mentioned Soul Sisters, her mom unloaded. She'd always seemed threatened when Sam shared what she was learning about the Bible—and this time she was riled enough to shut the whole thing down.

Sam rolled over on her back, staring at the ceiling, tears falling to the side. Did her mother mean it? Would she never be able to spend time with Miss Stephanie again? Never visit her house and play with the little girls? Those times at her house were the best Sam could remember. And Soul Sisters had become a favorite part of her week as well. She didn't say much, mostly listened. But then she'd look up the things they'd said in the Bible her Grammie gave her.

How could her mom *do* this? It wasn't like *she* was going to spend time with Sam. Was she supposed to go back to being by herself?

Her tears subsiding, she rolled onto her side and reached for her journal on the floor—and heard a text come in. She hoped it was Miss Stephanie, though she wouldn't know what to say.

She found the phone on the bed and stared at it. The text said, Hey Sam can you talk? But whose number was it?

As if reading her mind, another text came.

It's Ben. Leavn football practice, thinking abt u. U there?

Her stomach dipped, and she sat up. Really? Ben Willoughby was thinking about her?

She heard Miss Stephanie's voice in her head, telling her not to answer him. But how could she *not* respond? That would be rude. Plus . . . she was dying to know what he wanted to talk about.

Nervously she typed back, I'm here. Yes, I can talk.

Seconds later her phone was ringing.

CHAPTER TWENTY-EIGHT

Saturday, September 25

L ibby had on her event-planning hat, taking notes at her client's kitchen table. "Intimate setting . . . festive yet elegant . . . evening time frame . . ." She looked up. "How many people?"

Janelle did a slow shrug. "That's where we're stuck."

Libby set down her pen. "The number affects size and type of venue, as well as other aspects. You brought me all the way out here, and you have no idea how many you're inviting?"

"All the way out here?" Janelle said. "Driving forty minutes to see family is a big inconvenience for you now? Wow."

"I didn't mean it like that," Libby said. "But I came because you asked me to help plan your wedding—" She stopped. "That's why you asked, isn't it? Not just because I haven't been here in a while." Libby looked at her. "You're not even ready to plan your wedding."

"You're right," Janelle said. "You haven't been here in more than a month, and I was concerned. I knew you'd come if I asked for help with wedding plans. But you're wrong on the last count—I *am* ready to plan, if I can figure out the number."

"Okay." Libby picked up her pen again. "What do you two envision in your heart of hearts?"

"What we envisioned at first was small, just Kory and me and the kids."

"Why not go with that?"

"I tossed it out there, but I got all kinds of grief from family." She sighed. "So we decided we should invite more family. How much more is the question."

The pen went down again. "Jan, I know they mean well. I'd love to celebrate with you too. But this is a second marriage for you both, and you should give yourself permission to start it off the way you want to. Don't make plans based on what other people say."

"That's good advice." Janelle gave an apologetic shrug. "But now I do feel like I wasted your time, because I should share this with Kory and see if he wants to revisit the 'just us' ceremony idea."

"No problem." Libby got up. "Just let me know when you're ready to move forward." She rummaged in her purse for the car keys.

"You're leaving?"

She heard a jingle and pulled them out. "Yeah, I'm heading back."

"But you know everybody will want to see you. They should be back shortly."

Libby hadn't told her, but the fact that they were all at an away football game had played a factor in her deciding to come. She had planned all along to be gone before they returned. She looped her purse on her shoulder. "Just tell them I missed them, and I'll be back soon."

"Libby . . ." Janelle's eyes showed concern. "Why don't you want to spend time with us? What's going on? You must be seeing someone."

Libby shook her head. "I haven't gone this long *without* seeing anyone in a long time."

"Work keeping you busy?"

Libby shrugged. "Had an event last night, but no busier than usual."

"Is it me, then? Did I do something?"

The question stopped Libby. She had distanced herself on purpose, but she didn't want Janelle to think she was somehow to blame.

"It's not you. It's me." She sat back down. "I'm just"—she searched for the right word—"*driven* right now. It's hard to explain. I'm working through some things, and to be honest, if I'm in Hope Springs it gets complicated. So . . ."

Janelle stared at her. "That totally made no sense to me. Working through *what* things?"

Libby hesitated. "Working through . . . the Bible."

Her cousin's entire countenance changed. "Are you serious? That's awesome, Libby. How did that happen?"

"See, that's why Hope Springs makes it complicated—one of the reasons, anyway. I don't need you asking a bunch of questions or assuming it means this or that. This is personal for me."

"So . . . I can't even know how it happened?"

Libby wasn't sure she wanted to say, but she'd started in now. "Kinda began on a weekend I spent with Aunt Gwynn, Keisha, and Aunt Floretta."

"What?" Janelle looked as if she couldn't find the words. "You planned a trip to New Jersey and didn't tell me? You spent time with Aunt Gwynn . . . and didn't tell me? When was this?"

"Over a month ago," Libby said. "It was spontaneous, and surreal. The entire weekend, the conversation, the meals, even little impromptu things seemed meant for me, at just the right time." She caught herself. "I know I'm not making sense again."

"Actually, now you're making perfect sense. It was God."

"I can't quibble with that." Libby rose from her seat again. "But on that note—before you ask more questions—I've got to go." She headed for the door.

Janelle followed. "I won't ask anything right now. But I'm really excited for you. I can tell you're in a different place."

They walked together to Libby's car as a caravan of cars came toward them. Stephanie and Lindell parked first, followed by Todd, Becca, and their kids. Kory had apparently driven Dee, Tiffany, and Daniel. And parking next to them was Marcus, with Charley, Travis—and Trina. Everyone in the crew had on Hope Springs Tigers shirts or at least royal blue and gold.

Stephanie came toward her. "Libby's in Hope Springs? And trying to sneak off before we got back? What's up?" She hugged her.

"I was here on business." Sounded nice and official. "Helping Janelle with wedding plans. But I couldn't stay long."

"Hey, stranger." Becca gave her a warm hug. "We've had a change of season since you were here last."

"I know. I'm terrible."

Trina came over next, chatting it up in her Hope Springs football shirt. Did Travis get that for her?

Libby gave a quick glance in his direction. He was the only one who hadn't joined them. Looked like he was searching for something in the car. More like stalling.

"I'd better be going," Libby said.

"You should stay," Todd said. "We're about to put some hot dogs and burgers on the grill."

Libby felt strangely out of place. Is this what things were like now? Trina was a regular part of the circle?

"Thanks, Todd," she said, "but I can't." She smiled. "Maybe next time."

A quick round of good-byes ensued, and the crew moved inside both houses.

Janelle lagged behind. "He thinks it's better this way," she said, "if he gives you your space."

"You don't have to make excuses for Travis." Libby opened her door and got in. "He didn't speak. So what."

Janelle leaned into the car. "Have you thought of telling him about this journey you're on?"

She frowned. "No. Why would I? I don't keep him apprised of my life."

"But I know he prays for you," Janelle said. "I really think he'd want to know."

"That's funny. His actions just showed the exact opposite." Libby started the car. "I'm not telling him where I am, and I don't want you to either."

Janelle didn't move.

"Yes?" Libby said.

"I'm praying."

Any other time, Libby would've tossed the comment away as cliché. But in this moment, it meant something to her. "Thank you," she said.

Libby drove away, trying not to wrestle with the image of Travis and Trina. Why should she? They were a couple. And given Travis's age and desire to marry, they likely had a clear trajectory.

She played it out in her mind . . . Travis married. Travis in his boyhood home with a wife. Travis at New Jerusalem with a first lady. The Travis she'd known for more than thirty years, with whom she'd always had a special connection in one way or another . . . committed to someone else.

CHAPTER TWENTY-NINE
Friday, October 1

M arcus opened the passenger door when Charley pulled to a stop. "This is the first Friday night we haven't been together."

Charley shook her head at him. "That is so not true. We were just at the football game together."

"That's not together, together," he said. "That's assistant principal and coach amongst a crowd of rowdy teenagers, acting professionally. *Together* is different."

"You're just spoiled."

"And I'm okay with that!"

"Next time I'll tell Stephanie, Janelle, and Becca not to plan a girls' night on our night. But I have to admit, I'm looking forward to it." She nudged him. "Anyway, you get a guys' night out of the deal since they're all hanging at Todd's while we're next door."

"Yeah, but we get the kids."

Charley looked as if she were trying not to laugh.

"All right, I'll muddle through," Marcus said, sighing.

"Poor guy."

"I need a kiss to make it, though."

"Really?"

"Really."

Charley smiled. "Only if it's completely necessary."

He held her face and looked into her eyes, his heart dancing as always when he was close to her. He had no clue how he ever thought this couldn't work. Never had his soul been this intertwined with any woman. Their lips touched softly and they pulled closer, deepening the kiss, then gently pulled back.

"If you hear a double knock on the door in two hours," he said, "that's my code to let you know I need another dose." Marcus stepped out.

"What about a serenade outside the window?" she said.

He bent back down. "Don't think I won't do it. You'll just have to be embarrassed."

She laughed as he closed the car door and walked up to the house to grab a few things before heading to Todd's. He stopped first in the kitchen. That hot dog at the game had worn off, but scanning the inside of the refrigerator, he didn't see many options. He got a bottle of water and closed the door, hoping there'd be something to eat at Todd's.

He took the stairs by twos up to his bedroom and heard a knock on the door.

"Come in," he called, heading back down.

The door opened, and when Marcus looked down, Skip Willoughby was standing in his foyer in a windbreaker and slacks.

Marcus walked downstairs and extended his hand. "Mr. Willoughby, I'm surprised to see you tonight."

The older man didn't shake his hand, but closed the door behind him.

"Marcus, I'm surprised as well," he said. "Surprised you're still seeing my granddaughter despite the clear statement that it went against my wishes as head of the family. I find that disrespectful."

Marcus rapidly marshaled his bearings. Had this man come to his house to confront him?

"No disrespect intended, sir." Marcus looked him in the eye. "If I recall, it was Charley who expressed to you that she wanted to continue seeing me."

"Charley is young and on the rebound from a failed engagement. I don't expect her to see things clearly. But I had hoped you understood my meaning when I said I did not approve of this relationship."

"Sir, I don't know what to say," Marcus said. "Charley and I . . . care deeply for one another. We didn't plan for it to happen—"

"Is that so?" His voice was eerily calm, his eyes piercing. "You didn't plan to smooth-talk my granddaughter so you could seduce her? I saw you two just now in the car. I swear, if you get her pregnant—"

"Mr. Willoughby, I'm sorry, but what I find disrespectful is that you would come into my house and falsely accuse me." Marcus could feel his adrenaline surging. "I have no intentions of 'seducing' Charley. For your information, we're not sleeping together. We're trying to honor God—"

"Don't give me that. If you were honoring God, you'd honor her mother and me by leaving her alone."

Marcus squared his stance. "But Charley doesn't want that. I don't want that, and there's nothing you can do about it." He moved around Skip and opened the door. "Sir, it's time for you to leave."

Skip slowly pushed the door again, reached beneath his jacket, and drew out a gun. In the blink of an eye, it was aimed at Marcus's temple, and every muscle in his body froze.

"That's where you're wrong," Skip said. "I can and will do something about it. You think you can rise up against my authority in this family?" His tone took a menacing turn. "Surely you're aware of my deep connections in this town. If you do not end your relationship with Charley, you will find yourself out of a job." He cocked the weapon. "And if you still persist, well . . . I suppose we'll all admire that you're so enamored with her that you're willing to lay down your life for her."

Marcus had never been so scared and so incensed in his life. He spoke through gritted teeth. "Are you threatening my life?"

"I'm trying to spare your life."

"You would kill me?" Marcus cut his eyes over at him. "Are you crazy? You'd never get away with it."

"That clearly wouldn't be your concern, now would it?"

"Mr. Willoughby, I'm calling the police as soon as you're gone."

"Your word against mine and a dozen others," he said. "I'm at a bar with family and friends celebrating another win in an undefeated football season."

He uncocked the gun and put it away. A moment later he was gone.

Marcus exhaled hard, his heart pounding out of his chest. *Skip Willoughby just threatened my life. What on earth am I supposed to do?*

❧

"You're telling that girl right there good-bye, that's what you're going to do," Gladys said.

Marcus's parents had driven from Raleigh the moment they heard, joining the rest in Grandma Geri's living room. Having heard the full story, his mom had been quick with her verdict.

"You've got to be kidding me." Gladys was pacing the room. "Is there even a question? My son's not gonna put his life on the line for this girl. Ain't *no* girl worth all that."

Charley was on the love seat beside him, head cast downward, spent from crying. Now she looked numb.

Gladys looked at Marcus. "What did the police say?"

He was spent himself. "Haven't called them yet."

Gladys turned to her husband. "Warren, did you hear your son say he hasn't called the police yet?" She turned back to Marcus. "Why not? That man needs to be locked up for attempted murder." Gladys's hand went to her forehead like she had a migraine. "My blood pressure is up, I can feel it."

"Aunt Gladys, it's not attempted murder, which is a felony," Travis said. "It's misdemeanor assault. They wouldn't exactly lock him up for that."

"I want to at least see that man placed in handcuffs and hauled down to the station." Gladys was growing more upset. "If it was the other way around, and my son put a gun to Skip's head, do you not think he'd be in jail right now?"

"Now that's a good point," Stephanie said. "I hadn't thought about it that way."

Gladys looked around the room. "Can somebody please tell me why the police haven't been called?"

Charley looked up. "I asked Marcus to wait." She sighed. "I don't know what possessed my grandpa to do this, but I'm sure he only meant to scare Marcus. I know he wouldn't follow through on those threats." She looked teary again. "I think I can handle him myself. I just . . . would hate to see him in trouble with the law."

Gladys's hand went to her hip. "Okay, I see. You're still on some prairie in La La Land, and we're over here in the real world. You didn't even *know* your grandfather like some of us did, but now you think you can 'handle' him?" Her head shifted to Marcus. "Did I not *tell* you this girl would complicate your life?" She shook her head. "Call the police *now*."

"I have to agree," Warren said. "This is serious, son."

"Absolutely," Travis said. "The fact is that Skip Willoughby came into my house with a gun, pointed it at Marcus's head, and threatened his life. There needs to be a police report to that effect."

Gladys turned to Todd. "He's your elder. What's your counsel?"

Todd hadn't said much beyond his initial shock. He started with a long sigh. "I'm still stunned," he said. "No matter what happens with the law, this has far-reaching implications as far as I'm concerned." He looked at Marcus. "But I don't see how you could *not* call the police."

Charley turned toward him. "Marcus, can we talk about it some more? This will cause such a rift in my family."

Marcus ran his hands down his face. "Your grandfather held a gun to my head, and you're worried about your family?"

"Marcus, please. I'm as upset as you are, but—"

He released her hand and stood. "There's no way you could be as upset as I am. There's no way you understand how it feels for a black man to have a white man put a gun to his head." He uttered an empty laugh as he dialed 911. "I should've called the police the minute he left."

"911. What's your emergency?"

Marcus eyed Charley as he spoke. "I'd like to report an assault with a deadly weapon."

CHAPTER THIRTY

Friday marked the eighth day since Sam and Ben's first phone conversation. She knew it was silly, but she'd been keeping track, making mental tallies each day. Or more precisely, each night. They rarely interacted at school, but he'd called her consistently in the evenings. She'd never had a boy show interest like this, talking more than an hour some nights. When he called tonight and asked her out, she didn't think twice. She must be really special to him if he wanted to spend time face-to-face.

Sam squirted a light mousse into her hands and ran it through her hair. Brushing the outer layer, she smoothed her hair into a ponytail and secured it at the base of her neck, letting the curly spirals hang down. She didn't have much makeup—and rarely used what she had—but she had it all laid out before her tonight. Powder base, eye shadow, eye liner, blush . . . She applied each carefully, then remembered mascara. Flipping to the cabinet behind the bathroom mirror, she found her mother's. With a steady hand, she thickened her lashes. Perfect.

She stepped back and examined herself, loving the look of the dark wash jeans Miss Stephanie bought with a brand-new shirt from last week, courtesy of her mom. Hank had taken her mother shopping, but this shirt was too big when she tried it on at home. She offered it to Sam, and Sam wondered where she'd ever wear it. A chic white shirt with a tailored V-neck and long shark-bite hem, it seemed too nice for school. But now she was glad it was hers. She primped a little, feeling pretty . . . and sexy.

A giggle rose inside. Sexy? Her? But Ben had said it enough that maybe she should believe it. He made her feel an entirely different way about herself—beautiful and alluring.

She opened the cabinet mirror again and tried on different shades of her mother's lipstick. The peachy one looked pretty, so she went with that, lining her lips. She should take a picture for her Facebook profile. She was probably the last in her school to join, but she was glad she finally did. It was sort of fun keeping up with what everyone was doing. She tucked the lipstick back in—

"What's going on in here, Sam?"

She jumped, staring at her mother in the mirror. "I didn't hear you come in."

"Apparently." She looked at her watch. "It's eleven o'clock at night. Where do you think you're going?"

"I thought it'd be okay." *Since you weren't home.*

"I told you, Sam. No sleepovers, no visits, no nothing at Stephanie London's."

"I'm not." She turned around. "It's a guy."

Her mother came closer, with a smile that said she was curious. "My Sam's got a date? With who?"

"His name's Ben Willoughby."

"The football player? I've heard about him. He's interested in you, huh?"

Sam's head lowered slightly. "I don't know. Maybe."

"Well, obviously, silly. You're on his mind on a Friday night, aren't you?" Her mom leaned against the wall. "Turn around, let me see you."

Sam did so. Felt good to have her mom's approval.

"My little girl's growing up," she said. "Look at those curves."

"Mom . . ."

"Here, let me fix your shadow. Subtlety is key."

Her mom took a tissue and blotted some of it out, adding small strokes of a different color in the outer edges.

Sam watched the transformation in the mirror. "Thanks, Mom."

A horn sounded outside.

"That's him." She got her purse from the living room. "Oh." She turned. "When do I have to be back?"

Her mom waved away the question. "Don't worry about it. I trust you."

"Okay. Thanks."

"Have fun, baby."

Ben's music blasted from the sporty Mustang. He turned it down only slightly when she got in. As bulky as he was, he was a commanding presence inside.

"Hey." He checked her out. "You look hot."

Sam smiled faintly and reached for her seat belt. "Thanks." Being alone in person like this felt strange.

He drove off, his right hand reaching for something on the floor. He brought a beer can to his mouth and guzzled it.

"You're drinking and driving?" She glanced down and saw several empty cans.

"No big deal," he said. "I do it all the time."

She watched him drain it. "So . . . where are we going?"

"Back to my house."

Her mood fell. When he'd called he said they were celebrating the football win. She figured someone from school was having a party. But since he'd been drinking, maybe the get-together had been beforehand. "What're we doing at your house?"

He smiled, head bopping to the music. "Hanging."

Moments later they were there. Ben got out, slammed his car door, and waited for Sam. They walked together to the house, and Sam suddenly wondered if Coach Willoughby was home. What would she think of Sam being at her house, with her brother?

Ben let them in and threw his keys on a side table. Heading straight upstairs, he turned midstride. "Can I get you something to drink or something?"

"No, I'm fine."

"I've got some more beer."

"No thanks."

"Cool, come on. We're going up to my room." He bounded up the stairs.

She followed slowly. "Your mom doesn't mind?"

"She's out with friends."

"Is your sister home?" Sam asked.

"Nah, she's out too."

Ben obviously hadn't bothered to prepare for company. Clothes were strewn across his bed, over an armchair, even on the floor. An entertainment center was the main focus, with a TV and video game machine—she wasn't sure which one—plus other electronic gadgets. There were video games everywhere, along with DVDs, sports magazines, and books.

Sam lingered by the door, not sure where to sit.

He sprawled across the bed, kicking his shoes off and throwing the clothes to the floor. "You can sit on my bed. I don't mind."

She picked up a couple of DVD cases from the floor and sat on the edge of the bed, reading them. "You want to watch a movie?"

"Sure, we could." He got more DVDs from a shelf for her to look at. "What do you want to watch?"

"Um . . ." She kept looking. "I haven't seen *Red Tails*. I'm a history buff, so that seems interesting." She looked at him. "What about that?"

His nod vacillated as he leafed through the pile beside her. "Have you seen *Friends with Benefits*?"

"No. What's that about?"

He gave her a look, as if she should know.

She read the back and felt the heat rising on her neck. "I don't know about this one."

"Aw, come on, you'll like it."

He jumped up and started clicking buttons. The TV turned on and a DVD popped out. He put the new disc in and rejoined her, the bed sinking down as he lay on his side. "You should take your shoes off and get comfortable."

She slipped off her flats.

He gave a slow grin. "But you're still not comfortable. Come lie up here beside me."

She shifted, moving parallel to him. On their elbows—his body behind hers—she felt the strangest conflicting sensations . . . heart pounding like she'd stumbled into a danger zone . . . and pounding in exhilaration. She was sure of it—Ben would be her first kiss.

The first few minutes into the movie, Sam felt Ben playing with her ponytail. He took the band off and let her hair fall free.

"Man, you're sexy this way," he said.

He ran his fingers underneath, massaging her scalp. Then he inched closer and draped a leg over hers.

The heart pounding increased.

"Ben, I don't think—"

"Shh."

He rubbed her leg, then her arm. She tried to focus on the movie, but he turned her body toward him.

"You're so beautiful," he said. "I don't think you know how beautiful you are."

He kissed her forehead and her nose, and just like that, he was kissing her lips.

My first kiss.

Despite the alcohol on his breath, it was tender at first, then a little forceful. She moved her head to take a breath, and he brought it right back. Seconds later she tried again. "Ben, we should slow down. Let's watch the movie."

"We're making our own movie." He smiled. "We're friends, right? With benefits."

He kissed her neck, his hand moving under her shirt.

She sat up now, everything pounding danger. "Ben, seriously." She moved her hair from her face. "I'd rather just watch the movie. Or maybe we should go downstairs."

"I'm not going anywhere. You feel too good."

With a strong hand he brought her back down, pushing her shirt all the way up, kissing her.

"Ben, please stop. Please."

He unbuttoned her pants and started tugging on them, and her heart constricted.

"No! Ben, no! I'm a virgin!"

She rolled over, and he grabbed her, manipulating her like a rag doll with a fraction of his strength.

Tears streamed down her face as he shifted the weight of his body on hers. "Noooo . . . please, noooo . . . oh, God, help me . . ."

❧

Sam sat on the bed fully dressed, legs pulled to her chest. The tears came and went, but not the shaking. She couldn't stop the shaking.

She stared at the bed, nauseated by Ben's snores—nauseated, period. She needed to vomit. Would be better than these dry heaves. And she needed to go to the bathroom. And she needed to get away from Ben. She never wanted to see him again. How would she face him Monday morning? Whenever she saw him, whenever she heard a mention of football, she'd want to throw up.

She rocked gently back and forth as the tears started again. *Why did this happen to me?* And why this sick twist, that she now felt imprisoned, unable to get home?

"I just want to go home . . ."

She rolled her eyes over to Ben. She'd prodded, pushed, even screamed at him to wake up, but he was passed out. Now that he'd ruined her life, the least he could do was get her home.

I'm not a virgin anymore. She was sick from that too. She'd read about the woman at the well, the one Stephanie and Janelle had showed her. One night in bed she'd looked at the chapter again, where Jesus told the woman she'd had several husbands and was with a man who wasn't her husband. Sam knew right then and there she didn't want that. She and that woman might've been alike in some respects, but she wanted that aspect to be different. She wanted to keep her virginity for one man, a special man, her husband.

Not a selfish drunk like Ben Willoughby.

Why didn't I listen to Miss Stephanie?

Stephanie. Sam could call her for a ride home. Her eyes found the clock. 1:20 a.m. How would she explain needing a ride in the middle of the night from Coach Willoughby's house? She sighed. No one here had come home yet, at least not that she'd heard. She could call her mom, but that would definitely be a last resort. She couldn't face her right now.

No option was good, but one thing was clear—she wasn't staying in this room another minute.

Slowly she climbed off the bed. She hurt, and she felt dirty, and every step reminded her of it. She got her purse and opened the door, listening for sounds. Hearing nothing, she found a bathroom and went, using only the light from the hallway. She didn't ·

want to see herself in the bathroom mirror. She couldn't. But in the darkness she splashed water on her face and pulled her hair back in place. She couldn't bear anyone else knowing what she'd gone through.

She walked downstairs and sat on the bottom step. Someone had to come home soon. She'd never met Ben's mom, and she'd be embarrassed to meet her in the middle of the night like this. But she didn't care. She had to get home.

Several minutes passed, and Sam heard a car outside. She tiptoed to the front window and looked out. *Coach Willoughby!*

Sam opened the door immediately and walked out, just as two other cars pulled up . . . and a *police car?*

Coach Willoughby caught sight of her and came toward her. "Sam? What are you doing here?"

Sam forced a lightness into her voice. "I . . . Ben . . . brought me here just to hang out. But now he's asleep, and I can't get home."

"What?" The coach frowned. "That doesn't make sense. Why were you hanging out with my brother?"

"Charley, we need you over here," a woman called. "The policeman's got some questions."

Coach Willoughby looked the other direction, where a policeman had gotten out of his car and approached the others. "Be right there, Mom."

The coach took out her phone and dialed a number. "Steph, Sam's at my house, and the police just pulled up so I can't leave. Can you come and take her home? . . . I don't know . . . Yeah, you need to come now." She looked at Sam. "Stephanie will be here in five minutes."

"She was already up?"

Coach Willoughby nodded wearily. "It's been a long night for a lot of us."

Now everyone was out of the cars, angry voices rising.

"Sam, will you be okay right here waiting for Stephanie?" Coach asked. "I need to see what's going on over there."

"Sure."

Sam took a big breath and sat on the front step, holding herself as she waited.

CHAPTER THIRTY-ONE

Stephanie couldn't jump in her car fast enough, heart racing the entire way to Charley's house. What in the world was Sam doing there? *Why was she with Ben at one in the morning?* And why couldn't *Ben* take her home?

She felt her hand squeezing the steering wheel. Better be because he'd left town. Because if he tried anything with that girl, Stephanie would kill him.

As she approached the house, she saw drama unfolding with a policeman, Charley, her mom, and Skip Willoughby. There'd been a flurry of phone calls that precipitated that. After Marcus called the police, Charley got a call from her grandfather, who'd apparently gotten a call from the sheriff, a personal friend. The sheriff had wanted Skip to come down to the police station; Skip arranged for a meeting at his house.

As much as Stephanie wanted to know what was happening over there, she spotted the main object of her concern on the front step. And when Sam spotted her car, she came quickly down the steps and into the street. Stephanie threw the car in park as Sam opened the passenger side door and got in. She reached for her seat belt and clicked it, barely looking at her.

"Thank you for coming, Miss Stephanie."

Her voice was so thin that Stephanie stared at her a moment. "No problem at all." She drove off, noticing the pretty shirt Sam was wearing, one she'd never seen. "So . . . I'm surprised you're here, visiting Ben so late." She glanced at her. "How did that happen?"

Sam stared downward.

"Sam?"

The girl turned toward the passenger window. Stephanie caught her wiping tears.

Lord, something has happened, and everything in me is saying it's something awful. Please give me the strength to help Sam. Give me the words. Help me not to break down or do something rash—because, Lord, if Ben . . . She took a breath. I love this girl, Lord. I know You love her more. Help me to be what You want me to be for her in this moment.

Stephanie pulled in beside Sam's mom's Oldsmobile, hoping she was asleep so they'd have some time. She cut her lights.

"Sam, come here, sweetie." Stephanie tugged at her gently and opened her arms. "Come here."

Sam reached for her and broke down in such sobs that Stephanie began crying herself. She held her, stroked her hair, rubbed her back.

"I'm so sorry," Sam blurted suddenly. "I'm so . . . sorry."

"Sorry for what, sweetheart?"

"You told me to stay away from him, and I didn't listen. I didn't listen."

Stephanie dabbed her tears and looked directly at Sam. "I need you to tell me what happened."

She looked down, racked with emotion. "I can't."

"Sam . . ." Stephanie lifted her chin with a finger. "Yes, you can. Tell me everything." She reached for a box of tissues on the floor in the back and gave her one.

Sam blew her nose and stared out the side window. After at least two minutes, she said, "He called me after the game tonight, said he wanted to celebrate."

Stephanie heard the backdrop in that one statement. Ben had already been working her.

"I thought we were going out somewhere"—her breath caught as the sobs came from her chest—"but we went back to his house and watched a movie in his room."

"What time did he pick you up?"

"Eleven thirty."

Jerk. Probably had already been out with another girl for the real after-game celebration.

"Okay, so you watched a movie . . ."

"*No.*"

Stephanie waited.

"It was only on maybe ten minutes, and he started feeling on me and kissing me. And . . ."

Stephanie's stomach tightened.

". . . and . . ." Sam let out a low wail. "He started taking off my clothes . . . and I told him no . . . I told him I was a *virgin*, and he didn't care." She blew her nose again. "I scratched his back hard, but he wouldn't get off me. He was too heavy . . . so heavy . . ." She turned red eyes to Stephanie. "It *hurt*."

"Oh, baby girl . . ." She embraced the younger girl, tears flowing down Stephanie's face faster than she could wipe them.

"I feel so ashamed. I was trying to look cute. I wanted to look *sexy*. If I hadn't—"

"Uh-uh." Stephanie looked at her. "You're not going there. You can look cute all you want. This is the bottom line—he had no right to touch you. This was *rape*. What he did was criminal." She pointed down the street. "We need to go back to that police officer outside the house and tell him what happened."

Stephanie thought of the irony. *They can haul away both of those jokers.*

"No, no." Sam was shaking her head again. "I'm not telling anyone else. *Please* don't tell anyone. It's too humiliating." She stared downward, still shaking her head. "I *hate* my life. I hate that I never had a dad. My Grammie was taken from me. *You* were taken from me. My virginity was taken from me." She rolled the tissue around her finger. "My mom doesn't care about me. She was more excited about my going out with a boy than going to a Bible study. I'm just . . . *sick* of my life. It's not worth living."

Stephanie put her hand on her shoulder. "You have *everything* to live for, Sam. I've told you before and I'm telling you again that you have no idea how much God loves you. He *loves* you. Life can be horrible at times. People can do horrible things. Moms and dads might not be all that they should. But I want you to keep your focus on God. He never fails."

"Miss Stephanie . . ." Sam looked at her. "He failed tonight."

Lord, what am I supposed to say to that? I'm not good at this stuff.

"Sam, all I can tell you is I believe the Bible—it took me awhile, but I do—and the *truth* is that God never fails. It doesn't mean He controls our every action. We're sinful people. We do sinful things. And He allows that. But you know what?"

Sam stared at her.

"Those sinful things let us know how much we need Jesus," Stephanie said. "*I* need Jesus, right now, because I hate Ben for what he did, and I'm supposed to love him and pray for him. Ben needs Jesus—clearly. And, sweetheart, you need Jesus. That's been my prayer for you, Samara." Stephanie squeezed her shoulder. "That your eyes will be opened to the truth of your desperate need of Him—just like the Samaritan woman at the well."

Sam was quiet a moment. "I don't know about anything right now. But I know I'm not going back to that school. I can't face him."

"Sam," Stephanie said, "you need to talk to your mother about all of this. She needs to know what happened. And you should talk to her about going to the police."

"I'm not telling her."

"Do you want me to talk to her?"

"That wouldn't help. And anyway, she wouldn't care."

"Oh, Sam, yes she would. Let's just—"

"No." She shook her head for emphasis.

Stephanie blew out a breath and tapped on the steering wheel, debating her next step. She suddenly threw the car into reverse.

"What are you doing?" Sam asked.

"I have to take you to the police station." Tears started again. "I have to."

"I'm not telling them anything," Sam said. "You can't make me."

"Sam, this makes no sense. You can't let Ben get away with this. Anyway, if you change your mind—and you will if I have anything to do with it—this is for your protection, for the police to have the evidence they need."

Stephanie had never been to the police station, but she'd passed it enough in town to know where it was. She pulled into a parking spot—and thirty minutes later she was pulling back out.

"I told you I wasn't saying anything," Sam said. "I just want to put it behind me." She added, "And I wish you hadn't told them it was Ben Willoughby. They probably have kids at my school. People will know."

"They're professionals, Sam. They'll keep it confidential." She looked at her. "I just wish you would have cooperated." She got an idea. "I know," she said. "We can go to the hospital in Rocky Mount and do a rape kit. That way—"

"Noooo." Sam began crying. "I would've walked home from Ben's house if I knew you were gonna do this. Please, just take me home." She was sobbing now, the weight of the evening hitting her again. "I want to go to bed. Please!"

Stephanie wanted badly to at least take her to her house, let her be loved on by her and Janelle. If Sam's mom wasn't home, she would've done just that.

She pulled in front of Sam's house again, checking the clock on the dash. "We'll talk again in the morning," she said. "I want you to really consider telling your mom. She needs to know."

Sam sighed. "Fine, I'll think about it."

"I love you, Samara." Stephanie didn't know why she was suddenly using Sam's whole name, but she liked the sound of it. "And see, I wasn't taken from you. As God would have it, I'm still here."

Sam reached for her and held her tight. "I love you too, Miss Stephanie. Thank you."

"Look for my call later this morning."

"Okay," she said. "And, Miss Stephanie, please promise me you won't tell anyone what happened."

Stephanie sighed. "I don't know if I can do that."

"Please. You have to."

"I'll respect your wishes," she said, "but only until we talk again. I really don't want him to get away with this."

Sam got out and went into the house.

Stephanie drove off, her mind in a million directions, her heart torn to shreds.

CHAPTER THIRTY-TWO

Saturday, October 2

Charley was dead tired. With so much going on, this wasn't the time for a Saturday morning volleyball game. She'd been up half the night dealing with the fiasco her grandfather started—which he said *she* started because of her relationship with Marcus. The scene with the police officer alone consumed much time.

"Mr. Willoughby, I think it'd be best if you come down of your own volition," the officer had said. "I know you don't want me to do it by force."

"You would slap handcuffs on an old man? You'll lose your job," Skip said.

"Actually, sir, I don't think I will. The sheriff is the one who told me to bring you in."

"Jack and I go way back," Skip said. "He knows there's nothing to these charges. I don't know why you all are wasting my time."

"It's merely procedure, sir," he said. "We can't ignore the report that was made."

Her grandpa finally went, seeing the benefit of doing so in his own car, and was ultimately let go after being charged with a misdemeanor. An hour of argument at home followed, in which her grandfather denied Marcus's version of events—"I didn't stick the gun in his face; I just showed him I had one on me"—and alternatively argued he had a right to do what he needed to do to protect his family.

Charley had awakened bleary-eyed, further upset because Marcus's phone kept going straight to voice mail and he hadn't answered her texts. They had a ritual of texting before bed and first thing in the morning. But today she was looking for more than a good-morning ritual. She wanted him to know she had no hard feelings about involving the police. She even agreed with it now. The whole thing was a mess, but she hoped they could weather it together.

And then there was Ben. What was going on with him and Sam? She didn't even know they were in contact with one another. And had she known, she would've told Sam to stay away from him. She'd knocked on his door before she left at eight thirty this morning, but he was still sleep. Stephanie wasn't answering her phone either. She'd have to wait until after the volleyball match to find out what happened.

"Awesome, Mary!" Charley said. "Keep it going!"

The Hope Springs crowd cheered as Mary served her third straight ace, putting the team up by thirteen. They were only two points away from winning the final match. Charley had benched most of her starters and put some of her backup in the game to give them some playing time. Mary was proving herself in the opportunity.

Mary served again, and the libero on the opposing team got this one, passing it to the setter, who set it to the middle hitter, who spiked it against Hope Springs. The opposing team cheered the point and got ready to serve.

"That's all right!" Charley walked along the sideline, clapping to keep them—and herself—energized. "Side-out, girls, side-out!"

One of the players passed Kelsey a phone. Kelsey stared intently at it, growing visibly upset. Tia pulled out a phone and looked at hers. And seconds later the entire bench was gathered around, looking animated and horrified.

Charley walked over. "Girls, you know my policy. No phones during the game. No tweeting, texting, or Facebooking."

Tia looked up. "Coach, this is some serious stuff right here."

"Put the phones away," Charley said.

The crowd cheered a long series of volleys that ended with the point for Hope Springs.

Charley pumped her fist. "Game point! Come on, Hope Springs!"

She looked back at the bench. None of them were paying attention to the game, engrossed still in those phones. She called over, "Fine. From here on out, you will give every phone to me prior to the start of the game."

Hope Springs won the final point easily, and the entire team got up to shake hands with the visiting team.

Charley shook hands with the visiting coaches and shared a few words with them, encouraging their players as well. When she turned back around, almost every team member had a phone in hand. In the bleachers, the opposing fans were filing out. But the scene among Hope Springs students was beginning to mirror the one on the bench, as they were either riveted to a phone in hand or gathered around the phone of another.

But only one person was crying—Kelsey.

Charley strode over to her. "Kelsey, come with me to the athletic office."

Phone clutched in her hand, Kelsey walked alongside, and all eyes seemed to follow.

Charley turned to her the moment she stepped in the office and closed the door. "What is going on that's captured everyone's atten-tion? And why are you upset?"

Kelsey cut her eyes away. "Ask your brother."

"*Ben* has something to do with this? Is this about another fight between you two?"

Kelsey flicked a tear, her predominant emotion clearly anger. "He's still mad about me going out with Roger, which was because *he* went out with someone else." She pulled something up on her phone. "So now he put *this* on my Facebook wall, for all of our friends to see."

Charley took the phone. Ben had indeed posted on her wall. It said, This is what payback looks like, you slut. By the way, enjoyed her much more than you.

A forty-seven second video was attached. Charley clicked Play and saw Ben on top of some girl, with sensual music added for effect. She pushed Stop.

"I'm not watching that foul video." Charley gave her the phone and paced the room, so angry she didn't know where to start. "How is this even *allowed* on Facebook?"

"It's not," Kelsey said. "People post all kinds of stuff that's not allowed. If it gets reported, it might get deleted. But thousands of people have seen it by then." She sighed her disgust. "I can't believe he called me a slut for everybody to see."

Charley looked at her. "That's not nearly the worst part of this. He took *video* of himself and some girl—who knows if she knew she was being taped—and *posted* it." She held out her hand. "Give me your phone again."

Charley clicked through several Facebook screens until she'd reported the post and the Facebook user in violation of the rules, Ben.

"Wait a minute," Charley said suddenly. "Why didn't you delete this the minute you found it? Then other people wouldn't have seen it."

"He posted it to a dozen other walls—and people are sharing it like crazy." She huffed. "And when I find out who that girl is . . . probably Alisa. He was flirting with her at the after-game party last night."

Charley gave her back her phone. "I have to go."

Her sights were set on home, but seeing numerous students in the gym, still milling around phones, she reacted.

"Listen up." Her voice echoed. "You're looking at and gossiping about real people with real lives and real feelings. If you've posted that video to your own page, I'm asking you to do the right thing and delete it. Now. Don't spread it around."

If one person listened, she'd be shocked. Still, it needed to be said.

Charley burst through the door at home and doubled up the steps to Ben's room. She'd seen his car outside, but the room was empty.

She stopped in the upstairs hall. "Ben! Where are you?"

"What?" he called. "I'm in the kitchen."

She'd hurried right past him. Hastening back down, Charley entered the kitchen, where her mom and Ben were eating lunch—Ben only somewhat. He seemed more preoccupied with the laptop on the table in front of him than with the sandwich off to the side.

"Checking comments on your vile post?" Charley asked.

Ben sat back, looking satisfied. "I hear the whole gym was captivated. Sorry if I distracted your players."

"This is sick and slimy even for you, Ben."

Her mom looked up. "What's this about?"

"Ben posted a video of himself and some girl having sex. On Facebook. All the high schoolers were looking at it at the game."

Her mother put down the newspaper. "You did *what*? I don't

even know what to—Ben, what on *earth* would possess you to do such a thing?"

Ben didn't respond, so Charley responded for him.

"He was mad at Kelsey and called it payback."

"Delete that video right now," Dottie said.

Ben sighed. "Mom, you don't know how Facebook works. Wouldn't matter if I deleted it. I only posted it an hour ago, and hundreds of people already shared it."

"What does that mean, 'shared it'?" Dottie asked.

"Means they posted it too, so all their friends could see. It's gone viral."

Dottie stared in disbelief. "Do you know what you've done to your reputation?"

"Who *cares* about his reputation?" Charley said. "This probably improves his reputation among his twisted friends. I'm worried about the girl in the video."

It dawned on Charley that Sam was at the house just last night, but no way could she be the one in the video. As surprising as it was to see her with Ben, Sam would never have had sex with him, Charley was sure. But there were plenty others he'd been out with and could easily have sneaked to his room.

She turned to Ben. "Did you give any thought to the girl? You've ruined her life."

"Have not." Ben was dismissive. "You can't even tell who she is."

"Still," Charley said. "Viral or not, I think you need to delete every post that you personally put out there."

"Absolutely," Dottie said. "Take them down right now."

Ben gave in with a groan as he turned back to his laptop. A couple of clicks later he did a double take. "Oh crap!"

"What?"

"That stupid geek, Leonard." Ben was reading. "He's got a

comment on the video. Says he took a screen shot, enlarged it, and figured out who she is."

"Oh no . . ." Charley felt sick. "Tell me Leonard didn't post her name."

Ben nodded slowly. "He did. And by the look of all the follow-up posts, now *that's* going viral."

"Do I know her? Is she a Hope Springs High student?"

Ben stared at the screen. "It's Sam."

CHAPTER THIRTY-THREE

S tephanie had jumped into the car once again after a phone call about Sam. But this time she had a posse with her— Lindell and Janelle, and they'd picked up Marcus on the way. Stephanie was sure she'd get pushback from Sam's mother about seeing her. Whether it made sense or not, she felt that a group— especially one that included the assistant principal—would let the woman know how serious this was. Given Sam's tendency to seclude herself, she probably wasn't yet aware of the video, but it was imperative that Stephanie let her know—then figure out how to cope with it.

"This street right here, Lindell," Stephanie said. "Turn here."

"No, the whole thing blew up this morning," Marcus said. He was in the backseat talking to the principal. "Right . . . Absolutely. Definitely a fiasco." He blew out a sigh. "You think news organizations might get hold of it? I hadn't thought about that . . . Okay, will do."

"What did he say?" Stephanie said.

"He wants me to call him back once we see how Sam's doing,"

Marcus said. "We're meeting later this afternoon to determine what administrative action should be taken."

"Every time I think about it, I just want to cry," Janelle said.

"I can't believe it." Marcus had said it about a hundred times. "I really cannot believe Ben did this."

"I don't put anything past him," Stephanie said. "I have no words for how I'm feeling right now."

She hadn't told them that the video was actually of a rape. She'd promised Sam she wouldn't say anything until she talked to her. Stephanie had called her right before she found out about the Facebook post, but she hadn't answered.

"That's her house," Stephanie said, pointing. "Huh. Her mom's car isn't there. I hope Sam's home."

They filed out and looked as Charley's car came crunching over the gravel. She'd said she would meet them there.

They all walked to the door.

Stephanie knocked. "Sam, you in there?" She waited. Knocked harder. "Sam? Are you home?" She turned to the others. "What if she already knows about the video? She might be too humiliated to open the door."

Marcus knocked this time, his fist making a louder sound.

Stephanie pulled out her phone and called again. No answer. "Where could she be? She hardly goes anywhere."

"Is there a home she could go to if she wanted to escape all this?" Janelle said.

"Just ours." Stephanie looked over at the front window. "That's Sam's bedroom."

She stepped into the dirt and brushed against the bush in front of the window, trying to peer in. The blinds were partially open, and she saw a cell phone on the bed. And the bed was unmade. Stephanie's heart pounded.

"I've never seen her go anywhere without her phone," Stephanie said. "And she's a neat freak. Says she doesn't feel right unless her bed is made." She walked back over to them. "I'm trying the door."

"We can't just walk into the girl's house," Lindell said.

"I have to. Something is wrong." Stephanie didn't want to reveal what Sam said last night—that life wasn't worth living. And that was *before* knowledge of the video.

"This door is locked," Stephanie said. "I'm going around back."

"Steph," Janelle said, "I'm a little nervous about creeping around this girl's house. Maybe we should come back or call later when we're sure someone's home."

Stephanie ignored her. She jiggled the doorknob on the back door, and it opened. "I'm going in."

The door opened to a narrow, dim hallway off the kitchen. Stephanie heard footsteps behind her as she walked through the kitchen, past a bathroom and living room, then to the left where Sam's bedroom was. The door was closed.

Stephanie knocked. "Sam? Are you in there? It's Miss Stephanie." She turned the knob. "It's *locked*?"

She stared at it, thinking. Then, "This is a flimsy door. I know we can kick it in."

Marcus looked at her. "I'm with you. I've got a bad feeling."

At Marcus's swift kick, the lock popped and the door flew open.

They walked into an empty room. Stephanie sighed, glancing around at the bedroom furniture and decorations, wondering what to do next.

"Oh, God!"

Stephanie turned. Janelle had fallen to her knees, hands to her face in shock after opening the closet door. Stephanie's entire body tensed as she walked to where Janelle stood.

"No!" Stephanie wailed. "No! Oh, God, no!"

She was still wailing as Lindell hurried past her to the closet.

"Call 911," he shouted.

Marcus put his arm around Stephanie, gently pulling her aside.

Seconds later Lindell had carried Sam's body to the bed and was performing CPR.

Charley was talking to the 911 operator. "An ambulance is on the way," she told them. She went back to answering questions.

Lindell stopped the CPR and slid to the floor, face buried in his hands.

In silent sobs, Stephanie knelt by the bed. "Sam . . ." She stroked her hair. "I'm here. It'll be all right. Help's on the way. Sam, please, I know you hear me. *Please* hear me."

Charley and Janelle were holding hands, heads bowed, praying. Marcus was pacing.

Stephanie kept talking to Sam, stroking her hair, until the ambulance came. Marcus went to open the front door and let them in.

As the paramedics rushed in, Stephanie moved out of the way so they could tend to her. Her eyes caught Sam's phone on the bed. Curious, she picked it up and flipped it open, awakening the screen, surprised to see that her phone with prepaid minutes had Facebook.

Stephanie brought it closer. Sam's profile page was open, her wall flooded with recent comments.

Ur the real slut, not Kelsey, one girl wrote.

Another, Why do you act all quiet in school? Ur just an undercover whore.

Stephanie's blood boiled.

Didn't know Ben liked black girls, one guy said. Gotta ask what dark meat is like. lol

Charley came beside her. "What's on there?"

"Facebook posts. She knew." Stephanie threw the phone on the bed. "I can't read any more of that filth."

She found a piece of paper and left a note by the front door for Sam's mother to go to the hospital. Hopefully she'd be home soon.

But Stephanie knew already—it was too late.

Stephanie left the Rocky Mount hospital at 5:14 p.m., the moment she heard Sam had been taken off life support and pronounced dead. She didn't want to hear a single word or engage with anyone. She knew Lindell understood.

She got in her car and zoomed out of the parking lot, taking the route back to the highway. But she wasn't headed to Hope Springs. She would keep driving and driving. If she knew the way, she would drive all the way back to St. Louis. Where life made sense. Where people worshiped together. Where you didn't get a gun stuck in your face for dating a person who looked different.

Where she didn't have to worry about her heart getting ripped out because she'd gotten so close to a young girl.

Is that what this was about, Lord? It wasn't enough to stay in St. Louis in my own selfish world. You had to bring me to Hope Springs so I could experience what it felt like to extend myself, to love another, and to witness a tragic end? I had to experience what it was like to pray for someone, then watch her suffer in such a despicable way? Oh, and for added measure, I got to see prejudice up close. Nice.

"I should've stayed in St. Louis!" she yelled at the top of her lungs. "I *hate* Hope Springs."

The image of Sam's body came to mind, and just that fast, her emotions turned back to overwhelming sadness. Her eyes filled with tears. *Sam, I wish you had called me. I wish I could've been there for you . . .*

Her mind went through what Sam must've been thinking and feeling, how much she must've been hurting to actually go into that closet . . . *Lord, this is so painful . . .*

Would the tears ever stop? When she pictured the scene today, she cried. When she pictured Sam running through the house with Tiffany on her back, she cried.

And she cried when she recalled Sam's mom, Teri, at the hospital, hearing the news.

When Teri had arrived, no one on the hospital staff was available immediately to speak with her. Stephanie approached, and Teri was clearly not pleased that Stephanie knew what was going on and she didn't. It only got worse when she learned that they'd come to her house, let alone *entered* her house. But when Teri grasped what Sam had done to herself, she broke down.

Stephanie went further, telling her what had happened last night and this morning with the video. Teri walked away, lost in her grief. After a nurse came and got her, they didn't see her again.

Now Stephanie's phone rang, and the only reason she gave it a thought was because she recognized the ring as Cyd's.

She answered. "Lindell must've called you."

"He did. I'm so sorry, Steph," she said. "I know how much Sam meant to you. This is absolutely devastating."

Stephanie nodded, as if Cyd could see.

"When was the last time you talked to her?" Cyd asked.

"I was with her last night."

"Oh, wow," Cyd said. "So you were one of the last people she talked to. That's a blessing."

Stephanie stared at the road stretching out in front of her. "How is that a blessing? It obviously made no difference."

"You don't know that, Steph."

"I don't?"

"I'm just saying, from everything you told me, you made an impact."

"Yeah. Okay. Next time I guess I should make less of an impact." She sighed. "I'm not trying to be difficult. I'm just wondering, maybe if I hadn't come along, and Sam was living life as usual, maybe she would've been on a different track that didn't lead . . . here."

"I don't believe that." Cyd had her resolute tone. "You can't tell me that your presence in her life was anything but positive. Still, what happened is beyond heartbreaking."

Scenes from today pierced her again. "Cyd, I've got to go."

"I understand," her sister said.

"And, Cyd?"

"Yes?"

"Can you pray for Sam's mother?"

"She was actually already on my heart, but what made you ask?"

"I just figured, if that sweet girl made such an impact in my life in two short months, I can imagine how much her mom must be hurting."

Stephanie's phone beeped with another call. She took a glance but didn't recognize the number.

"Okay, really gotta go now," she said. "I'd better see who this is." She clicked over. "This is Stephanie London."

"Ms. London, this is Officer Fraser. I believe we met briefly at the police station last night."

"Okay. Yes?"

"Ma'am, we need you to come back down to the station to give a statement."

"Regarding what?"

"Regarding an alleged crime of sexual assault upon one Samara Johnston."

CHAPTER THIRTY-FOUR
Sunday, October 3

Charley knocked hard on Marcus's door early Sunday morning. "Come on, Marcus," she muttered, "you have to be home. Answer."

She'd knocked twice already, and in the interim, what had been a steady rain was starting to blow in gusts, pelting her even as she stood on the covered porch. The two of them hadn't yet had a real one-on-one conversation. With yesterday's tragedy, there was more than enough to keep them occupied, talking past one another. She had no way of knowing where their own relationship stood. But would he leave her out here?

She heard footsteps, and the door opened. Marcus had on long gym shorts and a wrinkled shirt, and looked as if he was trying to get his bearings.

"How long have you been knocking?" he asked.

"A few minutes."

He took her hand and helped her inside. "Wait a minute."

He ran upstairs and returned with a towel, handing it to her.

"Thanks." She dried her face and hair.

"It's seven in the morning, Charley. What's going on?"

"Ben was arrested less than an hour ago."

"What? For what? Something with that video?"

"Well . . ." It was hard to say. "He's been charged with sexual assault."

Marcus ran his hands down his face. "They're saying this was rape, what was in the video?"

"Marcus, I feel terrible. I should've seen it." The thought of it pained her. "I knew there was no good reason for Sam to be at my house late Friday night. But she didn't look like anything was wrong. She simply asked for a ride home. And I was distracted with the police and my grandpa. So I called Steph to come get her."

"Where was Ben?" He took the towel from her and threw it on a step.

"Sleeping. Can you believe that? He'd fallen asleep." She was disgusted by even the little pieces of the story. "I don't know, Marcus. If I had known, we could've dealt with it right then and prevented all the other . . ." She closed her eyes. Yesterday was still so hard.

Marcus led her into the kitchen, and they sat at the table.

"You can't beat yourself up over this," he said. "Who reported the crime?"

"I called Steph before I came here. Apparently Sam told her Friday night but swore her to secrecy. Steph even took her to the police station, but Sam wouldn't talk. But once she . . ." She blew out a sad breath. "Anyway, Stephanie told her mother at the hospital and left it in her hands. Teri called the police."

Marcus sat back, taking it all in. "How did the arrest go down?"

"No negotiations or calls beforehand this time," Charley said. "Two officers banged on the door with a warrant for Ben's arrest. And they confiscated his computer and other equipment."

"How did your mom react?"

"She broke down, said Ben would never do that, then the next minute berated Ben *for* doing that. I don't think she's even grasped everything that's happened." Charley sighed. "Really seems like my family is falling apart. And there's absolutely nothing I can do."

"You're a bright light in that family, Charley. They need you, whether they know it or not."

She looked at him. "I would think you'd counsel me to keep away from them, after what happened to you."

"Travis spent two weeks preaching about loving those who are hard to love." He looked intently at her. "That came to me at the hospital when I thought about how upset I was at your grandfather and at Ben—and I only knew about the video—and at the students I see every day in the halls who wrote foul things on Sam's wall . . ." He stared off for a moment. "I don't want to love any of them. But they'd have no hope at all without love—God's love. That's what you have to keep showing your family."

"Right. I can't even look at Ben. Or my grandpa."

"Charley, when all is said and done, your brother might be going away for a long time. He'll lose everything he has and probably every friend he has. Do you know what a difference it'll make if you're still in his life?"

Charley was quiet for a moment, then looked at him. "What about you? Are we still in each other's lives?" She paused. "I wasn't even sure if I should come here this morning."

"After your brother's arrest?" he said. "Of course you should've." He paused. "I admit I needed some space after what happened with your grandfather, but we're still friends. Don't ever doubt that."

Still friends . . . Charley suddenly felt like crying. What more could happen this weekend? "Do you feel like our relationship has shifted?"

Marcus was slow to respond. "I don't see how it could *not* have shifted. I saw in very real terms how complicated life can be simply by crossing color lines. We've been raised in two different worlds. We have different backgrounds, different backdrops when it comes to analyzing a situation. And you know what else I thought about?"

She fought the tear that brimmed on her lid. "What?"

"What if we got married and had a daughter? She'd be biracial, just like Sam. She might feel like an outcast, just like Sam. Can you imagine?" He shook his head. "I finally see what my mom was saying. Life is hard enough without intentionally complicating it."

Charley stood, nodding. "So we're over. Just like that." The tear spilled.

Marcus went to her. "We're not *over*. I'll always consider you—"

"A friend. Or wait, sister. Back to the beginning."

"Charley, that's not fair," he said. "I wanted it to work. You know I did. I care for you. Life just caved in on us in a big way."

Charley walked around him, ready to leave, then turned near the door.

"What happened to walking by faith? What happened to trusting God?" She flicked a tear. "I thought this relationship was going to be all about *Him*. If you ask me, you're walking by sight."

Charley walked out, closing the door behind her, relishing the downpour that drenched her. It felt just about right.

CHAPTER THIRTY-FIVE

Stephanie decided she was going to Calvary Church this morning—and only because she had an attitude. She didn't particularly want to go to church at all. Her first plan had been to stay in bed, where she could catch up on sleep she'd missed the past two nights. But instead of sleeping, she was grieving decisions she could have made. Like bringing Sam home with her when they left the Willoughbys' so she wouldn't have been alone the next morning. Or calling her earlier on Saturday. Or somehow forcing her to make that police statement.

Having driven herself sick with that, her mind took a different turn—to her anger at Skip Willoughby. He had actually threatened her cousin's life with a pistol. The same man who'd called a boycott of the joint services. And helmed a family where the likes of Ben Willoughby could flourish . . . and yeah, Charley too, but no need to mellow the mental rant.

Stephanie couldn't understand how this man had been a Calvary elder for decades. And as she thought about it, she realized that she'd never been to the church, other than to the funeral last year for Todd's father. What was the atmosphere like? Since Skip had also helmed the church, in a sense, would his influence show?

She didn't expect him to show up, but she'd be waiting for one person to look at her crosswise for being there—just so she could blame Skip and keep her attitude.

She and Lindell walked into the sanctuary ten minutes early.

"Wow, remember the last time we were here?" Stephanie whispered. "It was packed."

"Yeah," Lindell said, "because members of both churches had come to pay their respects to Jim Dillon."

"There aren't any ushers to seat people."

Lindell looked around. "No need."

True. Most of the pews were only two-thirds full.

Definite second glances came their way as they walked the aisle to a seat. Well, it was a natural response. They were the only black people in the building. She didn't count second glances as crosswise. Crosswise came with attitude.

Becca saw them from up front and waved them forward.

"Great." Stephanie spoke under her breath. "Now we'll really be on display."

"Weren't you the one who told Charley *she* needed to sit up front at New Jerusalem, just to make it fun?"

"Whatever."

They slid into the second pew, directly behind Becca.

"Good morning," Stephanie and Lindell said.

Claire turned fully around with a grin. "What are y'all doing here?"

"Joining *you*, Miss Claire." Stephanie touched her nose.

Ethan stood in the pew and reached for Stephanie to pull him back there.

"Sit down, buddy," Becca said, helping him. "You two didn't tell us you were coming." She sat sideways, arm draped over the back of the pew.

"It was last-minute," Stephanie said. "Full disclosure—I came to check it out in light of everything I'm learning about Mr. Skip Willoughby. The bonus is I get to hear Todd."

Becca gave a knowing look. "I hope Todd's fingerprints are the ones you see here."

A middle-aged couple came to the pew. Stephanie and Lindell turned their knees so they could get past.

When they were seated, the woman asked, "You two new in town?"

"Actually, we are, sort of." Lindell shifted toward them. "We moved here in August."

Stephanie waited for her to find a way to tell them they'd happened into the wrong church.

"Well, welcome to Hope Springs and Calvary," the woman said. "I'm Rose Talcott, and this is my husband, Paul."

Mr. Talcott rose again and shook their hands.

Lindell did the same. "Lindell London and my wife, Stephanie. Nice to meet you."

After he'd sat back down, Lindell poked Stephanie and whispered, "That's what you get."

The choir entered from the back and started the service in song. Everyone stood, and Stephanie noticed that Todd had entered the pulpit area as well. They sang three hymns before Todd came to the podium. He looked like he hadn't slept much this weekend either.

He stood in silence for a moment, looking out among them. Then he spoke. "I want to take some special time this morning to pray for the family and friends of a beautiful young girl, Samara Johnston . . ."

Stephanie nodded. What a blessing.

"I'm sure most of you heard about her very sad and tragic end yesterday," Todd continued. "It breaks my heart when a young person—"

Voices were heard in the back of the church, growing louder.

Stephanie turned. Skip Willoughby was in the rear, resisting obvious attempts by an usher to move him toward a seat.

Skip strode to the front of the church, directly to the podium. Todd, looking calm yet assertive, shielded the microphone while they had words. Skip looked defiant, pressing his point practically in Todd's face.

The result—Todd stepped aside. But he didn't return to his seat.

Skip moved to the mic, clearing his throat. "Thank you, Pastor Todd, for allowing me this moment to address members of Calvary. This church has always been family to me, and family pulls together in time of need." He looked out among them, clearly weighing his words. "I know you all heard lots of talk this weekend. People have been slandering my good name. And yes, to clear up any confusion, I was indeed arrested—for a misdemeanor, without cause . . ."

Stephanie folded her arms with a disgusted sigh.

"I'm not at all concerned about the legalities. I have no doubt my name will be cleared. What I *am* concerned about is the sense my family and I are getting that you may be putting stock in these claims." His gaze was steely as he moved it from one side of the church to the other. "Don't think we haven't heard the whispers. But don't forget that by law, everyone is innocent until proven guilty."

Stephanie looked to see what response he was getting. So far . . . silence.

"Which brings me to my next point." Skip gripped the sides of the podium. "There's more slander afoot, about my grandson. I'm not talking about the dumb prank he pulled online. I'm talking about slander that led to his arrest this morning."

She leaned over to Lindell. "Is he saying my statement to the police was slanderous?"

"I just left the police station," Skip said, "and I came straight here to ask for your support in this. You will hear all manner of accusations regarding some girl." He waved a hand as if it were trivial.

"I don't even know this girl. She's not one of us at Calvary. In any event, I'm determined that my grandson's entire life will not be ruined over this."

Todd moved to the podium, ready to end it.

Skip raised a finger at him to wait. "I have one last thing to say. My father and I helped build this church. Our leadership here spans several decades. I hope and expect to have the support of every one of you as we endure a very difficult time in our family. Thank you."

The church was silent as Skip walked back down the aisle toward the door.

"This girl Mr. Willoughby doesn't know," Todd said, "whom most of us don't know, is the one we were remembering before we were interrupted—Samara Johnston. Let's pray."

The church doors opened and shut as Skip left.

⁂

"Kory, can you pass the mashed potatoes, please?" Stephanie said.

Kory passed the bowl to Janelle, who passed it across the table to Stephanie. Stephanie scooped some onto her plate and handed it to Lindell, who sat at one end of the table.

Lindell looked to the other end. "Marcus, can you pass the gravy when you're done?"

"Sure thing," Marcus said.

With frequent stops, the gravy boat moved from Marcus on down to the other end, to Charley.

Stephanie had already invited her to dinner before the events of the weekend. When Charley begged off, Stephanie told her their friendship transcended whatever happened with her and Marcus— and she planned to keep it that way.

Travis held up a serving bowl. "Anyone else want some of this cabbage?"

"I'll take that," Kory said. "Thanks."

And that was about all the conversation they had. Everyone still seemed somber from the prayer over the food, which had led to a prayer in memory of Sam—that God would cause her life and story to impact the kids at school—which led to a sharing of stories about her. Stephanie was surprised by how many they had in the short time they'd known her. The only thing that got passed around the table during that time was a box of tissues.

"Mommy!" a voice called from the kitchen.

"Excuse me," Janelle said, rising from the table. "I've told Tiff not to yell across rooms, especially during dinner."

Since there were only eight chairs at the dining room table, Tiffany, Daniel, and Dee ate together in the kitchen, which they preferred. Said they liked having their own conversation.

Janelle returned to her place next to Kory, just as the front door opened and closed.

Libby appeared, looking cute in a straight skirt and wrap top. She smiled. "I see my timing's perfect. I'm starving."

The men voiced greetings while the women got up to hug her.

"You snuck up on us," Janelle said.

"But it was a nice surprise sneak," Stephanie said.

Stephanie got Libby a plate while she went to wash her hands. When she returned, she assessed the table. There was one open seat—and it was next to Travis.

Stephanie watched as she took the spot, making friendly conversation with Marcus on her end of the table.

"Thanks," Libby said, as a steady flow of food was passed down to her. "Shades of Grandma Geri. This looks delicious."

"Janelle's trying to step into Grandma's shoes," Stephanie said. "You should see her. Cooking's her new love. Either that or she's trying to make sure Kory doesn't go anywhere."

Kory smiled. "I don't think she's worried about that."

He and Janelle stole a glance at one another.

Stephanie was eyeing them. "Okay. What?"

They looked at each other again, Janelle's eyes questioning. Kory gave her a nod.

"Well," Janelle said, "we had actually planned to get married yesterday."

All eyes were definitely on them now.

"After talking with Libby last time she was here, then talking with Kory, we decided to go with the original 'just us' wedding—with the kids, of course—and we'd already scheduled a time to meet Travis at the church yesterday afternoon." She glanced over at her pastor. "But when everything unfolded . . ."

Libby served herself a helping of roast beef. "Wow. You would've been Mr. and Mrs. right now."

"Secret wedding, huh?" Marcus said.

"I don't know if it was secret so much as you weren't invited," Stephanie said. "Hold up . . . or *me,* for that matter." She narrowed her eyes at Janelle and Kory. "How y'all gonna have a 'just us' wedding in this family? That's not gonna work."

"Works just fine." Libby was spooning potatoes. "I encouraged her to do it. We can celebrate with them afterward."

"*You* can celebrate with them afterward." Stephanie pointed her fork at them. "I'll be watching. And if I see the two of you and three little people sneaking off, I'm following. It'll be a 'just us and Stephanie' wedding."

Janelle laughed. "At this rate, maybe we'll be married by spring."

"What made you show up out of the blue today, Libby?" Marcus said.

"Exactly what Janelle was referring to," Libby said. "Everything that happened this weekend. She filled me in, and I was devastated. I had to come." She looked at Marcus. "How are you feeling? I can't imagine my life being threatened like that."

Marcus glanced at Charley, who was focused on her plate.

"When I think about what happened with Sam," he said, "I can get over a gun in my face. Not that I'm dropping charges. If nothing else, Skip Willoughby needs to learn he can't go around bullying people."

"Oh my goodness, that reminds me." Libby had forked up some food but set it back down. "Aunt Gwynn said back in the day, Skip Willoughby paid a visit to Todd's granddad and made it known that there would be consequences if the relationship between Aunt Gwynn and Jim didn't end."

"What? That's the exact same thing he did with us," Marcus said.

Charley looked sick.

"When did you talk to Aunt Gwynn?" Stephanie said.

"Oh. Yeah. Haven't filled you in yet." Libby looked around Travis to see Stephanie better. "I spent an impromptu weekend in Jersey and really bonded with them. I'll tell you more later, but, wow, I hadn't put her story together with Marcus's until just now."

"I know it might seem like a small thing," Stephanie said, "but I'm still bothered by the flippant way he regarded Sam during the service."

Stephanie had shared it earlier with the others and filled Libby in now.

Her frustration was palpable. "I mean, it was like she was nothing," Stephanie said. "Makes me so sad when I think of how special she was and how no one seemed to treat her that way, even now. When people think of her, it'll be about the girl no one knew or the girl in the video or the girl who committed suicide." She sighed. "I don't want her to be remembered like that."

"Then change the story," Libby said.

"What do you mean?"

Libby sipped her lemonade. "We talk about it in our planning meetings. When people leave our events, we want them telling the story *we* want them to tell. So we supply the right touches that leave an impression." She paused, thinking. "In this case, I could see you maybe writing about who she really was, an article for the school newspaper, a blog, anything. It would not only change the narrative that's out there; it could be healing as well."

As her thoughts churned, Libby spoke faster. "Janelle said Sam went to Bible study with you all. It would be powerful if you brought Jesus into it that way—taking it to another level. You could honor her memory and also point people to Christ."

Libby got some surprised looks for that one too.

Stephanie cocked her head on an elbow. "Okay, so that's what you've been up to all this time you've been away? Getting deep and spiritual?"

"I don't know about deep," Libby said, "but it's probably time to share with you all that there's been a definite change." Libby took a breath. "I've committed my life to Jesus, and I started attending church in Raleigh. Came straight from there to here today."

There seemed to be a delayed reaction. Then everyone jumped up at once to hug her.

Travis was last. He stood and spoke so no one else heard. Libby stared hard at him, then left an almost full plate and walked with him out the back door.

CHAPTER THIRTY-SIX

We've been here before.

That was Libby's first thought as she and Travis lowered themselves into the swing on the back porch. Nearly a year ago, when they'd gotten back in touch after more than a decade, they'd hashed out past grievances in this very spot.

The swing swayed slowly back and forth as they stared in different directions. It was still light out, but cloudy and semi-cool, the intermittent rain having ushered in a slight breeze.

Hunched over, forearms on his thighs, Travis glanced at her. "Why didn't you tell me about the change in your life? Before now, that is."

She stared at the slats on the porch. "It was personal for me. I was on a journey, reading the Bible, studying other resources . . . I didn't want any interference."

He looked away, out into the yard. "Interference . . . that's what I would've been?" He turned back to her. "We talked about this, Libby, at the reunion. Talked about committing your life to Jesus, but at the time you weren't ready. I told you I'd be praying for you, and I have. Then you have this big spiritual awakening"—he gestured with his hands—"and I get to find out weeks later in a group announcement?"

"Is something wrong with that?"

Travis raised himself slightly. "If you want to know the truth, I'm a little hurt by it. I thought we had something more special than that."

"Why?" Libby gave him a bewildered look. "You're the one who said we shouldn't be friends. Why would you think I owed you anything?"

"And why did I say we shouldn't be friends? It was because I had feelings for you I couldn't act on because you weren't walking with the Lord. Then you start walking with the Lord . . ." He looked away, frustrated. "A phone call would've been nice."

"Every time I see you, you look rather happy with Trina," Libby said. "I didn't want to get in the middle of that."

He looked back at her. "Now Trina's the excuse?"

"Trina's the reality."

He got up, sending the swing out of rhythm. Walking to the edge of the porch, he sighed and looked up into the clouds. After a long moment, he said, "I'm sorry."

He turned around. "I made this about me. Instead of focusing on why you didn't tell me, I should've been rejoicing with you." He leaned against the porch rail. "Like I said, I've been praying, and I thank God that He drew you that way. The little you described is awesome. I love that you dug in the way you did. It's like . . . you discovered the treasure."

"That's exactly what it was like," Libby said. "I grew up hearing Bible verses, but suddenly they came alive to me, and they *were* like treasures." Her eyes brightened. "I remember reading in the gospel of John—and I can't remember exactly how it's said—but it was about becoming a child of God, and it said being born, not of blood . . ." She stared off, trying to remember.

"Or of the will of the flesh," Travis said, "or of the will of man . . ."

Libby finished it. "But of God." She said it with awe. "How many times have I heard that? But that time, I was, like, wow . . . that's what being born again is all about. When *God* does it. Then all these other verses about being 'recreated' came at me—like the verses in I John about being born of God." Libby stopped. "I could go on and on. It was so good."

Travis was staring at her. "I'm standing here thinking that all these years I've known you, we've never once had a conversation like this."

Libby reflected on that. "I told Aunt Gwynn that my heart had been broken from the one relationship that was meaningful to me. But as I think about it, it's like you said. We weren't having conversations like this. So I wonder what I thought was so meaningful about it."

"I don't think it's so hard to figure out." He joined her again on the swing. "There was always a spark between us—sometimes nearing explosion—and also a deep affection and caring. It wasn't grounded in the right things, true. But the special connection has always been there."

She didn't know if she wanted to know, but she had to ask. "You think . . . still?"

"I know still."

"But like I said, Trina is your reality now, and—"

"Libby, look around. Do you see Trina?"

He paused for her answer, but she only looked down.

"I actually invited her here today."

Curious, Libby turned back toward him.

"Janelle invited me to dinner after church. Trina was also at church, and they're friends, so Janelle said I could feel free to invite her too. And I did, but she said no."

"Why?"

"She said she saw the dynamic last week when you were leaving and everyone but me went to greet you. She said that wasn't like me, and that I wasn't myself afterward—just like after we saw you at Mama Jay's." He paused. "I was really sorry about that, by the way."

Libby simply let him continue.

"So she asked me pointedly if there was romantic history between us, which opened up a long conversation that ended with her saying I didn't feel the same connection with her that she felt for me." He hesitated, looking at nothing in particular. "She said I still had feelings for you."

"What did you say?"

"I couldn't say anything. I knew she was right. But I thought to myself, *Great. I'll never have a serious relationship if I can't get over these feelings I have for a woman I can't be with.*"

"It makes sense to me now," Libby said. "We were in two different worlds. I was still in darkness. You were in the light." The magnitude of it all struck her. "I understand why you couldn't be with me."

Travis stared at her for long seconds. "But that's not the case anymore."

Libby felt his words deep in her heart, and at the same time, her mind was poised to reject them.

"Travis, I'm not the woman you deserve. You changed right after college, but I've had another ten years of living in ways that . . . well, weren't pleasing to God. You need a woman who's—"

"What, perfect?" he said. "She doesn't exist. And if she did, she wouldn't want me because I'm not perfect. What matters is we've both been changed by the grace of God." His gaze penetrated. "You are *more* than I deserve. Just the thought that God would give me the one person I've been crazy about my entire life."

"Really?"

"Are you kidding? I was crazy about you when we were running around in this very backyard, and you were telling me to stop bugging you."

"Yeah, literally." Libby laughed faintly. "Chasing me with those stupid worms."

He took her hand. "Come here."

"Where are we going?"

He led her down the steps and into the yard.

"But the grass is wet, Travis."

"You'll live."

They walked beyond the main backyard over to a clearing and stopped at the water tower.

"Remember this?" he said.

Her mind traveled back in time. "That night you found me during hide-and-seek, and per the rules—rules you boys had changed up—the one seeking could pick one person they found and kiss them."

"And I picked you. But you would only let me kiss you on your hand. Like this." He was holding her hand still and lifted it, kissing the back.

Goose bumps danced up Libby's arm. "I'm pretty sure it didn't give me that feeling, though."

"You don't think so?" He kissed the inside of her hand.

"No. I'm certain."

He put his arms around her and brought her close, gazing into her eyes. "I'm just wondering if you have that same aversion to a real kiss right now."

She could feel his heart beating against hers. "It's not like we've never had a real kiss."

"But like our conversation, I think this will be more meaningful too."

His lips brushed hers, and as the kiss deepened, she knew it was true. This kiss was more meaningful than any they'd had—because it was much more than a kiss. For the first time, she sensed hope and promise between them. She didn't know where it would lead, nor did she fear where it would lead. Another first . . . she would trust God with the outcome.

CHAPTER THIRTY-SEVEN
Monday, October 4

VIRAL FACEBOOK VID LINKED TO TEEN'S SUICIDE

"Are you serious? Front page of the local section? Let me see that." Stephanie took the newspaper from Marcus and leaned against the kitchen counter, reading.

Janelle walked in looking harried, searching for her car keys, ready to run the kids to school. She did a double take at Marcus. "What're you doing here on a weekday morning?"

"We closed the school today," Marcus said, "although I'm about to go in for a meeting regarding our response in terms of the media, grief counselors, etc. I got the morning paper and wanted to make sure you all had seen it."

Janelle looked over Stephanie's shoulder and gasped. "It's in the paper?"

"I was shocked too," Stephanie said. "Not that it's strange for something like this to make the news. Given the facts, the headline wrote itself. But being such a part of what happened, it *is* strange to see it written up like this." She pointed at a paragraph. "And look, it says Sam's mother found her and called 911."

"They got one thing right, though." Marcus poured a bowl of cereal. "It names Ben Willoughby as the one responsible for making and posting the video, and talks about his arrest."

"Wow, they even tie in that he's the grandson of Skip Willoughby and reference *his* arrest this weekend," Janelle said.

Daniel came in. "Mom, we've been waiting outside. We're gonna be late."

"We're leaving right now. Tiffany and Claire are out there?"

Daniel gave her a look.

"Okay. You did say *we*. Let's go." She looked at Stephanie. "Save that so I can read the rest."

"See, this is what I've been saying." Stephanie laid the paper down. "They covered everything in that article from cyberspace bullying to teen suicide statistics to the Willoughby family. But very little about Sam herself."

"I noticed that." Marcus wiped some milk from his lip. "I'm guessing they rushed out the story before they could amass a profile of her."

The side door opened and banged close, footsteps moving quickly inside. It was Todd. "Hey, Becca said to turn to Channel 29. They said they're about to cover a tragic story in a small town that's left a community devastated, and they showed Sam's picture."

"It made national news?" Marcus said.

The three of them hurried to the family room, and Stephanie turned it on. They were returning from a commercial break. The anchor focused on two political stories and an international story, then—

"We are just getting word of a tragic story that unfolded this weekend in the small town of Hope Springs, North Carolina," the anchor said, "involving an alleged sexual assault of a teen that was apparently *videotaped*"—the anchor, who was female, couldn't hide her disgust—"and, believe it or not, placed on Facebook."

Sam's picture came onscreen as the woman continued with the video going viral and the teen committing suicide as an apparent result.

"We'll have updates on this story as we get them," she said.

"Unbelievable," Stephanie said. "Seeing Sam's picture in the corner of the screen like that . . ."

"I'd better get to school," Marcus said. "Now that the story's national, we'll be getting even more media requests."

As he prepared to leave, Stephanie turned to Todd.

"I didn't get a chance to tell you how much I loved your message yesterday," she said. "Even though it wasn't directly related to what happened, the points you made about our eternal hope and this not being our home were right on time."

"It was a tough message to give," Todd said. "I didn't know Sam—only had small talk with her here a couple of times—but she seemed like a special girl." His countenance changed a little. "And I'm sorry you had to witness that scene by Skip Willoughby. If it bothered me, I'm sure it bothered you."

"Oh, it bothered me all right," Stephanie said. She hesitated. "You don't have to answer if it's confidential, but I'm wondering if the church will take any action where he's concerned. Does he get to maintain his position as elder?"

"The elder board and I are meeting with him tomorrow," Todd said, "and I'll say this—under the qualifications for elder spelled out in the Bible, there are grounds for him to be disqualified."

"Huh. That's really ironic."

"What do you mean?"

"You know Libby was here yesterday. And she was giving me details last night about a conversation she had with Aunt Gwynn about Skip Willoughby."

He looked at her intently. "Tell me about it."

Stephanie did, down to the detail about Willoughby telling

Todd's granddad that the relationship between his son and Aunt Gwynn was evidence that *he* didn't meet the qualifications for pastor, and that he'd be removed if he didn't put an end to that relationship, among other possible consequences.

Todd's jaw was tight. "Who heard Skip Willoughby say that?"

"I gather your dad did, and shared it immediately with Aunt Gwynn. Once Skip issued that ultimatum, your grandparents and mine put pressure on them to separate."

Todd stared at her, but Stephanie knew he didn't see her. "I have to go. I'm calling Keisha so she can put me in touch with her mom. I need to hear this firsthand."

He left out the side door, and Stephanie headed back to the kitchen, heart and mind heavy. She had just finished loading the dishwasher when a knock sounded at the front door.

She went and opened it, surprised to see Sam's mom. "Miss Schechter . . ."

Sam's mom walked in. "I hope it's okay for me to come. I just . . ."

She started shaking, and Stephanie took her into her arms as she broke down. A few inches shorter than Stephanie, she sobbed into her chest, and all Stephanie could say through her own tears was, "I know . . . I know . . ."

"I'm sorry," Sam's mother said. She took a step back, wiping tears, chest heaving still.

"I can't even imagine how you're feeling," Stephanie said. "Let's sit down."

Stephanie led her by hand to the sofa, grabbing the box of tissues from the coffee table and placing it between them.

Sam's mother blew her nose, then wiped more tears. Stephanie waited.

"I guess I want to say thank you for . . . for what you did for my little girl. I was reading this yesterday"—she dug into her purse and pulled out a journal—"and she said . . . she wished you were her mother."

"Oh, Miss Schechter, I'm so sorry. I never meant for her to—"

"No, no." She shook her head. "And call me Teri. No, it's my fault. She wrote everything in there. I had no idea. All about what a terrible mother I am. I mean, she didn't *say* that. She made excuses for me half the time. But when I read the things I said and did, I said to myself, what kind of mother was I?" More tears came. "And there's nothing I can do about it now."

"Teri, please don't do this to yourself. Any mistakes you made are behind you now."

She was shaking her head again. "They're not behind me." She sniffed. "A reporter called yesterday and said something about me finding her and calling the ambulance. He just assumed I had, and I didn't correct him." She was lightly wringing her hands. "I didn't want to admit I was with my boyfriend. When she needed me most, I wasn't there . . . again."

"There was no way you could have known she needed you," Stephanie said.

"You did." She gave Stephanie a quick glance and went back to focusing on her hands. "You were tuned in. And the bad part is I cut her off from you because I was jealous that she liked you better."

"No, Teri, that's not true. She loved you. She wanted to please you. I was simply able to be there for her as a friend."

"Well . . . that's sort of why I'm here," she said. "I wondered if I could ask you a favor."

"Anything," Stephanie said.

"I'm planning a memorial service at the funeral home for Friday. I wondered if you could give the message . . . or whatever they call it . . . say some words about Sam."

Stephanie's eyes widened. "Oh, I'm not a minister or any kind of speaker. I couldn't do that."

"But you knew my Sam, and she loved you." Teri looked at her. "Doesn't have to be fancy. Just words from your heart."

Stephanie suddenly had a different reason for turning it down.

Just thinking about it made her emotional. There was no way she could get through something like that. Still, how could she say no to speaking from the heart about Sam?

She sighed. "Okay. I'll do it."

"And I have a bigger favor."

"Okay . . ."

"You know how sometimes on the news when something happens, a family friend talks to the news people?"

Stephanie had no clue where this was going. "Yes, I'm familiar with that."

"I wondered if you could be the family friend."

It took a moment for her request to register. "You want me to talk to the news people?"

"I can't take all the phone calls, and some of 'em even come to the house. I don't know what to say or how to say it." She looked intently at Stephanie. "You would represent my Sam well."

"Teri, I don't have experience with that. I've never been on the news, wouldn't know how to handle the questions . . . That's way too much."

"I just thought," she said, "you could tell people who she was."

Whether she knew it or not, Teri had aimed straight for Stephanie's heart. She also heard Libby's words from yesterday. *"You can tell her story."*

Stephanie nodded. "When you put it that way," she said, "I'd love to represent Sam. I'm honored that you trust me to do that."

"I want to warn you," Teri said. "There'll be a lot of calls and such."

"I know. Let me get my phone, and we'll exchange contact information."

She got it, and the women took one another's phones and put in their own information.

"I want you to have this." Teri put the journal in her hands. "That'll tell you who Sam was like nothing else."

Stephanie held it gently. "You want me to . . . *have* it, as in keep it? I can't do that."

"Yes, you can." Teri got up to leave. "When you read it, you'll see why you can." She headed for the door.

"Teri, can I ask you a question?"

She turned. "Yeah?"

"What happened that turned you against the churches in town?"

"It's a pretty straight story," she said. "I got pregnant senior year in high school, and my momma sent me to Hope Springs to live with my grandma, who went to Calvary. I got stares for being pregnant, and more stares when they saw Sam had some color to her." She took out cigarettes and held them. "I stopped going. Decided to try New Jerusalem. Got stares like people were wondering if I took a wrong turn or something." She threw up her hands. "I said, I don't need none of y'all."

Stephanie nodded. "I would've said the same thing. But I sure wish you'd give either one a try again. You're more than welcome to come with me to New Jerusalem one Sunday. If you get one stare, I'll punch 'em in the nose."

Teri's eyes smiled. "I see why Sam loved you." She opened the door—"I'll be in touch"—and was gone.

Stephanie stared at the journal in her hands. She'd curl up with it in a quiet place with some hot tea . . . and a box of tissues.

CHAPTER THIRTY-EIGHT
Wednesday, October 6

C harley walked in from a long and heart-wrenching day at school, their first since the tragedy. On her way upstairs to her room, she heard animated voices in the kitchen and stopped. Sounded like her mom and Grandpa Skip were going at it with Ben. No telling what the latest was. She went to see.

"How could you be so stupid?" Grandpa Skip was saying. "You've ruined your life. You know that, don't you? Bad enough you were expelled from school, football future gone. Now this? Your life is over."

Ben sat slumped at the kitchen table, arms crossed, legs fully extended, saying nothing.

"Son, what do you have to say about this?" Dottie said. "Tell us you have a defense. Tell us it's not what it seems."

Ben cut his eyes over at her. "I don't know what you want me to say. It is what it is, Mom."

Charley was standing in the middle of the kitchen. "What's going on?"

Her mom turned to her. "Your brother's attorney just left.

Apparently the video that was confiscated from Ben's room clearly shows him forcing himself upon that girl despite her pleas for him to stop." She looked at Ben. "Of course he edited all of that out when he posted it online. Oh, and the other nice revelation was that he'd recorded himself and Kelsey too." She eyed her son. "Probably the same night he claimed they were only watching a movie."

"You are an absolute idiot," Grandpa Skip said. "You filmed your own crime. You *handed* them evidence against you."

Ben was stoic, refusing to look at him.

Charley joined them at the table. "So what happens now?"

"Lawyer's talking plea agreement," Dottie said. "But Ben will likely still have to serve several years."

"I don't know if we give up like that, though," Grandpa Skip said. "I believe in fighting to the bitter end."

"You've got to be kidding, Skip," Dottie said. "If he takes it to trial, he'll get nailed. It'll be about more than the sexual assault. It'll be about the video and the suicide. They'll throw the book at him." Her head fell in her hands. "I can't believe this is happening. It's an absolute nightmare." She looked at Charley. "We got more hateful phone calls today from area codes all over the country. I don't even know how they're getting our number. I'm afraid for Ben's life."

"That Stephanie London's to blame, if you ask me," Skip said. "How did she get a voice in this thing, anyway? The minute she started carrying on about this girl's life, the media blew it up into a big sympathetic story." He looked up at the television in the kitchen where the news was on but the sound turned down. "Why do you keep this on? It's maddening."

"I want to hear what they're saying," Dottie said. "*I'm* moved by this poor girl's story. We're saying Ben's life is ruined. At least he's still got a life." She turned to Ben. "How could you *do* that to her?"

Skip stared at her. "This is not the time to get emotional, Dottie. We've got to stay focused on the task at hand—"

"Well, what exactly is the task at hand, Skip?" Dottie said. "Protect Ben at all cost? Or no, protect the family. Right? Because everything's justifiable if done in the name of protecting family. Even threatening a young man's life with a gun to his face."

"I told you I only *showed* him the gun."

Charley was ready to get up and leave. She couldn't bear to hear any justification for what he'd done.

"*Showing* the gun was despicable enough," Dottie said. "But I'm sorry, I have a hard time believing your version of the events after talking to Marcus."

"What?" Charley turned to her mother. "When did you talk to Marcus?"

"I met with him at the school today," Dottie said. "And that was *after* I met with Pastor Todd."

Skip looked incensed. "Now wait a minute, Dottie. Just what do you think you're doing?"

Dottie gave an exasperated sigh. "What I'm doing is getting a handle on my family." Her voice broke. "For too long, I looked to you to lead this family in George's stead. I *trusted* you. But my eyes are opened now, Skip. You haven't even led Calvary well." She looked pained. "I talked to Todd about the decision to remove you as elder—"

"Which they won't get away with," Skip said.

"And he gave me an earful about a visit you paid to his grand-dad over thirty years ago. Remember that? About the relationship between Todd's father, Jim, and Gwynn Sanders next door?"

"Of course I remember it. What about it?"

"What about it? You said the relationship had to end. And it worked, Skip. It ended. And do you know what the result was?"

Skip only looked at her.

"The result was that Gwynn left, had her baby up north, and neither she nor her daughter have had any real relationship with the rest of their family."

Skip's expression was dismissive. "Surely Todd doesn't have a problem with the fact that I intervened. If it weren't for me, his dad and Gwynn would've gotten married, and Todd would've never been born."

The look in her mom's eyes was one Charley had never seen. "That's just it, Skip. It's not up to you to determine people's futures. I guess you think it all worked out just fine that Charley and Marcus broke up. So what if you threatened a man's life to make it happen."

Charley had to interject. "What happened with you and Marcus?"

"I asked for his side of the story," Dottie said, "and despite what he'd been through, he was calm and respectful. Said he'd never had a moment of fear like that in his life, gun aimed at his temple, his life at the mercy of another."

"Give me a break. It wasn't that dramatic." Skip looked away. "I never would've pulled the trigger."

Dottie threw up her hands. "So you're admitting you aimed it at him?" She sighed and turned back to Charley. "Sweetheart, I apologized to Marcus, and I'm apologizing to you, for my part. He seems to be a wonderful man. I'm sorry for not embracing him from the start. Maybe the two of you could've weathered all of this if you'd had more support."

Charley had thought the same herself. "I appreciate that, Mom, but I don't know. Maybe I was being naïve to think it could work."

The television screen caught her eye. "Hey, look, there's Stephanie." Charley looked for the remote. "I haven't caught her on TV yet."

Skip groaned. "I'm heading home."

Charley found it and turned it up.

"You had gotten close to her in the last two months of her life," the reporter was saying.

The camera had a close shot of him with Stephanie, but Charley could tell they were in front of Sam's house.

"Yes, that's right." Stephanie faced the reporter. "I was a substitute teacher at the high school, and the very first day we had lunch together. A little while after that, she began spending time at my home."

"When we see her picture with that infectious smile and that gorgeous curly hair, it's hard to believe she was apparently quiet, shy, and practically friendless. What drew you to her?"

"This is so wild," Charley muttered. "Stephanie's on CNN."

Stephanie smiled at the memory. "At first my heart went out to her because she was alone," she said. "But as I got to know her, and she started coming out of her shell, and that infectious smile turned to infectious laughter, I fell in love with that girl. And what I loved about her was she didn't mind being a girl, acting silly, playing dolls with younger girls. She was just . . . so sweet . . ." She fought the emotion. "I'm sorry. You'd think I'd stop getting choked up talking about her."

"Not at all," the reporter said. "Her story moves me, and I never met her." He paused. "I'd love for you to share with us the special way you're remembering her."

"And I'd love to do so," Stephanie said. "Sam's mom was kind in allowing me to learn even more of Sam's heart through her journal." She held it up. "In it Sam wrote that she wished the two churches in town had continued their joint services, because she felt a sense of belonging there. If you don't mind, I'd like to read a short quote."

"Absolutely," the reporter said.

"'I don't know a lot about how these things work, but it doesn't seem like it should be a hard thing for Christians to come together. Why couldn't there be unity?'" Stephanie closed the journal, and her hand went to a red ribbon on her chest. "So in honor of Sam, we're wearing these unity ribbons. It would be easy for a town to be forever fractured after a tragedy like this, to carry hatred toward certain individuals, to cling to division. Instead, we're praying for people to honor God by coming together." She smiled. "And we chose red because it was Sam's favorite color."

The reporter nodded at Stephanie, then looked directly at the camera. "And Sam is being remembered another way. When people heard she still slept with a teddy bear at night, they began leaving teddy bears on the front stoop, which has spilled over into the yard." The camera shifted to a wide angle, revealing an abundance of bears and flowers. The reporter picked one up. "A note on this bear reads, 'Sam, I wish I had sat with you at lunch.'" The reporter looked visibly moved as he sent it back to the studio.

Charley wiped a tear.

"Excuse me." Dottie rose from the table, looking shaken, and left.

Charley heard sniffing and looked across the table. Ben's head was down, his shoulders heaving. She went and sat beside him.

"Ben? You wanna talk?"

"I did that to her," he said. "I did that to her!"

He slung a pile of papers across the table and onto the floor and got up, fists balled, looking like he wanted to beat the air. Instead, he opened a drawer just to slam it shut. Then he picked up a glass and cocked it back—

"Ben, stop!" She ran over to him. "Put that down. It's okay, Ben. Put it down."

He lowered the glass and himself to the floor. "I did that to her . . ." His whole being sobbed. "I was drunk, Charley. I'm not making excuses. But I was drunk and thinking how I could get Kelsey back." He didn't bother to stop the tears. "I didn't mean to hurt Sam. But that's the bad part. I don't think I even *thought* about it. I used her. I *hurt* her." He turned tortured eyes toward Charley. "I thought I was hiding her identity when I edited the video. I didn't mean for it to . . ." He threw his head back with a groan. "Mom was right. My life might be ruined, but at least I've got a life. I don't care what happens to me, Charley. I don't care."

She held him, rocking her football-playing brother back and forth like a baby. So many words sat poised on her tongue, ready to shoot at him, ready to agree that every foul thing he thought about himself was true. But she stifled those words.

She would simply hold him and cry with him.

CHAPTER THIRTY-NINE

Friday, October 8

S tephanie held the phone in the crook of her neck and
clutched her robe tighter as she walked through the house,
spying new faces. *Who are these people?*

"That's right," she said into the phone. "All floral deliveries are
being redirected to Children's Hospital in Rocky Mount. Thanks."
She almost hung up but brought the phone back quickly. "You know
we're keeping the red ones, though, right?"

"Yes, ma'am," the local florist said.

"Okay, great."

She walked into the dining room. "How's it coming, girls?"

Tiffany, Claire, and Dee were on their knees in chairs, hunched
over the table as they labored over a white poster board.

"Look!" Claire said, pointing. "We put a blowed-up picture in
the middle."

Becca smiled, helping the girls angle and affix the pictures.
"Blown-up, sweetheart."

"Aww, I love that," Stephanie said, "How'd you get it that big?"

"Kory went to a photo shop this morning and got various enlarge-
ments," Becca said.

Teri had given what pictures she had, which weren't many, so blowing them up made a huge difference.

"Ooh, I love this one too." Stephanie pointed to a picture of Sam and the girls the night of the girls' sleepover. "I remember taking that."

The girls had cried when they were told Sam died. They hadn't been told how. Although the school district had closed all Hope Spring schools for the day in honor of the memorial service, the girls wouldn't be going. Their parents didn't want to take the chance of their hearing what happened.

"I'm so proud of you girls," Stephanie said. "This looks beautiful."

Stephanie's phone rang in her hand. "Sara Ann, sorry, forgot to call you back."

"No prob, I know you're busy," Sara Ann said. "Just wanted to double-check. Did your voice mail say the punch *has* to be red? Because they're telling me it's gonna be more like pink."

"Well, no, it doesn't have to. We just want the color red to pop up in as many places as it can today, so I thought red punch would be cool. But no worries."

Sara Ann spoke to someone in the room. "We can make something work," she told Stephanie. "Now that I know why, I'll make sure it happens."

"Thanks, Sara Ann. And thanks again for asking Lila to keep the diner open and serve everyone like this. It's amazing."

"Sam is our Soul Sister," Sara Ann said. "This is nothing."

Lindell came up behind her as she hung up. "Steph, you need to start getting dressed. Service starts in two hours."

"I know." A text message dinged, and she glanced at her phone. "I'm trying to make sure everything comes off beautifully." She sighed. "Why did Teri ask me to do this? The speaking part was already over the top, but then to plan the service too? It's not like I know what I'm doing."

"Teri was having a hard time handling arrangements when it was being held at the funeral home. Once it got moved to the school, it was way too big for her to handle."

"For me too!"

"Not true," Becca chimed in. "God's grace has been all over you this week, with the interviews and with the planning of this service."

Stephanie pictured that big gym and herself standing at the front of it. "I pray His grace is all over me this afternoon when I speak. I don't want to break down, but I don't want to be unemotional either. I don't want to read it, but I don't want to be cavalier, like, 'I got this.' You know?"

"Babe." Lindell looked at her. "God's got this. Go get ready."

She lowered her voice. "By the way, who are those people in the living room?"

"Remember Teri said a reporter from a national paper asked to interview you two? He's here with a camera guy."

"I thought they were meeting us at the gym."

"They want to talk to you beforehand," Lindell said. "That's why you need to get moving."

A flurry of voices got louder and came nearer.

"Who is that?" Stephanie said.

She walked toward the sound. Janelle was heading toward her, and behind her—Cyd, Janelle's parents, and Libby's dad, Wood.

Stephanie looked shell-shocked. "What is this? What's going on?"

"I went to get them from the airport," Janelle said. "They wanted to be part of this."

"But you didn't even know Sam," Stephanie said.

Cyd hugged her. "Sweetie, most of the people who will be here today didn't know Sam. But you've made us want to celebrate her life."

Aunt Estelle hugged her next. "And you've made us want to celebrate what God is doing in this town in bringing people together. I've been riveted by the news and how big this story has gotten, including the story of this town. *My* town." She looked around. "I hope you've got some extra red unity ribbons around here."

Stephanie wiped tears. "Y'all could've at least told me you were coming. This day is emotional enough."

"I need all the women to move that way." Lindell made his hands a megaphone. "Continue all conversation while getting dressed. We have a schedule to keep. Thank you."

Stephanie glanced around. "Where's my Chase?"

Cyd smiled. "Home with Dad. I decided to get a ticket last-minute."

"Oh, so y'all didn't hear me?" Lindell got behind them and prodded them both in the back toward their proper destination.

Stephanie looked around the bedroom at her family who'd gathered there—Cyd, Janelle, Aunt Estelle, and Aunt Gladys, who'd arrived minutes before. All of them wore white with a touch of red somewhere.

They were each hurrying, stepping into heels—red heels for Cyd—or dabbing on lip gloss, when a soft knock sounded on the door.

"Come in," several of them said.

It opened, and Teri peeked in. "Are you sure? Is it okay?"

"Teri, absolutely." Stephanie brought her before the group. "Everyone, this is Sam's mom, Teri."

Stephanie introduced the members of her family, and each of them gave her a long hug.

"How are you holding up?" Aunt Estelle asked.

Teri nodded at Aunt Estelle, and kept nodding until the tears flowed. "I don't know if I can do this."

Aunt Estelle grabbed her hand, Stephanie grabbed the other, and the rest gathered around.

"Lord, we pray Your strength upon Teri," Aunt Estelle said. "We can't imagine the weight of what she's been carrying this week, the horror of losing a child, the unanswered questions and never-ending what-ifs. But, Lord, You said Your yoke is easy, and Your burden is light." She rubbed Teri's back. "I'm praying for Teri to give You her burden and, in exchange, walk in the grace that You so freely provide. Let this be a time of drawing near to You. I pray You wrap Your arms around her and cause her to feel the lavishness of Your love. Carry her through this day and the weeks to come with Your strong hand. In the mighty name of Jesus, we pray."

"Amen," rang out in the room.

"Thank you." Teri stayed in the circle, squeezing their hands. "Thank you. I know I needed that."

Lindell knocked and poked his head in. "The reporter's going to ride with you and Teri to the service and talk to you on the way. Caravan's leaving in fifteen."

"Okay," Stephanie said. "Thanks, babe."

Teri wiped her face with her hands. "Guess I need to get myself together." She looked at them all. "I have on this white skirt and blouse, but I don't have any red."

"Yes, you do," Janelle said. "That red ribbon on your shirt speaks loud and clear." She smiled. "But if you want extra, we've got everything here from red hair ribbons to red belts." Janelle took her aside to help her.

A knock sounded again.

"You said we had fifteen," Stephanie called.

The door opened, and Libby walked in. Behind her—Aunt Gwynn and Keisha.

The room was silent. The last time Stephanie and the others had seen Aunt Gwynn, she had entered the house with attitude, gave a rant, and left. Her older sisters, Estelle and Gladys, walked toward her.

"You're really here?" Aunt Gladys said.

Aunt Gwynn nodded, her eyes smiling. "I'm really here."

The three sisters hugged in their own little circle. Aunt Estelle, who'd been strong moments before as she prayed, was in tears.

"I can't believe this," Aunt Estelle said. "I can't believe you're here." She turned around. "And Keisha."

Time seemed to stand still as everyone hugged everyone, Teri included.

"How in the world did this come about?" Aunt Gladys asked. She looked up, shaking her head. "Will wonders never cease?"

Surprisingly, Aunt Gwynn went to Teri first. She took both of her hands.

"When I heard about your Sam, I was reminded so much of my Keisha's upbringing—struggling to belong, to figure out who she is, to find her place in this world." Aunt Gwynn's eyes were warm. "And her heart's cry in that journal has been my own heart's cry for Hope Springs. In fact, I did cry when I heard Stephanie read her quote on the news, asking why there couldn't be unity in the churches."

Aunt Gwynn glanced over at her sisters and back to Teri. "I've been back to Hope Springs one time in almost four decades, and I came in bitterness. I'm back today because of Sam and the hope she's inspired that there could actually be unity."

Teri stared at her, taking it in. "That's incredible. Thank you."

"Thank *you*," Aunt Gwynn said, "for raising such a special young lady."

Minutes later they filed out of the room, Stephanie feeling a mix of emotions. *Lord, I hate that we're going to this memorial service. I hate that we'll be talking about Sam in the past tense. I hate everything about last weekend, and I will never understand it.*

She took a breath. *But I need my focus to be on You. Please . . . have Your way today.*

CHAPTER FORTY

L ibby and more than a dozen relatives arrived early at the high school, the landscape filled already with hundreds of people. The line began at one of the entrances and snaked down the sidewalk and around the parking lot. News reports had mentioned that family and friends would be wearing white with a red accent. Many in the crowd had done the same. The image was striking, especially against the backdrop of a sunny, cloudless sky.

A limousine service from a neighboring town had offered the use of as many as five cars. Since Teri's family was small, she insisted that the Sanders family make use of them. The drivers dropped them off at the front, and an officer escorted them all inside. Stephanie and Teri went a different direction from the rest, who headed to the gym.

The scene inside was captivating. There were rows and rows of chairs with a big red bow tied around the back of each, and up front, a dazzling array of flowers—all of them red.

"Who tied all those bows?" Libby said. She mentally calculated the time it must have taken in her event-planning brain.

"I'm not sure," Janelle said. "But a lot of people were volunteering to help however they could."

"Students did it." Charley gazed at the sight. "The varsity and JV volleyball teams spearheaded it."

Two guys serving as ushers came to man their posts as time neared for the doors to open. They handed Libby and the others a program. Sam's picture was on the cover—the one that had been shown on the news—with her full name and dates that reflected a life cut much too short. Libby opened it and skimmed the order of service, noting Todd's and Travis's names on the program.

Family members moved to take their seats behind the first two reserved rows as people started flowing in. Libby spotted Travis, though, and backed out of her row to speak to him.

"Save my seat," she told Janelle.

Travis was talking to a guy Libby recognized as the owner of a funeral home in Hope Springs. As Libby understood it, a private graveside ceremony would take place later this evening. She waited for them to finish and approached him.

"Hey." She hugged him, then looked into his eyes. "How are you doing?"

He took a moment to answer. "I don't know. This is incredibly sad. So incredibly sad," he said again. "It hit me hard when I walked in." His eyes brimmed. "I just wish I could wind back time and rush into that house and save her. You know?"

"I know."

She hugged him again, and he held on extra seconds. She felt him wipe a tear.

He sighed. "How did the reunion go with Aunt Gwynn and Keisha and everybody?"

Libby had told him of their plan to fly in. "Really good. But we'll talk about that later. I know you need to focus." She squeezed his hand. "I'm praying for you."

"I needed this." His gaze penetrated. "Thank you."

Walking back, Libby saw Janelle talking to a group of women, probably from her Soul Sisters Bible study. Trina was among them, and Libby caught her looking straight at her.

She spoke when she got near enough. "Hi, Trina, how are you?"

"I'm doing well." The smile wasn't bright like prior times. "How about yourself?"

Libby nodded thoughtfully. "On a day like today, it would be hard to complain about anything."

Trina nodded in agreement. "Amen."

Libby took her seat and couldn't help glancing behind at the people pouring in, many of them teens. Marcus had positioned himself near the entrance, talking to many of them. Charley was in a different area, hugging the girls who were in tears.

Janelle returned to her seat beside Libby, and Libby turned to her.

"I just realized," Libby said. "Aunt Gwynn and Keisha are here."

Janelle quirked a brow. "A little too much sun for you out there?"

"And your parents are in town too," Libby said, "plus my dad. How often does that happen?"

"Let's see," Janelle said. "It's happened once in my lifetime."

Libby gave a single confirming nod. "There you have it."

"There I have what?"

"You and Kory should get married tomorrow."

Janelle showed surprise at the thought. "But nothing's planned."

"Nothing was planned last week either," Libby said, "except to just do it." She looked at Sam's face on her program. "I don't know about you, but I'm really struck by the need to make the most of every day God gives us."

CHAPTER FORTY-ONE

Stephanie and Teri held hands with Todd and Travis as the pastors took turns praying for friends and loved ones, especially Teri, for the service, for those in attendance, and beyond.

Teri looked them both in the eye when they were done. "When I had to make arrangements," she said, "I thought I had nowhere to go but the funeral home. I felt like I might want to call on a pastor, but I didn't know you. And I figured I had no right, seeing as we didn't go to church. The two of you doing this just . . ." Her head dropped. "Thank you."

"I think God went ahead and made these arrangements," Todd said. "He knew what He had in mind. We're humbled to be able to take part."

"And we're glad to have met you, Teri," Travis said. "We hope the connection continues long beyond today."

Miss Collins, an office secretary at the high school, walked into the classroom. "They said to tell you all it's time."

Teri reached a shaky hand toward Stephanie, and together they walked down the hall, past a line of people still filing into the gym. They both paused at the sight of the crowd and decorations inside, which they hadn't seen, but someone guided them to the front row.

Todd went straight to the podium up front and looked out over the crowd. "People are still being seated in the back, but we're going to go ahead and get started," he said. He waited a few seconds. "One hardly knows how to begin a service like this. You have come from near and far to remember the life of a precious girl, Samara Renee Johnston. Many of you come with questions. That's appropriate. Many are angry and casting blame. That's understandable. Some are even angry at God. It's okay to acknowledge that." He paused. "When tragedy hits, we struggle with how to respond. And honestly, that struggle won't end today. We're not here to give you all the answers. We don't know all the answers. We're here to remember Sam's life and to reflect on her death insofar as it sounds a warning as to how we ought to treat our fellow man. And we're here to point you to One who has all wisdom and knowledge, whose understanding is limitless, and who is able to give peace and strength, even in times like this."

Todd gestured to the robed choir members who'd assembled on his right. "In honor of Sam, we have reassembled the joint choir for New Jerusalem and Calvary Church, which we're calling the Unity Choir. They will sing two selections for us."

Stephanie listened with her eyes closed, needing her soul saturated.

After the second song, four of Sam's classmates came forward. When they contacted Stephanie, she remembered them as the ones who'd been sitting with Sam at lunch one day. Stephanie had let Teri decide if they should be on the program, and she was quick to say yes.

Three of the teens read Scripture verses. The fourth had written an original poem encouraging people to be the one to look for the outsider or the loner in a crowd and to befriend them. After another choir selection, Travis came forward.

"When I first heard about the events that led to Sam's tragic end, I was very angry," he said.

Stephanie saw heads focus forward as people seemed to be surprised at how Travis began.

"Yes, I'm a pastor," he said, "but I'm human. And I was angry. How could someone treat this girl this way?" He spoke slowly, deliberately. "How could others pile on, publicly humiliating and demeaning her? How could people be so sick?"

The gym was silent, the only sound a baby crying in the distance.

"But then I remembered my own sin sickness," he said. "I remembered things I did in my past, before I knew Jesus, that hurt and demeaned people. And I remembered things I did *after* knowing Christ that I regretted."

Stephanie could tell Travis was feeling this in a deep place.

He sighed. "A weekend like the one we just had puts our sin natures on blast. Like a siren, it lets us know something is wrong deep in our souls. It lets us know we are in desperate need of a Savior. And I'm going to tell you about that Savior . . ."

As Travis shared the gospel, Stephanie prayed silently that Teri and others would hear and believe. And then she started feeling jittery—one more song, and it was her turn . . .

She walked up with her notes and set them on the podium. Eyes scanning the breadth of the gym—and the news cameras   her nerves got the best of her. *Lord, please help me.* She looked down at her opening sentence, and it sounded stupid.

Looking out at the crowd again, she took a big breath and turned her notes facedown. She took the wireless microphone from its stand.

"I could say a lot of glowing things about Sam," she said, "things like, she was so sweet and nice, so quiet and shy, so diligent and hardworking . . . But if you're here, you probably already know that. So I think I'll share who she *really* was. Because I found out one night."

Stephanie walked away from the podium. "One evening when her guard was down, and she might've had a sugar high from too much sweet tea, Sam said, 'You'll never guess what I really, really want to be.' I said, 'If I'll never guess, then just tell me what you really, really want to be.' She grinned and said, 'I'm too embarrassed to say.' I said, 'Sam. Say.'"

Stephanie smiled, mostly to herself, remembering the moment. "Miss Quiet-and-Shy Samara Johnston said, 'I really, really want to be the next American Idol.' I said, 'Sam! I didn't know you could sing!' She said, 'Because I *don't* sing. At least for people.'"

The audience chuckled slightly, as did Stephanie. "I didn't want to alarm her," Stephanie half whispered, "but I knew at this point we had a problem." She smiled, continuing in her regular voice. "I said gently, 'Sam, if you want to be the next American Idol, you have to sing . . . for actual people. So here's what we'll do. We'll practice on actual little people.'

"So I assembled a three-judge panel of five-year-olds"—she stopped as she walked across the floor—"I bet y'all think I'm joking. Totally true story. I told Sam she could sing any song she wanted." She paused again. "Now, at this point, honestly, I'm thinking it's cute she's got this pipe dream, but I've watched enough singing competition auditions, complaining, 'Come on, *nobody* in this child's life told her she couldn't sing?' So I was already formulating ways I could nicely respond . . ."

Stephanie put a hand to her hip, shaking her head. "Y'all. She bust out with her song, and she. Could. Sing. She could actually . . . *sing*."

Emotion snuck up on Stephanie, and she paused a moment.

"I think there was much more where that came from." She swiped tears. "I think Sam had many hidden talents and dreams that would've come out with a little coaxing and an overdose of sweet tea." She laughed softly as more tears came. "It's such a gift that many of those things were revealed in the pages of her journal. But nothing in that journal impacted me like what she wrote her last night on this earth.

"It was disturbing, rambling, and poignant all at once. The first words were, 'I hate this world. I hate my life. I hate the pain.'" Those words gripped Stephanie even now. It took her a moment to continue.

"And she said . . . she said she'd read where Jesus said, 'My kingdom is not of this world,' and she wanted to be part of *His* world, His kingdom. And it seemed like she was getting on her knees as she wrote, telling Jesus to please save her, to please let her be part of His kingdom." She swiped some more, but stopping the tears was fruitless. "The last thing she wrote was this . . ."

Stephanie went back to find it in her notes. "'Jesus, I want to live with You forever, and I want to go now. But I'll try to hang on . . .'" She looked down at the podium for several seconds, then looked up. "Hours later she logged on to Facebook. And then she just couldn't hang on . . ."

I don't know if I can finish, Lord. This is so hard. She wasn't even sure *how* to finish. She'd strayed from her message and wasn't sure where to go from here.

Her eyes landed on a section of seating, and she headed that way. "This is where I first met Sam"—she stood by the row—"at a combined service of Calvary and New Jerusalem. It was Sam's first joint service. In fact, it was her first *church* service other than when her mom took her as a baby. And she was looking forward to coming back. But the joint services ended because of a lack of unity."

Stephanie walked slowly back up front, talking as she went. "The one time Sam went to church would be her last. She didn't know if she belonged at the 'black church' or the 'white church.' She wasn't sure she belonged at either."

Back at the podium, she surveyed the crowd. "I don't know if that bothers anyone else, but it sure bothers me. When we aren't what Jesus calls us to be, it affects other people. If we can't love enough, can't be 'one' enough to worship with one another, it affects other people."

Stephanie knew she needed to wrap it up, but her adrenaline was going.

"You know what else bothers me?" she said. "And I know I'm about to get in trouble, but I don't care. In honor of Sam, I'm saying it—the fact that we even have a black church and a white church in this town bothers me."

She was surprised to see a few people stand in agreement.

"They were founded like that in the 1800s," she continued. "Have we not progressed beyond that?" She started walking again. "Where does the Latino family go who comes to town? Where does the Asian brother or sister go?" She paused. "Where does the biracial girl go? Call me crazy, but I believe we can change."

More people stood, including teens, with a smattering of "Amens."

Stephanie looked out at them. "I believe we can come together, not just today in honor of Sam—which is beautiful—but every day going forward, in honor of God. I'm crazy enough to believe that with God, all things are possible."

Everyone stood now with loud applause. Stephanie returned the mic and gathered her notes from the podium to sit down—and her heart started racing.

Then she grabbed the mic again. "I think I want to *do* something crazy . . ."

CHAPTER FORTY-TWO

Stephanie couldn't believe she was leading a crowd of people down Maple Street. Head high, arm linked with Teri's, every step felt steeped in purpose and conviction. She had no doubt this was inspired—she never walked, and certainly not in heels. Yet the idea had come to her clearly to announce a unity prayer walk that would proceed along Maple and end midway between the two churches, a total distance of about seven blocks. Stephanie had told them, "I don't care if only ten of us go. If you care deeply about praying toward unity, let's gather after the service and do it."

The instructions had been simple. They would pray silently as they walked, and they'd pray in a circle once they reached the destination. But Stephanie was starting to wonder how large this circle would be. Every time she looked behind her, the crowd was growing bigger.

A cameraman ran past them and turned, walking backward as he filmed the procession of mourners who had reason to hope. Next officers on motorcycles zoomed by, redirecting traffic as the group spread more and more into the street.

Teri turned wide eyes to Stephanie. "This is amazing. I had no idea you planned all this."

"I didn't," Stephanie said. "This is all God."

Stephanie was so taken with everything happening around them she'd almost forgotten the charge. She set her mind to praying and imagined what it would look like if she could see all the prayers rising from Maple Street to heaven.

When she got midway between the churches, she picked a spot and stopped, which happened to be in front of somebody's home. A woman walked out, clearly stunned by the mass of people moving up the street.

"What's going on?" she said.

Stephanie met her in her walkway, unsure of the reaction she'd get. The woman had to have been aware of the memorial service . . . but what did it mean that she hadn't gone?

"I'm sorry," Stephanie said. "We're coming from the service for Samara Johnston. It's a prayer walk for unity between the churches." She hesitated. "Are you a member of Calvary?"

"All my life," the woman said. She appeared to be in her fifties. "I couldn't go to the service for that poor girl because I had to take Momma to the doctor." She looked down the street. "You say it's a prayer walk for unity?"

"Actually, we're stopping right here between the churches to pray now." Stephanie saw more and more people coming, forming a circle. "I hope it doesn't bother you too much. We shouldn't be long."

"Won't bother me at all," she said. "I'm joining you." She walked across her front yard. "Hey! Y'all can make the circle larger by standing in my yard. Come on up here!" She turned to Stephanie. "I'll tell the neighbors to do the same."

Stephanie smiled. "Thank you so much."

Walking back, Stephanie saw the circle trying to take shape.

Most of her family was in one section, Teri with them. Stephanie linked hands with Lindell to one side, Teri on the other. Aunt Gwynn linked with her sisters, Estelle and Gladys, Keisha with Janelle and Cyd. Marcus and Charley were near as well, though not near one another.

Stephanie grew more and more worried as the circle widened, and they moved farther and farther back. People were still coming. How would they accommodate everyone?

But one woman stopped short of their circle and formed another. The idea caught on and spawned at least four additional circles, smaller but large in their own right.

Charley suddenly moved from her spot, looking as if she'd seen something. She left the circle, searching, and minutes later returned with her mom. Stephanie watched as they came toward them.

Her mom spoke, eyes on Teri. "Miss Schechter, my name is Dottie Willoughby." She paused. "This is about the hardest thing I've had to do in my life. I didn't attend the memorial service. Honestly, I was too ashamed. But when I got word of what was happening down here, I had to come." Her eyes were moist. "I am so very, very sorry about Sam. I will never understand your pain. I'm just . . . so sorry . . ."

Teri reached for Dottie's hand. "It's not your fault. You're hurting too."

They held one another, clutching tighter as they cried together.

Teri took Dottie into the circle as a chain of whispers passed and people realized what was taking place. Charley was visibly moved, taking her mom's hand—then Stephanie watched as Marcus moved from his spot and walked over to Charley.

Charley looked surprised. Marcus didn't say a word. He simply grabbed her hand and stood beside her.

Todd and Travis entered the big circle, Travis carrying a bullhorn he must've gotten from an officer.

He lifted it to his mouth. "If we can have your attention, please . . ." He turned a different direction. "Attention, everyone, please."

Travis and Todd spoke to one another as they waited for the crowd to quiet down.

"To say we are overwhelmed is an understatement," Travis said. "Pastor Todd and I were just asking one another why we hadn't come up with the idea of a unity prayer walk. We've been praying for unity, and for God to move in a special way with these two churches. But an idea like this never entered our minds." He turned toward Teri. "For God to do this on a day like today . . . We'll never forget it."

He passed the bullhorn to Todd.

"Unity is the prayer," Todd said. "By your presence here, is it safe to say we're all in agreement that we want God to bring unity in the hearts of members of Calvary Church and New Jerusalem Church?"

An amazingly loud cheer went up.

Todd nodded. "Amen. Okay. But here's a harder question. For the members of these churches, are you all willing to put *your* will aside and accept God's will for us, whatever it might be?"

Stephanie watched Dottie say "Yes" with the rest of the crowd.

"And are you willing to keep praying until we sense what God's will is?" Todd asked.

"Yes" and "Absolutely" rang out.

He handed the bullhorn back to Travis, who said, "Todd and I are about to pray. But first I want everyone to take in this sight, all of us wearing red ribbons of unity in honor of Samara Johnston." He looked around at the crowd. "Let's not lose sight of the fact that red also symbolizes the blood that Jesus shed so we *could* dwell in unity, so we could be healed from deep within."

Travis gazed out among them. "Let us not forget that red is the color of hope."

CHAPTER FORTY-THREE

Charley watched the circles slowly breaking up and the people lingering as if they wanted—no, needed—to remain in this moment. And it didn't escape her that Marcus had not yet let go of her hand.

He guided her to the outskirts of the crowd and paused several seconds, staring into her eyes.

"I got it wrong," he said. "I made last weekend a cautionary tale, a warning to avoid the complications of crossing color lines. But hearing Sam's heart in her journal all this week . . . that wasn't the lesson at all." He spoke deliberately, with the weight of all that had happened. "She would tell us to avoid the status quo. She'd tell us to be led by love, to be who God called us to be. I lost sight of that, of *Him*, like you said."

"I'm not sure what you're saying," Charley said.

"I'm saying I want to continue building our relationship."

Charley sighed. "Marcus, so much has filled my heart in just these last two hours that I haven't begun to process." She looked into his eyes. "I'm sure it's the same for you. There's no way you can know what you're really thinking or feeling right now."

"That's not true." His fingers entwined in hers, he brought her a little closer. "I know exactly what I'm thinking and feeling. I love you, and I can't let complications get in the way of the most meaningful relationship I've ever had. I don't want to start or end my day without connecting with you. I don't want to see you at school or church and pretend— Charley, what's wrong?"

"I don't know." Tears had begun streaming down Charley's face. "I guess . . . it's been so much. Losing Sam, about to lose my brother, feeling like I lost my grandpa—the one I thought I knew, anyway— and losing you." She stared up at him. "I never thought I'd hear you say you love me."

He ran a finger down her face, tracing a tear. "I do. I love you. More than I thought possible."

He took her into his arms and held her, both of them cherishing the closeness for several seconds.

"I love you too."

Marcus pulled back so he could see her. "But how could you really know what you're thinking or feeling right now?"

"What a ludicrous statement. Where did you get that?"

"Charley! Marcus! You don't want to miss this!"

They turned and saw Stephanie waving them over. Standing in a cluster around her were Tiffany, Claire, and Dee, each holding the string of a red helium balloon, and Jackie, Marcus's teenage cousin who had been watching the little girls at the house.

Charley and Marcus went to join them.

"Where'd you girls come from?" Charley said.

Claire was taking in the sight around her. "We saw everybody on TV and wanted to come," she said.

"And Jackie bought us red balloons at the party store!" Tiffany said.

"Balloons?" Marcus said.

Becca chimed in. "They wanted to have their own little memorial service." She smiled at the girls. "The plan was to go outside, say a few words, and send the balloons up in Sam's honor."

"Aww." Charley felt teary again.

"But when they caught all this on the local news"—Jackie gestured around her—"they wanted to come down and do it here, with the family." She blew out a sigh. "It was something getting over here. Had to park way down Main and walk the rest of the way."

"You girls ready?" Janelle asked. "Maybe you should stand in the middle of all of us."

They looked at one another, a little uncertain, then shuffled a few feet toward the middle of the mini-circle of family members.

"What should we do now?" Dee asked the other two.

Claire shrugged. "I don't know." She turned to Todd. "Dad, what should we do?" she called. "You're the pastor."

Amid light laughter, Todd came forward. "I think you girls should say whatever you want. This is your time to remember Sam." He stepped back.

The girls whispered among themselves. Then Claire started. "Sam . . ." Her voice quavered. "We miss you so much. And . . . we love you . . . so much."

Claire looked to Dee, who waited, looking downward. Then with sad eyes, she said, "You were our bestest fourth friend. And you never got tired of pushing us on the swing."

She elbowed Tiffany, who was swiping a tear from the side of her eye. "I can't believe . . . I'll never see you again." Tiffany pressed a fist against more tears. "You were like . . . my big sister."

Charley looked at Janelle, who had tears streaming as she listened to her daughter.

"But Mommy said I'll see you again one day," Tiffany said. She looked at Janelle. "Right, Mommy?"

Janelle nodded. "That's right, baby."

"Jackie has to take the ribbons off first," Claire said, "so they don't tangle any birds or anything."

The girls held their balloons carefully while Jackie untied the ribbon from each one, then they lifted the balloons high above their heads.

"One, two, three!" they shouted together. "For Sam!"

They released the red balloons, and the group watched them sail upward, a small yet glorious sight moving slowly, farther and farther away from them . . . to the sky.

Marcus put an arm around Charley. "I will never forget this day, and especially what we just saw right here."

"Me too." Charley was still gazing upward. "And every time I see red it'll come to me—the color of hope."

READING GROUP GUIDE

1. After a lot of prayer, Stephanie and Lindell decided to make a radical life change and move to Hope Springs. But on the eve of the move, Stephanie thought she must be crazy. Have you ever felt strongly that God wanted you to make a radical change, only to be visited by fear and doubt? How did you move beyond that fear and doubt?

2. Members of both New Jerusalem and Calvary resisted the joint services, and for some, it was a matter of race. How do you feel about worshiping with people of a different race or ethnicity?

3. Marcus admitted to Stephanie that he might feel a little something for Charley, but his preference was for a black woman. If you're single, do you picture your ideal mate with a certain color skin? Would you be willing to submit it to God?

4. In the "Love Reigns" lesson, Travis said sometimes you have to decide to love, despite how the person feels about you or what people may say. Has there been a time in your life when you *decided* to love someone? Explain.

5. Keisha challenged Libby to draw near to God and see for herself what His Word is about. And Libby took up the challenge. Have you ever done a deep study of the Bible to learn truth for yourself?

6. Marcus told Charley that life had caved in on them as he ended their relationship. Charley felt he was walking by sight, not by faith. In the midst of trials, how do you keep yourself from walking by sight? In other words, how do you keep your focus on God?

7. Because of her past, Libby said she wasn't the woman Travis deserved. If you've dedicated your life to Jesus, do you have a hard time seeing yourself as He sees you, as a new creation?

8. At the memorial service, Travis said at first he was angry at those who played a part in the tragic events. But then he thought of his own sin sickness. When the behavior of others causes you anger or disappointment, do you consider your own sin? Do you reflect on the fact that we are all in desperate need of a Savior?

9. In her message, Stephanie said, "When we aren't what Jesus calls us to be, it affects other people." Do you agree? How have you seen this play out in your own life?

10. Travis said, "Let us not forget that red is the color of hope." In the midst of the trials and tribulations of life, do you remember that, because of His shed blood, you have an inexplicable hope in Jesus?

AN EXCERPT FROM *FAITHFUL*

Cydney Sanders jumped at the ringing of the phone, startled out of slumber. She rolled over, peeked at the bedside clock, and groaned. She had twenty whole minutes before the alarm would sound, and she wanted every minute of that twenty. Only her sister would be calling at five forty in the morning. Every morning she called, earlier and earlier, with a new something that couldn't wait regarding that wedding of hers. Not that Stephanie was partial to mornings. She was apt to call several times during the day and into the evening as well. Everything wedding related was urgent.

Cyd nestled back under the covers, rolling her eyes at the fifth ring. Tonight she would remember to turn that thing off. She was tired of Stephanie worrying her from dawn to dusk.

Her heart skipped suddenly and she bolted upright. *The wedding is tomorrow.* The day seemed to take forever to get here, and yet it had come all too quickly. She sighed, dread descending at once with a light throbbing of her head. She might have felt stressed no matter what date her sister had chosen for the wedding. That she chose Cyd's fortieth birthday made it infinitely worse.

She sank back down at the thought of it. *Forty*. She didn't mind the age itself. She'd always thought it would be kind of cool, in fact. At forty, she'd be right in the middle of things, a lot of life behind her, a lot of living yet to do. She'd be at a stride, confident in her path, her purpose. She would have climbed atop decades of prayer and study, ready to walk in some wisdom. Celebrate a little understanding. Stand firmly in faith. Count it all joy.

And she'd look good. She was sure of that. She'd work out during her pregnancies, and while the babies nursed and sucked down her tummy, she would add weights to the cardio routine to shape and tone. As she aged, her metabolism could turn on her if it wanted to; she had something for that too. She would switch up her workout every few weeks, from jogging to mountain bike riding to Tae Bo, all to keep her body guessing, never letting it plateau. Her husband would thank her.

He would also throw her a party. She wasn't much of a party person, but she always knew she'd want a big one on the day she turned forty. It wouldn't have to be a surprise. She'd heard enough stories of husbands unable to keep a party secret anyway. They'd plan it together, and she would kick in the new season in high spirits, surrounded by the people she loved.

Now that she was one day away, she still had no problem with forty. It was the other stuff that had shown up with it—forty, never been married, childless. Now, despite her distinguished career as a classics professor at Washington University in St. Louis, she was questioning her path and her purpose and dreading her new season—and the fact that she was forced to ring it in as maid of honor in her younger sister's wedding . . . her *much younger* sister.

She was still irritated that Stephanie kept the date even after their mother reminded her that October 18 was Cyd's birthday.

"Why does that matter?" Stephanie had said.

The only thing that mattered to Stephanie was Stephanie, and if she wanted something, she was going to make it happen. Like now.

She cared not a whit that she was ringing Cyd's phone off the hook before dawn, waking Cyd and the new puppy, who was yelping frantically in her crate in the kitchen.

Cyd gave up, reached over, and snatched up the phone. Before it came fully to her ear, she heard her sister's voice.

"Cyd, I forgot to tell you last night—*stop*," Stephanie giggled. "You see I'm on the phone."

Cyd switched off her alarm. "Good morning to you too, Steph." She swung her legs out from under the warm bedding and shivered as they hit the air. The days were warm and muggy still, but the nights were increasingly cooler.

From a hook inside the closet, she grabbed her plum terry robe, which at Cyd's five-nine hit her above the knee, and slipped it over her cotton pajama shorts and tank. Her ponytail caught under the robe and she lifted it out, let it flop back down. It was a good ways down her back, thick with ringlets from air drying, a naturally deep reddish brown. Her face had the same richness, a beautiful honey brown, smooth and flawless.

Stephanie was giggling still as she and her fiancé, Lindell, whispered in the background.

I can't believe she woke me up for this. Cyd pushed her feet into her slippers and padded downstairs with a yawn to let out the puppy. "Do you do this when you're talking to Momma?"

Stephanie fumbled with the phone. "Do what?"

"Make it obvious that you and Lindell spent the night together?"

"Cyd, we are grown and will be married to*morrow*. Who gives a flip if we spent the night together?"

"Stephanie . . ." Cyd closed her eyes at the bottom of the stairs as all manner of responses swirled in her mind. Sometimes she wondered if she and Stephanie had really grown up in the same family with the same two parents who loved God and made His ways abundantly clear. Much of it had sailed right over Stephanie's head. Cyd had attempted to nail it down for her over the years, particularly in the area of relationships, but Stephanie never warmed to any notion of chastity, or even monogamy. In fact, when she'd called to announce her engagement six months ago, Cyd thought the husband-to-be was Warren, the man Stephanie had been bringing lately when she stopped by.

But Cyd had vowed moons ago to stop lecturing her sister and pray instead. She took a deep breath and expelled it loudly enough for Stephanie to know she was moving on, but only with effort.

"So, you forgot to tell me something?" She headed to the kitchen, where Reese was barking with attitude, indignant that Cyd was taking too long to get there.

"Girl, listen to this," Stephanie said. "LaShaun called Momma yesterday, upset 'cause we didn't include a guest on her invitation, talking about she wants to bring Jo-Jo. That's why I *didn't* put 'and guest' on her invitation. I'm not paying for that loser to come up in there, eat our food, drink, and act a fool. And why is she calling now anyway? Hello? The deadline for RSVPs was last month. Can you believe her?"

"Stephanie, was there a need to call so early to tell me this?" Cyd clicked on the kitchen light.

"Don't you think it's a trip?"

"Okay, yeah."

"I know! And you know Momma. She said, 'That's your cousin. Just keep the peace and let her bring him.' I'm tempted to call LaShaun right now and tell her both of them can jump in a lake."

Cyd headed to the crate under the desk portion of the kitchen counter. Tired though she was, Reese's drama tickled her inside. She was whimpering and pawing at the gated opening, and when Cyd unlocked it, the energetic twelve-week-old shot out. A mix of cocker spaniel and who knew what else, with dark chocolate wavy hair and tan patches on the neck, underbelly, and paws, she'd reminded Cyd of a peanut butter cup the moment she nabbed her heart at the shelter.

Reese jumped on Cyd, then rolled over for a tummy rub. Three seconds later she dashed toward the back door. At her age she could barely make it through the night without an accident. If Cyd delayed now, she'd be cleaning up a mess. She attached the leash and led her out.

"Well, what do you think?" Stephanie asked.

"About telling LaShaun to jump in the lake?" Cyd turned on the lights in the backyard and stepped outside with Reese, tightening her robe.

Stephanie sucked her teeth. "I mean about the whole thing."

"Well, Momma and Daddy are paying," Cyd said, since it seemed her sister had forgotten, "so if Momma doesn't mind Jo-Jo coming, why worry about it? You'll be so busy you probably won't see much of them anyway. No point getting your cousin *and* Aunt Gladys mad over something like this."

"Whatever," Stephanie said. "I should've known you'd say the same thing as Momma. I still might call LaShaun, just to let her know she should've called me directly, not tried to go through Momma."

"All right, go ahead and ponder that. I've got to get ready for class and—"

"I wasn't finished," Stephanie whined. "Did you talk to Dana?"

"I talked to her last night. Why?"

"So she told you about the shoes?"

"Mm-hmm." Cyd moved to different spots in the yard, tugging on the leash to get Reese to stop digging and do her business. A light popped on in the house next door and she saw Ted, a professor in the chemistry department, moving around in his kitchen. Many of her colleagues from Wash U lived in her Clayton neighborhood— six on her block alone.

"I wasn't trying to be difficult," Stephanie said, "but something told me to stop by her house yesterday to see for myself what kind of shoes she bought. You said they were cute, but those things were dreadful."

"Stephanie, they're flower-girl shoes. All flower-girl shoes are cute. Mackenzie tried them on with the dress when I was over there last week, and she looked adorable."

"The *dress* is adorable—because I picked it out—but those tired Mary Janes with the plain strap across the top have got to go. Is that what they wear at white weddings or something?"

"I don't know. Google it—'official flower-girl shoe at white weddings.'"

"Ha, ha, very funny. I'm just sayin' . . ."

Cyd led Reese back into the house, half listening as Stephanie droned on about some snazzier shoes with rhinestones Dana could've gotten and why she shouldn't have trusted Dana to make the choice in the first place.

She'd get over it. Stephanie did a lot of complaining about a lot of people, but there was no doubt—she loved Dana. Dana had been like family ever since she and Cyd met on the volleyball team in junior high, when Stephanie was just a baby. Stephanie had always looked up to her like a second big sister, and when Dana got married and had Mackenzie and Mark, Stephanie actually volunteered to babysit regularly. Those kids adored "Aunt Stephanie," and when it came time to plan her wedding, Stephanie didn't hesitate to include them . . . even though a couple of great-aunts questioned her appointing white kids as flower girl and ring bearer.

". . . so, long story short, I asked Dana to take 'em back and find some shoes with some pizzazz.'"

"She told me she's not hunting for shoes today. She doesn't have time." Cyd stopped in the office, awakened her computer screen with a shake of the mouse, and started skimming an e-mail from a student.

"She told me that too," Stephanie said. "So I'm hoping you can do it."

"Do what?"

"Find some cute shoes."

"I have to work." And even if she didn't, she wouldn't get roped into this one. She'd gone above and beyond for Stephanie already. This week alone, she'd taken care of several items Stephanie was supposed to handle. If her sister wanted to sweat the flower girl's shoes the day before the wedding, she'd have to do it alone.

"But your class is at eight o'clock. You've got the whole day after that."

Cyd donned a tight-lipped smile to beat back her annoyance. "Stephanie, you know that teaching is only part of what I do. I have a paper due for a conference coming up, and I'm already behind."

She unhooked Reese's leash and watched her run around in circles, delighted with her freedom. But when Cyd headed for the stairs, Reese fell quickly in step. No way would she be left behind.

"How can you even focus on work today?" Stephanie sounded perplexed. "Aren't you just too excited about the big event? Girl, you know this is your wedding too."

Cyd paused on a stair. "How is this my wedding too?"

"Since it looks like you won't be getting married yourself"— Stephanie had a shrug in her voice—"you've at least gotten a chance to plan one through me. You know, living vicariously. Hasn't it been fun?"

Cyd held the phone aloft and stared at it. Did Stephanie really think these last few months had been *fun*? She had involved Cyd in every decision from her dress to her colors to the style, thickness, and font of the invitations to the type of headpiece Mackenzie should wear—all of which *could* have been fun if Stephanie had really wanted her sister's opinions.

What Stephanie wanted was for Cyd to accompany her about

town to every wedding-related appointment, listen with interest as she debated with herself about gowns, floral arrangements, and what to include on the wedding registry, and affirm her ultimate picks. She also wanted Cyd to handle whatever she deemed drudgery. And Cyd didn't mind; as the maid of honor, she thought it her duty to address invitations, order favors, and the like. What bugged her was Stephanie's ingratitude, which wasn't new but had taken on a high-gloss sheen. It was Stephanie's world, and everyone else revolved around it, especially Cyd, since in Stephanie's opinion she didn't have a life anyway.

Now she was telling Cyd—matter-of-factly—that it looked like her sister wouldn't ever be getting married. Cyd wished she could dismiss it as she did Stephanie's other flippant remarks. But how could she, when her own inner voice was shouting the same?

Tears crowded Cyd's eyes, and she was startled, and grateful, when the phone beeped to announce another call. She didn't bother to look at the caller's identity.

"Steph, that's my other line. I've gotta go."

"Who would be calling you this early? Besides me, that is." Stephanie chuckled at herself. "Probably Momma. Tell her I'll call her in a few minutes. By the way, what did you decide to wear to the rehearsal tonight?"

"Steph, really, I've got to go. Talk to you later."

Cyd clicked Off, threw the phone on the bed, and headed to the bathroom. She couldn't bear more wedding talk at the moment, and if it was her mother, that's all she would hear.

She peeled off her clothes, turned on the shower, and stepped under the warm spray of water. Now that she was smack up against it—the wedding, the birthday—everything seemed to rush at her. She wouldn't mind being forty, unmarried, and childless if she'd expected it. But from a young age she'd prayed repeatedly for a husband—and not just a "Christian" but someone on fire for the Lord. And she'd believed deep in her heart that God would answer.

Cyd looked upward, past the dingy housing of the lightbulb, as tears mingled with water, questions with accusation.

I trusted in Your promises, Lord. You said if I delighted myself in You, You would give me the desires of my heart.

The tears flowed harder.

You said if I abide in You and Your words abide in me, I could ask whatever I wish and it would be done. Haven't I delighted *myself in You? Haven't I* abided *in You?*

ABOUT THE AUTHOR

Kim Cash Tate is the author of *Hope Springs, Cherished, Faithful, Heavenly Places,* and the memoir *More Christian Than African American.* A former practicing attorney, she is also the founder of Colored in Christ Ministries. She and her husband have two children.